THE
FIXER

Text copyright © 2023 Tara Crescent
All Rights Reserved

No part of this book may be reproduced in any form or by any electronic or mechanical means including information storage and retrieval systems, without permission in writing from the author. The only exception is by a reviewer, who may quote short excerpts in a review.

This book is a work of fiction. Names, characters, places, and incidents either are products of the author's imagination or are used fictitiously. Any resemblance to actual persons, living or dead, events, or locales is entirely coincidental.

Editing by Molly Whitman at Novel Mechanic, www.novelmechanic.com

Cover by Bookin It Designs, www.bookinitdesigns.com

v. 20240209

To being seen, protected, and loved.

THE FIXER

TARA CRESCENT

1
ROSA

The first time I meet Leo Cesari, I flash him.

Not intentionally.

My friend Valentina and I are going out to dinner. It's a double date with the guy I'm seeing, Franco, and one of his friends. I suggested it for two reasons. 1) I've gone out with Franco three times, and he bores me to tears. 2) Valentina needs to date more.

I realize Reason #2 is none of my business, but my friend is awesome. She's a badass hacker who works for the mafia, plus she's a single mom who's doing an amazing job of raising her daughter. If there's anyone who deserves to find someone who falls madly in love with her, it's Valentina.

If that kind of love even exists, a pessimistic voice inside of me pipes up. I make a face and squash it down. I'm an optimist. I don't think you can be a designer in the fashion industry, where failure is almost a certainty, and not be. But lately, the voice of doom has been rearing its head more often.

You have a plan, I remind myself. *One new date a month. Keep at it, and you'll find someone.*

I might not be super excited about the date—I'm fairly sure I'm breaking up with Franco after tonight—but that doesn't mean I'm not dressing up. I love clothes, and my closet is crammed with garments I've sewn and haven't had a chance to wear. Tonight, I'm going to wear a shimmering green cocktail dress made from translucent silk with a matching jade slip underneath. I'm zipping the dress up when I realize it's broken. The zipper pull has come free of the teeth, and there's no easy way to fit it back in.

Ugh.

I take off the dress to assess the damage. Just as I do, the doorbell rings. Valentina's here.

I head to the front door. "You wouldn't believe what happened," I say as I open it. "I tore my—"

Then I realize she's not alone. Standing next to her is a man I've never seen before.

I work in fashion, and there are a lot of good-looking people in my world. This man looks nothing like them. He's big, broad, and muscled. His left cheek is scarred, his arms are covered with tattoos, and there is a touch of gray at his temples. He looks *dangerous.* A shark in a sea of dolphins.

And I'm wearing a tiny slip that shows a lot of cleavage and nothing else.

"Umm," I blurt out. "Hi. My zipper broke."

"Yes," the hot stranger replies, his lips twitching. His piercing blue eyes rake over me in appreciative appraisal. I feel hot and cold all at once, shivery and shaky. I can't tear my gaze away from him. I'm a mouse hypnotized by a cobra, and I'm about to get eaten alive.

Valentina clears her throat. *Valentina.* For a moment, I forgot she was there. My cheeks heating, I drag my eyes away from the stranger and focus on my friend, who is looking at me with a knowing grin. "Rosa Tran, meet Leonardo Cesari. Rosa was in school with me and designs clothes. Leo works with me."

He's Mafia. That realization should snap me out of my daze—I have no desire to get involved with the criminal underworld—but it doesn't. I want to stroke his cheek and trace his scar with my tongue, rubbing myself like a cat against his stubble.

"Nice to meet you." I hold out my hand to shake his, and the strap of my slip slides down my shoulder, giving him a great view of my naked breast.

A gentleman would avert his eyes.

Not Leo.

He looks.

It's a male gaze, hot and carnal. He looks like he wants to push me down on the floor, tear my slip off, and thrust his hot length into me. No foreplay, no games. Just raw animal pleasure.

And I want it.

I've never felt this way before. I go on dozens of dates, but something has always been missing. I'm almost ready to believe that the sparks I'm searching for don't exist, but then I lay eyes on Leo Cesari, all muscles and darkness, and I realize that the fairy tales, the romance novels, and the movies were right. Leo is fire, and I am a moth, fluttering helplessly toward him. I don't know what to do with this violent cocktail of emotions churning inside me. "Sorry about the strip tease," I find myself saying. "My clothes don't usually fall to pieces on me."

Leo gives me a wicked smile that transforms his face. "No apology needed," he says, laughter coating every syllable. "I enjoyed it."

The moment the door closes behind him, I whirl

to Valentina. My body still feels feverish. "That's the Leo you work with?" I demand. "You never told me how hot he is."

"Leo isn't," she starts, and then she shrugs. "If you like the type, I guess. He's too old for you."

No, he's not, I want to reply. *He's perfect.*

That night, when I get into bed—alone—and turn out the lights, it isn't my date I'm thinking about when I touch myself. It's Leo, his piercing blue eyes staring into me, a small smile lurking at the corners of his mouth. And when I climax, it's to the memory of him saying, "I enjoyed it."

I SEE Leo for the second time six weeks later. I'm in a bacaro, and Valentina's daughter Angelica has just been kidnapped. Leo has a thousand things to do that day, but he still takes the time to walk me home.

We don't say much. Leo's face is grim, and as for me, I'm in shock. Who would kidnap a child? Why? I'm desperately worried, and my heart is pounding in fear.

"Will she be okay?" I finally ask at my doorstep.

It's a dumb question. He doesn't know the answer any more than I do. Anything he could say to me right now is a platitude, an empty reassurance to keep my fear under control.

"Yes," he says bleakly. There's a flat resignation in his voice. Almost like he's seen this exact scenario before, and he knows how it's going to play out. It's not going to end well, but he's going to do everything he can to prevent it anyway. I look into his eyes, and I see an inky ocean-deep darkness that threatens to drown him. "I will find her or die trying."

THE NEXT TIME I see Leo is in July at Valentina's wedding. My friend is getting married to Dante, the love of her life. I'm one of Valentina's attendants, and Leo is one of Dante's. He's wearing a tuxedo and looks every bit as good as I remember.

Better.

I haven't seen him in months. I don't know why. I get the sense he isn't doing well, but Valentina changes the topic every time I ask about him directly. I should have forgotten all about him. He's someone I've met twice in eight months, but I haven't been able to get him out of my mind. He's the object of my fantasies, a fairy tale prince in gritty armor. When I close my eyes, I remember the way he looked at me the first time we met, the raw hunger in his eyes, and I feel that keen ache of longing all over again.

We're seated together at the reception, but we don't get a chance to talk until late into the night. The band is alternating ballads with pop songs when Leo turns to me. "Not dancing, *principessa?*"

"*Principessa?*"

He gestures to my bridesmaid dress, a pale pink frothy confection dotted with sequins. "You look like a princess tonight, pretty and sparkling."

"I'm not sure if that's a compliment or an insult."

He tilts his head to the side. "Why would it be an insult?"

Because my parents think my choice of career is a mistake. Because Franco, the most recent man I dated, thought fashion was frivolous. I don't say any of that. "If I look like a princess," I reply, gesturing to Valentina on the dance floor, "what does she look like?"

He hesitates. "She looks... happy."

He sounds *off*. "And you look too melancholy for such a joyous occasion. Are you okay?"

"I shouldn't be here. If it weren't Dante and Valentina. . ." His voice trails off. "I don't like weddings."

"Why not?"

For a moment, I think he's going to tell me, but then he changes the topic. "It was a compliment," he says. "There's too much darkness in the world. Pretty and sparkling reminds us it's not all bad." He gets to his feet and stretches his hand toward me. "Care to dance?"

I don't know him well enough to probe, and besides, I'm not going to pass up the chance to dance with Leo. I take his callused hand, and we move to the floor. Just as we do, the song ends, and another begins, a slower melody about lost love.

Leo pulls me closer. His right hand engulfs mine, and his left rests at my hip, a light touch that only makes me want more. "No zipper mishaps today, I see. Pity."

My cheeks flush. I've had two glasses of prosecco already, and it's going to my head. Leo's nearness doesn't help. I'm very aware of his body, of how he looms over me. "You're teasing me."

A smile dances on the corners of his lips. "Only a little."

"Besides," I add. "If my zipper broke, you'd enjoy it."

His expression darkens. "And so would everyone else here," he growls. "No, *principessa*. I don't share. Trust me, if your zipper broke, anyone leering at you would do so at their own peril."

If you'd asked me before this conversation if possessive men turned me on, I would have laughed in your face. But there's no denying my reaction to his threat. My body is on fire, and I shiver. I want Leo. I want him more than I've ever wanted anyone. I gather up my courage and tilt my head up to look at him. "I'm going to get out of here and go back to my room. Want to join me?"

It's the first time I've said something like this to a man. The first time I've wanted to.

Leo gives me a long look, heat flaring in his eyes. I wait with bated breath for his response.

And then he says, "I don't think that's a good idea, Rosa."

His rejection feels like a slap.

For a moment, I can't hear the music of the band or the chatter of the other guests. I flush beet red, blood roaring in my ears. I've never slept with anyone before, but I'm not naive. I can tell when a man wants me. Leo is single and unattached, and from the bulge in his pants, he's definitely interested. "Why not?" I whisper.

"If I joined you in your room, we'd fuck," he says gruffly. His voice is harsh, and the words are crude, but they're meant to be. "We'd fuck on the floor, and we'd fuck against the wall. We'd fuck in the shower stall. I'd push your legs apart and lick your pretty clit until you came, and then, when you're in the grip of your orgasm, I'd shove into you so hard you'd scratch my back and scream my name. And it would be good."

He's trying to frighten me away with his words, but he doesn't know me. I'm not terrified; I'm turned on. "There's a 'but' in that sentence."

"But," he says. "Tomorrow morning, you'd want more. And I have nothing more to offer."

He's right about that: I do want more than a one-night stand. Even with Leo. *Especially with Leo.* "And you only want one night?"

Some unnamed emotion flits on his face. "Once upon a time, I wanted more," he says. He bends his head and kisses me, a gentle brush of his lips against mine. "But that time is in the past." He drags his thumb over my lower lip. "Stay away from me, *principessa*. I'm no good for you."

Then he walks away from me, and I don't see him again.

Until...

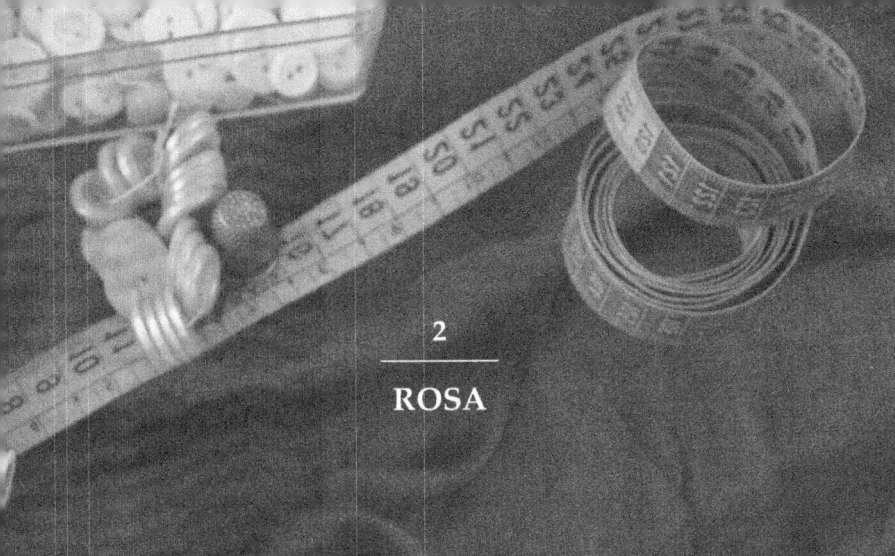

2
ROSA

"Are you seeing someone?"

My family isn't much for Christmas, but birthdays are a very big deal. I'm in Lecce to celebrate my mother's fiftieth. I arrived last night, and I've managed to spend the last eighteen hours avoiding this question.

My lucky streak has run out.

"No," I reply, trying not to think about Leo. "Is Hugh still dating Valerie?" When I came down for Christmas, my brother introduced me to his new girlfriend, but it's September now, and there's no guarantee they're still together. Hugh goes through women like I go through fabric.

"They broke up in January. Just as well. He's too young to be settling down." Elaine Tran is not to be dissuaded from her inquiries into my love life. "What about that man you were dating last year? Frank?"

"Franco," I correct. "We weren't serious. I'm not seeing him anymore." I glance at my phone discreetly. Where is Hugh? My brother promised to be home by five to rescue me from this exact conversation, but it's twenty after and he's nowhere to be seen.

"Whose decision was that?" my mother asks pointedly.

I take a deep, fortifying breath. Here it comes: the lecture. Any minute now, she's going to remind me that by the time she was my age, she was married and had already given birth to her first child. "Mine," I admit. "He wasn't right for me."

My mother throws up her hands in exasperation. "Why not? Was he unemployed? Homeless? Did he beat you?"

Unemployed, homeless, or abusive. In Elaine Tran's worldview, those are the only acceptable reasons to turn a man down. "No," I reply. "He has a good job, and I'm sure his apartment is very nice. It's in a great neighborhood. But he thought fashion was frivolous."

To be fair, even if Franco hadn't said that, we

wouldn't have lasted. He was more interested in his retirement portfolio than he was in me. Maybe I read too many romance novels as a teenager, but I want to fall in love. I want to be swept off my feet by a fairytale prince, someone who makes my heart race and my pulse pound.

Someone like Leo.

I shove that thought aside. Leo made it perfectly clear at Valentina's wedding that he wasn't interested in dating me. Enough wallowing. I need to let this stupid crush die and quickly.

My mother predictably takes Franco's side. "He's not wrong. You spend all your time in that silly shop of yours, sewing late into the night." She gives me a critical once-over. "Your skin is sallow, you have dark circles under your eyes, and you've put on weight."

Don't react. Do not react. "I like your dress," I say blandly. "Purple is a good color on you." Every year, I make my mother an outfit for her birthday. This year is a milestone, so I went all out. The fabric alone—a gorgeous, iridescent silk crepe—cost four hundred euros a meter. The skirt is cut on the bias, and to keep the silk from distorting, I hemmed it by hand. It took hours.

But my mother's face lit up when she tried it on. The effort was worth it.

Of course, Hugh could show up with wilted grocery store flowers, and she'll still think he walks on water. But that's just the way it is. My parents have always favored my younger brother, but I refuse to let it get to me. Life's too short for bitterness.

"You're trying to change the subject." My mother's voice is dry. "I suppose you think I'm haranguing you, and you're probably right. I worry about you, that's all. Fashion isn't the most stable of careers."

I got my love of sewing from my grandmother, who used to be a seamstress back in Hanoi. But as soon as my grandparents emigrated to Italy, she traded it in for a job as a bank teller. "Sensible hours, steady paycheck," she used to say. My mother has followed in her tracks, and so has Hugh. I'm the black sheep of the family.

She's not wrong to fret about my financial well-being. It wasn't too long ago that I was struggling to pay rent and sneaking into fashion shows and art gallery openings for free food and wine. Two years ago, I was sleeping in the back room of my shop because my business was barely profitable.

"You don't have to worry, mẹ. I'm doing fine." After Lucia Petrucci wore one of my creations to the Palazzo Ducale annual donor gala, business picked up dramatically. Things have never been better. I even applied to show in Milan Fashion Week a couple of weeks ago.

"It isn't just your business I'm worried about. It's also your personal life. At your age, I already had my first child."

There it is, just like clockwork. Damn it, Hugh, you were supposed to save me from this.

"Don't you want to get married, Rosa?" she continues.

"I do," I reply soothingly. I should leave it at that, but honesty compels me to add, "But I want to fall in love first, and that hasn't happened for me."

"Love," my mother says, as if it's a four-letter word. Which it is, I guess. "Once again, you have your head in the clouds. Look at your brother. He's only twenty-two, and already he has a well-paying job. You know what they gave him as a bonus? A brand-new car. A Lamborghini."

"What? They gave him a car as a bonus?" I ask sharply. This is the first I'm hearing about a Lambo, which is shocking. Boasting about Hugh's accomplishments is my mother's favorite thing to do.

But something doesn't add up. Banks do not hand out expensive Italian sports cars as bonuses to entry-level employees, and my mother knows that. This means Hugh's involved in something messy, and my mother is burying her head in the sand, pretending not to see it. "Which bank does he work for again, and exactly what does he do for them?"

Before she can answer, the front door flies open, and my brother bursts in. One look at him, and I know something's badly wrong. Blood pours down from a cut on his forehead, his shirt is torn and dirt-streaked, and he's shaking. "Where's bô?" he demands. "Is he still at the garage?"

"No, he's upstairs."

"Thank God." Hugh locks the door behind him, moves over to the windows, and closes the drapes. "Mẹ, I skipped lunch. Could you make me something to eat?"

It's a transparent attempt to get rid of her. My mother opens her mouth. It's obvious she has a thousand questions for my brother, but it's also obvious that she doesn't really want to hear the answers. "Rosa made phở. I'll heat it up."

The moment she leaves the room, Hugh whirls to me. "Rosa," he says. "Remember when you had trouble with your landlord, and a friend of yours helped out?"

I grow cold. The incident Hugh's referring to happened more than two years ago. My landlord started to harass me, and I told my friend Valentina, who got a Mafia lawyer, Daniel Rossi, involved. If my brother is looking for that kind of protection...

"What happened? Why are you bleeding?"

"It's complicated." He clenches his hands into fists. "My car blew up."

What? Oh my God. I put two and two together and get to an answer I don't like. "You got involved with the Mafia here, didn't you? What did you do?"

He doesn't answer my questions right away. "My new job," he finally mutters. "I might have fudged the details a little."

His evasiveness only makes me more nervous. "Hugh. What. Did. You. Do."

"I did the Mafia's bookkeeping and gave them financial advice. It's easy money, really. Most of these guys have trouble getting good help. Only thing, I might have lost some money."

"How much?" I ask, almost afraid to hear the answer.

"Ten million euros."

Panic slithers down my back. "What the fuck, Hugh?"

"When they find out, they're going to be furious. They're going to kill me." He suddenly looks really, really young and very, *very* afraid. "Can you help me, chi?"

A cold ball of fear settles in my stomach. Talking is difficult; I feel nauseous. If the Mafia blew up his car, that's probably only their first attempt at killing Hugh. Any moment now, they could make another. Someone could burst into the house and gun my brother down.

"I need to make a phone call."

3
LEO

It's September 7th.

My wife's birthday.

Patrizia would have turned forty today. I remember the last birthday I had with her, her twenty-first. I had flown her out to Tuscany as a surprise with money I didn't really have. It was a beautiful summer day. We sat on a green hillside, a picnic spread in front of us. The sky was blue, and in the distance, a farmer was tending to his vineyards.

We drank chilled prosecco out of the bottle and talked about the future. "This time next year," she said, looking at the engagement ring on her finger, "I'll be a married woman. Imagine that. Then we'll have children, and there'll be no more time for picnics and prosecco."

"There will always be time for picnics and prosecco," I replied. "I promise you that."

But my words were a lie, and my promise meant nothing.

She's dead.

Because of me.

And If I could rewind time, I would. I would find that girl on the hillside, and I would tell her to have nothing to do with me. All I will bring her is ruin and pain.

I skipped going to work today. I'm the head of security for the Venetian Mafia. Ironic, really, when I seem to constantly be doing a shitty job protecting the people I care about. It isn't a desk job, but I typically go into the headquarters every day. It beats staring at the walls of my studio apartment. But when I woke up this morning, I just couldn't do it. Drowning my sorrows in drink seemed like a much better idea. I started with a bottle of prosecco for breakfast in Patrizia's honor. When that ran out a few hours ago, I switched to vodka. It tastes vile, a mixture of sorrow and self-loathing, and that's just the way I like it.

The buzzer sounds. I ignore it. It sounds again, long and angry, like a hornet's nest. Dante Colonna's voice comes through the intercom. "Open up, Leo. I know you're there."

For fuck's sake, can't a man get wasted in peace? I stumble down the two flights of stairs and throw open the outside door. Dante Colonna, second-in-command of the Venetian Mafia, is standing there holding a picnic basket, his wife Valentina at his side. Dante and Valentina don't know about Patrizia—the picnic basket is nothing more than a wretched coincidence—but when I see it, pain stabs me, hot, sharp, and vicious.

"What are you doing here?"

Valentina looks taken aback at my surly tone, and I feel like an ass for snapping at her. Dante and Valentina are my friends; I've known both of them for more than ten years. But September is not a great month. Most days, I can push the pain deep inside and function, but in September, my failure to protect the girl I loved haunts me.

"You have plans tonight?" Dante asks. "We're inviting ourselves to an early dinner."

"Don't worry," Valentina adds. "I brought food."

I want to tell them to fuck off. Instead, I step aside and gesture them in.

Upstairs, we silently stare at each other. I didn't bother to shave today. My shirt is wrinkled, and I'm sure I reek of alcohol. Thankfully, both of them ignore my appearance. Instead, Valentina looks around the room.

It's not much, my apartment. There's a bed and an armchair, and that's about it. An old sheet acts as a curtain, blocking out the evening light. The kitchen is an alcove that houses a refrigerator and a burner stove. No oven, no dishwasher.

Pizza boxes and takeout containers cover the coffee table, and napkins litter the floor. Valentina looks a little shocked at the mess. "Leo, you're a slob," she scolds. "You're worse than Angelica, and that's saying something. When was the last time you cleaned?"

"Signora Sacchi is on vacation," I lie. My cleaning lady was supposed to come yesterday, but I asked her not to. I can't deal with people right now. "Where is Angelica?"

Nine months ago, Valentina's ten-year-old daughter was kidnapped by a rival family in Bergamo. The kidnapping happened on my watch. Another person I couldn't protect. Another way I've failed the people I care about.

Valentina opens the cupboard under the sink, looking for a garbage bag. "She's with Antonio and Lucia."

I stop her before she can start tidying up. Fishing out a pair of folding chairs from under the bed, I dust them off and set them up. "Sit," I tell my friends. "I'll take care of the mess." I throw out the takeout containers, wipe down the coffee table, and wash three dinner plates.

When I'm done, Valentina unpacks the basket. "I brought Vietnamese," she announces. "Fresh rolls, salted squid, and noodles with stir-fried beef in a curry sauce. I hope you're hungry."

This doesn't look like takeout. "You cooked?"

"Of course. I'm starving. Let's dive in."

The food is fantastic. I'm not much of a cook—the only dishes I can make are roast chicken and pasta. This though? A thousand flavors and textures burst on my tongue with every bite. It's almost enough to make me forgive the intrusion. *Almost.* "Thank you," I say. "Everything is delicious. To what do I owe this pleasure?"

"We're worried about you," Dante says bluntly. "You're still beating yourself up about what happened to Angelica."

"No, I'm not," I lie.

"Really? Then why was it that you wanted to know where she was earlier?" He gives me a pointed look. "You've been brooding for months, Leo. But the

Bergamo threat has been handled. Angelica is fine, and everything is okay. Nobody blames you for what happened, least of all Valentina and me."

They might not hold me responsible, but that doesn't absolve me of my guilt. "I don't blame myself."

Valentina switches from one unwelcome topic to another. "These are Rosa's recipes," she says. She tilts her head to the side and surveys me through narrowed eyes. "Speaking of Rosa, whatever happened between the two of you? I saw you dancing with her at our wedding, but I didn't notice either of you leave. Did you hook up?"

Dante's cough sounds suspiciously like a laugh. "You might as well tell her," he advises. "Evidently, every time the subject of you comes up, Rosa changes the topic. Valentina is dying of curiosity. Any minute now, she's going to hack into your email and search for messages between the two of you."

"I would never," Valentina responds indignantly. "I have *some* boundaries. Besides, Leo's going to tell me, isn't he?"

"Nothing happened between us." And nothing can. Rosa Tran is an optimist who believes in things like love and happily-ever-after, and I'm a dead husk of a man.

But when we danced, she made me want to feel again.

I pushed her away, and I don't regret it. Rosa is genuinely lovely—kind, generous, always quick with a smile and a laugh—but she's also twenty-five. She's got her whole life ahead of her, and I'm not enough of an asshole to ruin it.

"But you like her," Valentina prompts.

That's irrelevant. "What is it about newlyweds that turns them into relentless matchmakers?" I bite out. "It doesn't matter what I think about Rosa. Nothing is ever going to happen between us. In case you haven't noticed, your friend is *sixteen* years younger than me."

"There is a little bit of an age gap," she concedes. "But it's not like Rosa is eighteen."

This is getting ridiculous. Valentina is pushing way too hard. "It's not a little bit of an age gap," I snap. "It's a chasm." Maybe my friends think that a relationship is what I need to pull me out of my funk, but they don't know the truth. I was in love once, and it ended in disaster. I will never put myself on that path again. "For fuck's sake, I lost my virginity the same year Rosa was born."

"Too much information, Leo." Dante looks like he wants to punch me in the face. Tough shit. If he doesn't like me snapping at his wife, he should tell her to stop nagging me. And if he wants to start something, well, why not add more pain to this clusterfuck of a day?

Before the situation can escalate into disaster, Valentina's phone rings. She glances at the display. "What a coincidence. It's Rosa." She picks up the call, a smile on her face. "You'll never guess where I am right now."

Then she listens to what Rosa is saying, and the laughter is wiped off her face. "Hang tight," she says. "We'll be there in less than two hours. Whatever you do, don't leave the house, any of you."

"What's going on?" I demand as soon as she hangs up.

"Rosa is in big trouble."

4
LEO

Valentina insists on rushing immediately to Antonio's house. It's not until we're seated in his office that she tells us what's going on. "Rosa just called me," she says. "Her brother Hugh has gotten himself mixed up with the Mafia in Lecce. He's been doing their books and giving them financial advice, but it sounds like he just lost ten million euros of their money."

I bite off a swear. This isn't good. *At all.* Antonio leans back in his chair and shuts his eyes. "Fuck."

"Rosa said that her brother thinks they're going to kill him."

"They are," the padrino confirms. A shadow passes over his face. "Depending on how angry they are, they could kill his family as well."

"What?" Valentina breathes, horrified. "Why?"

I speak up. "The outfit that controls Lecce and all of Puglia, *Spina Sacra,* is as old-school as they come. Rigid protocols, elaborate oath ceremonies, and blood vendettas. If Hugh Tran's lost their money, they're going to make an example of him."

"Is there anything we can do?"

The padrino winces. "I don't like getting involved with Southern Italy," he replies. "They're all insane." Valentina opens her mouth to say something else, but before she does, Antonio continues, "I'll call in a favor and get her family out of there."

"But Hugh will still die?"

Antonio spreads his hands. "Valentina, I have no grounds to stand on here. Hugh Tran is not a member of our organization. Spina Sacra isn't going to back away because I want them to, and I cannot go to war over this."

He's right to be cautious. If we get into battle with Spina Sacra, it won't just be us versus them. The Spina Sacra is allied with the 'Ndrangheta and the Camorra, who are just itching for an excuse to come after our territory. In Milan, Ciro Del Barba will step in to help Antonio, not because of any love he bears for the man, but because he won't let the Sicilians take over Northern Italy. And in the background, the Russians will hover like vultures, ready to take over the country once we've destroyed each other.

No, Antonio can't stop this. The cost is too high.

"But if we pay back the ten million euros he lost. . ."

"It's not the money," Dante says regretfully. "It's the principle. I'm sorry, sparrow, I really am. Rosa is like family to me as well, but there's nothing we can do."

Family.

The instant I realize how we could save Rosa's brother, I flinch. There's one way out of this mess, but I cannot. *I will not.* Not even to spare Rosa the pain of seeing her brother die.

Except I find myself speaking up. "Not nothing," I say. "There is one thing we can do."

I see the exact moment Antonio realizes the way out of this trap. He stares at me, a question in his eyes. Dante and Valentina are ignorant about my past, but the padrino knows every secret in Venice, mine included. "Leo?" he prompts. "I cannot force you to do this. This has to be your choice."

"What is it?" Valentina leans forward. "What could we do?"

I can't make myself say the words out loud.

Antonio glances at me and then steps in to explain. "If one of my inner team were to marry Rosa, I could claim that Hugh Tran is family and is therefore entitled to my protection." He turns to me. "Leo?" he asks. "Are you sure you want to do this?"

No. I'm not sure. I'm not sure at all. Everything in me rebels at the idea. I was married once. I *loved* Patrizia. It feels disloyal to even contemplate this crazy idea. She took a bullet meant for me, for fuck's sake. And now I'm betraying her memory by suggesting this travesty.

But I can't stand by and do nothing while Rosa's life gets ruined the way mine was. Plus, I owe Valentina and Dante. Their daughter got kidnapped on my watch. Angelica's thankfully suffered no aftereffects from the incident, but Valentina hasn't recovered as well. She hides it as best as she can, but I see the way she's on edge when her daughter is on a playdate. I see the way she flinches whenever the phone rings.

I can't make amends for my failure, but I can atone for it.

"Marriage?" Valentina sits up, shock warring with hope in her eyes. "Would that work?"

"It's the only thing that might." Antonio turns to me. "Think hard, Leo. This is not a temporary union.

This is a wedding in church, with the two of you making your vows in front of family and friends. This is the rest of your life. This is *forever*."

Forever is what I thought I had with Patrizia.

I'm never going to feel for Rosa what I did for my wife. We won't share a bed. We won't come together in passion. We won't lie on a hill on a warm sunny day and look at clouds and talk about our future, and we won't build a family together.

This arrangement with Rosa—it isn't a real marriage. It's a farce.

But it'll save her brother's life.

"I'll do it."

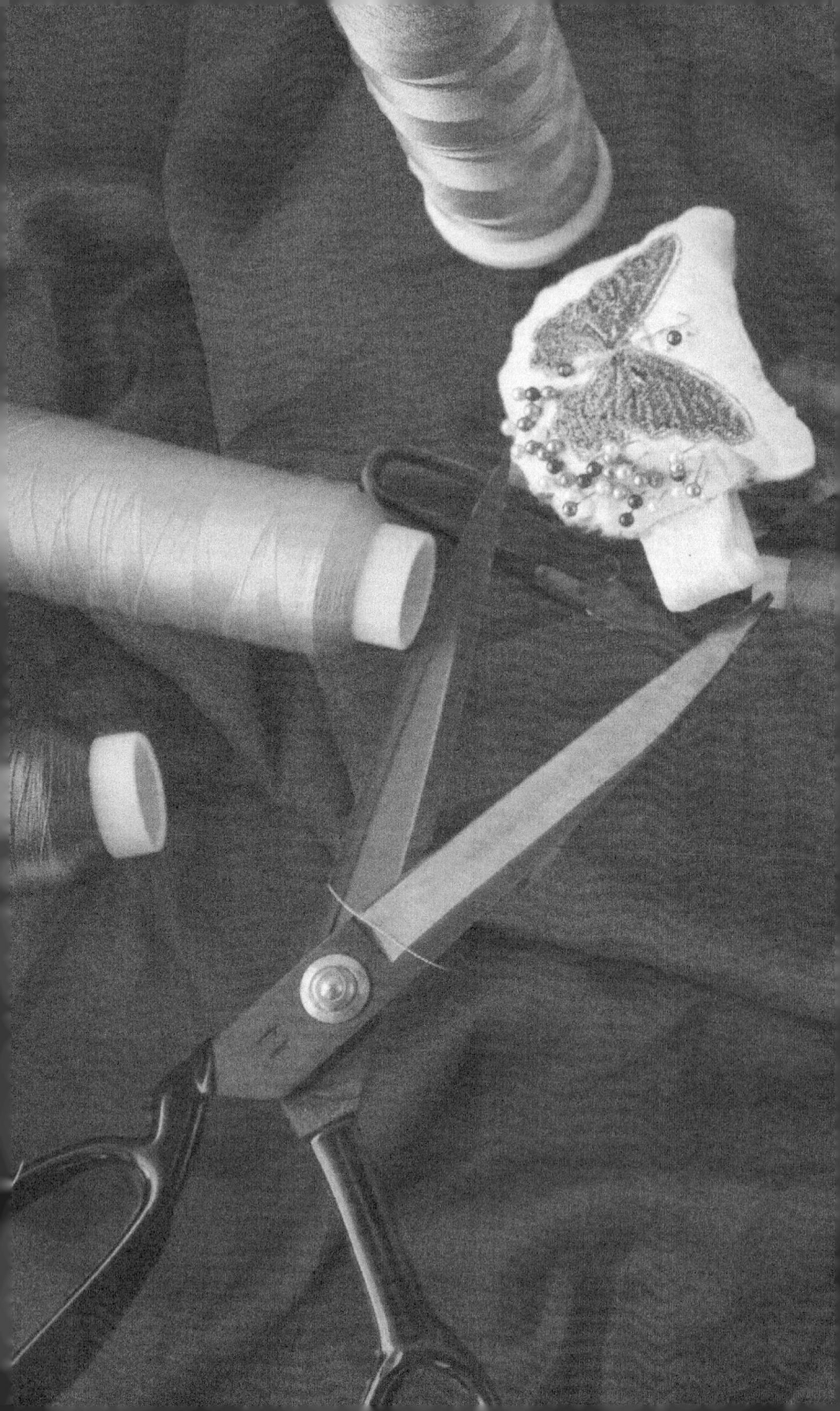

5

ROSA

The next hour is excruciating. Hugh alternates between pacing around the room and sitting on the couch, staring into space. He doesn't stop shaking. At one point, my mother tiptoes into the room with a mug of phở. He barely reacts.

"Has he told you what's going on?" she whispers to me.

"No." My mother's face is pinched and frightened, and as sorry as I feel for Hugh right now, I also want to slap him. This is her fiftieth birthday. All she wanted to do was go out for a lobster dinner, but I seriously doubt we're going to make our dinner reservation. "Don't worry, mẹ. It's going to be okay." I keep my fingers crossed as I reassure her. My mind is fuzzy with panic. God, I hope Valentina has a plan because I sure as hell don't.

"Worrying is a mother's prerogative," she responds. "I'll make something for dinner."

"Good idea." Cooking will distract her. "Do you want help?"

"You stay here," she says, giving Hugh another concerned glance. "Your father will help me."

She must be really worried if she's willing to risk unleashing my father in the kitchen.

I cross the room to the couch once she's gone. "Drink the phở while it's still hot."

Hugh nods. His hands close around the mug, but he makes no move to lift it to his mouth. "Talk to me," I urge. "What happened?"

He doesn't reply.

"Does the Mafia already know about the missing money?" I try again. "Is that why they blew up your car?"

He hesitates. "No," he says. "That was something else."

"Something else? What is that supposed to mean?"

He shakes his head. "Forget about the car," he says. "It doesn't mean anything." He takes a sip of the hot broth. "Rocco Santini doesn't know about the money. Not yet." He swallows. "I don't have a lot of time." He takes another big gulp of the broth, and awareness finally returns to his eyes. "You shouldn't be here. Not you, not the parents. Call a taxi, get to the airport. Take them back to Venice."

Right now, Hugh's judgment is suspect. "Can we trust the taxi drivers here?"

He starts to reply and then stops. "No," he says, defeated. "We can't. Even if they don't work directly for Spina Sacra, they won't oppose them. If Santini's put out the word..." His voice trails away.

Tears well in his eyes, and he averts his face. I settle next to him and put my arm around his shoulders. "I called Valentina. She told me to stay put. She and Dante will be here soon. They'll know what to do." He's still shaking; the phở has done nothing to warm him. "It's going to be okay," I say, offering the same empty reassurance I gave my mom.

"No," he says. I've never heard him sound so lost. So broken. "No, it's not."

NINETY MINUTES LATER, there's a knock at the door. My parents, who are in the kitchen, don't hear it. Hugh and I do, and we freeze.

Valentina said two hours. Is this her, half an hour ahead of schedule, or is this the Mafia come to shoot Hugh down in cold blood?

> **VALENTINA**
> Answer the door.

Oh, thank heavens. Relief floods through me, making me weak-kneed. I exhale the breath I didn't know I was holding, jump to my feet, and hurry to the front door. "Thanks for coming so quickly, Val—"

Then I look up, and the words get stuck on my tongue. Because it's not Valentina standing there.

It's Leo.

And he looks like he wants to murder me.

I gape at him for what feels like forever. "Leo?" I finally manage. I haven't seen him since our last disastrous encounter in July. "What are you doing here?"

The moment those words leave my mouth, I want to take them back. What a dumb question. I called Valentina for help, and Leo is the head of security for the Venetian Mafia. Of course, he's going to be here. He's probably the obvious person to call in a situation like this.

He stares at me for a long moment. Every time I've seen him, Leo's been in a suit. Today, though, he's dressed more casually in a long-sleeved white shirt, the cuffs rolled up to his elbows. Tattoos cover his muscled forearms. Before I met Leo, I couldn't understand why anyone would want to deface their body in such a way. Now, I want to stroke the dark ink with my fingertips.

Stop that, Rosa.

"We need to talk," he says, jerking his head at the black Range Rover behind him. "Get in the car."

Getting into a small, enclosed space with a man that sets my pulse racing? That sounds like a bad decision. "My family—"

"Will be fine. Antonio's negotiated a temporary ceasefire."

"Oh." I start to tremble. Ever since Hugh walked in an hour and a half ago and announced he was in trouble, I've been running on adrenaline. But it's draining now, and even though the evening's warm and balmy, I suddenly feel very cold. I hug my arms around myself. "They'll all be okay? Hugh, my parents?"

The hard expression in Leo's eyes softens for an

instant. "Yes," he says, and then his voice turns clipped again. "Now, get in the goddamn car."

I tell Hugh I'm heading out for a little bit, ignore his questioning look, and go outside. Leo is waiting by the Range Rover. He holds the door open for me, a gesture of chivalry I wasn't expecting, given he's practically barking orders at me, and then comes around the driver's side. He gets in, slams the door shut, and speeds off.

I study him out of the corner of my eyes as he drives. *Leo is furious.* His anger is a living, tangible beast occupying the space between us. Does he blame me for Hugh's mistakes? It's not like I have any control over my brother.

The silence quickly grows too much to bear. "Where are we going?"

"The beach."

"Why?"

He gives me a poisonous glare as if he's offended he has to explain himself. "We won't be overheard at the beach."

"That doesn't really answer my question," I point out reasonably.

He ignores that. I contemplate speaking again, but there are times when discretion is the better part of valor, and this is obviously one of them. I look out of the window instead and admire the scenery. The sun is setting, casting golden shadows over the countryside. We pass my mother's favorite nursery, and they're still open, their small parking lot filled with flowering plants. "We had a dinner reservation near the beach," I tell Leo. So much for staying silent. I wonder if anyone remembered to call the restaurant and cancel it. "It's my mom's fiftieth birthday. We were going to eat lobster." I make a face. "Well, she was."

He gives me a sidelong look. "You don't like lobster?"

"I don't like how they cook them," I reply. "I guess that makes me a hypocrite. After all, I'm not vegetarian; I eat meat. But tossing that poor thing in a pot of boiling water. . ." I shudder. He looks at me again, and his scrutiny makes me uncomfortable. "Anyway. I haven't seen you in a couple of months. How have you been?"

A smile briefly makes an appearance at the corners of his lips. "Are we making small talk now, principessa?" he asks dryly.

"I asked you why we were going to the beach, and you growled at me," I point out sweetly. I want to see that smile again. "Small talk seems safer."

He pulls into a parking lot and turns off the engine. "We're here."

I love the beach. *Love.* Leo opens my door, and I jump out and take a deep breath. Being here, inhaling the salty tang of the ocean and listening to the hypnotically soothing sound of the waves, helps my fear leach away.

Leo watches me with unreadable eyes. "Let's walk."

I trail after him to the small strip of sand. I'm dressed for dinner, not the beach. My dress is ankle-length and made from a hand-painted length of silk that absolutely cannot get wet, and my sandals have three-inch heels that will make walking impossible. I take three steps, then give up and kick the sandals off. Much better.

There aren't too many people about, just a small handful of families enjoying the late summer evening. We walk along the water's edge until we get to a deserted stretch, then Leo stops, looks around for curious eyes, and turns to me. "Your brother fucked up," he says bluntly. "Badly. Spina Sacra is not a forgiving outfit. Their head, Rocco Santini, will kill him, and then he'll come after your family."

The sand has lulled me into tranquility, but his

words jolt me out of it. I swallow hard. "My parents? He'll hurt my parents too?" I start to shiver. "Why?"

"To set an example." Leo takes off his shirt and drapes it around my bare shoulders. The fabric, a fine cotton, smells like a mix of cologne and laundry detergent. He's wearing a white T-shirt underneath that clings to his broad chest and carved biceps. The tattoos snake up past his elbows to cover his upper arms as well. It's the first time I've seen them; the first time I've seen Leo in short sleeves, and any other day, I'd be tempted to stare.

"I'm not saying this to scare you," he continues. "I'm letting you know the stakes."

Enough panicking, Rosa. Think. "But you're here, so there's something you can do?"

"Not me. We. This involves you as well."

"Anything," I say immediately. "I'll do anything to save my family. What do you need me to do?"

He stares at the ocean for a long minute. With each passing second, I get more nervous. "Leo?" I prompt, resting my hand on his arm. "What is it?"

"You and I need to get married."

"What?" My mouth falls open. The way he made it sound, I thought I was going to have to do something unspeakably horrible. "Married? Why?"

"If we were to get married, we can claim that

your family is under Antonio's protection. Spina Sacra will recognize the claim."

It's all making sense now. His anger toward me, his uncharacteristic surliness. He didn't even want a relationship, and now he's being railroaded into marriage? "But it's temporary, right?" I ask hesitantly. "We stay married until the heat dies down and then get a divorce?"

"No," Leo says harshly. "Not temporary. This is *forever*. We'll get married in front of our family and friends. You'll wear a beautiful dress and walk down the aisle on your father's arm, and we'll promise to love each other until death do us part."

He practically spits out the last sentence. I stop and stare at him. Oh, fuck. No wonder he looks pissed. "I don't understand. Why are you doing this? You don't even know me. What's in it for you?"

"I owe Valentina and Dante a debt," he says. "This will go a long way toward repaying it."

Oh.

A muscle ticks in his cheek. "Before you decide, you need to know something. In public, we'll need to pretend that we're crazy about each other. But in private, this won't be a real marriage in any sense of the word. We won't have sex, and we won't share a bed. I'm not interested in you. There's only one reason I'm doing this, and that's to save your brother."

I'm not interested in you. Hugh's life hangs in the balance, and given the stakes, I shouldn't let myself be wounded by Leo's matter-of-fact statement. "I'll try not to take that personally," I say lightly, shoving my hurt down. "But I don't understand something. If you don't want to sleep with me, then what are you going to do for sex? I'm assuming you're not signing up for a lifetime of celibacy. Do you have someone on the side?"

"What? No." He stares at me. "Of course not. Is there for you?"

You. "No," I reply. "But if there's no one else, then why celibacy? Two months ago, you were ready to fuck me on the floor, against the wall, and in the shower stall, all in the same night. What changed?"

He frowns. "You're not having the reaction I expected."

"In what way?"

He runs his hands through his hair. "I thought you'd be upset about being forced to marry me."

"Should I wail about how my life is over?" I roll my eyes. "I'm not an idiot, Leo. When we get married, my family falls under the protection of the Venetian Mafia. My brother gets to live." I smile up at him. "Also, I don't know if you've noticed, but you're pretty easy on the eyes."

He blinks in confusion.

"You, on the other hand, just get me," I continue. "Unless you're planning to use me as a punching bag, I'm definitely getting the better deal here."

He gives me a frustrated look. "You're selling yourself short," he says. "You're lovely. Any other man would be lucky to marry you. But, as I already told you, I have nothing to offer."

You're lovely. A throwaway compliment that shouldn't fill me with as much pleasure as it does.

"There can be no other lovers for either of us," he says. "Not for the first two or three years, at least. We need to pretend to be madly in love. After that. . ." His hands clench into fists. "As long as we're careful and discreet about it, I don't see a problem in either of us taking a lover."

I do. The thought of another woman touching Leo makes me see red. But that's Future-Me's problem. If I stop and think about all the ways this could go wrong, I'll be on the fast track to insanity. For the moment, this is the only way forward.

"I'm in, of course." As if that were ever up for debate. I could feel zero chemistry for Leo, and I'd still do it because the alternative is my family dying.

"Thank you for helping us. I'm never going to be able to tell you how grateful I am, but I'm truly, truly grateful." I square my shoulders. "What happens next?"

He looks at me as if he has no idea what I'm going to say next. Then his lips twitch. "We go back to your parents' house, where you'll introduce me to your family as your boyfriend," he says. "Then we'll go out for dinner. Over dessert, I'll ask you to marry me."

"Got it." At some point, I'm sure the sheer magnitude of what I'm doing will sink in, but for now, I'm going with the flow. "I'll make sure to act surprised."

6
LEO

Only one thought runs through my head on the short drive back.

I'm betraying Patrizia.

I stood in front of a priest with my first love at my side and promised to love, honor, and cherish her forever. *Until death do us part.* I meant those vows with every fiber of my being. But now, I'm spitting in the face of my promises. On my wife's fortieth birthday, no less, I'm asking another woman to marry me.

My phone dings with a text from Antonio.

> I'm meeting Santini at midnight. How did Rosa take the news?

I give my passenger a sidelong look. Rosa's reaction had been unexpected in the extreme. I thought I had her pegged: a romantic who believed in fairy tale fantasies of true love and happy endings, someone who lived in a bubble made of silk and satin, a pretty world filled with pretty things.

And all of that might be true, but there's more to her. When I revealed that the only way to save her brother was to marry me, she didn't flinch. When I told her that our marriage would be a farce, she didn't cry or carry on or wallow in self-pity.

Instead, she told me that she was getting the better end of the deal. She said, "I don't know if you've noticed, but you're pretty easy on the eyes."

Then she asked me if I was planning to be celibate for the rest of my life.

Fuck. I was not prepared for that question. I haven't thought this through, not at all. In the heat of the moment, I replied that I didn't see a problem in taking a lover after a few years, but that's a lie. Real marriage or sham, everything in me rebels at the idea of cheating on Rosa. And when I think about another man touching her intimately, I want to punch my fist into the wall.

> She took it well. I'm on my way to meet her parents.

> Good. You have a ring?

Shit. I totally forgot. I need to get my head in the game. Spina Sacra consists of half a dozen clans, and Rocco Santini heads up the most powerful. He's a dangerous man, slow to anger but ruthless when provoked. If his people aren't watching me now, they will be as soon as Antonio tells him I'm marrying Hugh Tran's sister. There's no room for error, no room for slip-ups.

> I'll get one.

I screech to a halt. Rosa quirks an eyebrow. "Why are we stopping on the side of the road?"

"We need an engagement ring." I pull out my phone and search for a jewelry store that's open late. "I can't ask you to marry me without one." Oh, good. There's a store not too far from here with decent reviews. I put the car in drive again and make my way there.

Rosa makes a face when we come to a stop. "This place," she says, her voice unenthusiastic.

"You don't like it?"

"I've never been inside, but the pieces in the windows are always. . ." She struggles for the right word. "Showy." A wry smile crosses her face. "I'm being ridiculous. Who cares what the ring looks like?"

"You don't?" If she doesn't, she's in the minority of women.

"Like you said, it isn't a real marriage." She forces a smile on her face, and guilt sloshes through me. She's young, only twenty-five. This morning, she had her entire life ahead of her, and now she's walking into a cage of her brother's making.

And I'm not making it any easier.

"We need to pretend otherwise," I remind her.

"I know." She takes a deep breath. When she looks at me again, her face is shining with joy. "An engagement ring?" she says, her voice high with surprise. "That's why we're here?" She leans over and kisses my cheek. "Oh God, Leo, I'm so surprised."

I asked her to sell it, and she's doing exactly that. But when her lips press against my skin, my heart skips a beat.

Fuck.

My shock is obvious, but Rosa misunderstands the reason for it. "I was in the theatre club at school," she says with a laugh. "This is just like that." She opens her door and gets out. "You coming?"

She smells like jasmine, soft and delicate, and makes me want things I cannot have. "Your lines need work," I snarl. "'Oh God, I'm so surprised?' Seriously?" I push open the door and gesture her in. "After you, principessa."

Her lips tighten in annoyance at the nickname. I probably shouldn't needle her, but I already know I'm not going to stop. This situation sucks, and I'm going to take my victories where I find them.

THE STORE IS ALMOST ready to close. The moment we enter, a suit-clad salesman immediately heads in our direction. I can see him assessing us, trying to decide if we're serious customers or browsers, if we have money to spend or if we're going to want the cheapest ring in the place.

I wonder what his conclusions are.

We're an incongruous pair. Rosa is dressed to go out for dinner. She's wearing a flowered ankle-length dress with slits up both sides, showing tantalizing glimpses of her tanned legs. Her shoulders are bare and sun-kissed, golden hoops gleam in her ears, and thin golden bangles adorn her delicate wrists. I, on the other hand, am wearing the first clean thing I could find on my way out of Venice. A cotton shirt that's been washed so many times it's practically transparent, faded jeans, and old sneakers.

This is an expensive store, and I look like a bum.

Unsurprisingly, the salesman directs his attention to Rosa. "Can I help you?" he asks, his eyes lingering a little too long.

I clear my throat. It's not bothering me that he's eye-fucking Rosa—really, it isn't—but to do it in front of me is inviting trouble. Even in enemy territory, this isn't something I'm going to allow. "We're looking for an engagement ring," I say icily.

The salesman hears the warning in my voice. He gives me a supercilious smile. "Our rings start at twenty thousand euros. What is your budget, signor?"

When I asked Patrizia to marry me, I saved and scrimped for months. In those days, I didn't make much money, and what I did went towards helping my mother with food and rent. After five months, I saved five hundred euros. It felt like a princely sum of money. With it, Patrizia and I went into an antique store and bought a diamond ring. The stone was tiny, but it sparkled like a star. Patrizia *loved* it.

Those memories engulf me and threaten to drag me under.

"I don't have one," I bite out. I'm supposed to be pretending to be in love with Rosa, but so far, I'm doing a terrible job of it. I smile fondly at her. "It's much more important that Rosa finds the ring she loves."

The salesman—Paulo—says something about true love. We sit down in front of the counter, and he leaves to fetch some rings to show us. The moment his back is turned, Rosa grabs my hand and pulls me down to whisper, "Twenty thousand euros? Leo, that's insane. Let's go somewhere else."

"It's fine." Her perfume wafts over me again, sweet and tantalizing. "I can afford it."

Paulo returns with a tray. "These rings just came in," he says. "These are round, brilliant cut diamonds, ranging in size from one to three carats." He gives me another condescending smile. "People sometimes think that a two-carat diamond costs double that of a one-carat, but—"

That's quite enough. I cut him off. "But in reality, they cost anywhere from three to four times more." I cast a dismissive eye over his tray of baubles. "None of these interest me. They're too boring. Too common." I lace Rosa's fingers in mine. "My girlfriend needs something special."

"Special," Paulo repeats. He can't figure out if I'm serious or full of shit, but he's taking no chances of letting a commission walk away. "Let me see what we have." He returns with another tray. On it, six engagement rings gleam against the black velvet. "These diamonds are colored," he says. "Colored stones are considerably rarer than the clear ones."

Rosa's fingers brush a pink diamond ring. Paulo notices. "Ah, yes. You have impeccable taste. This is a three-carat pink diamond mined in Australia in a halo setting surrounded by smaller pavé stones." He glances at me. "It is also extremely expensive. If you're looking for something cheaper, I can suggest a lab-grown gem—"

She can't take her eyes off the pink ring. And I need to get the hell out of this store before I choke and drown in the memories. I pull a card out of my wallet. "I'll take it."

7

ROSA

Leo tosses the jewelry box carelessly over his shoulder when he gets back into the car and lapses back into a brooding silence. It lands on the back seat.

As for me, I'm trying not to freak out.

My engagement ring is beautiful. Large diamonds leave me cold—I never wanted a giant rock on my finger. I prefer smaller, more delicate pieces of jewelry, pieces that aren't so expensive that I spend my life in terror of losing them. But there was something about the pink diamond. I couldn't take my eyes off it.

But the price... Oh God. Leo whipped out a black credit card and handed it to the salesman like it was *no big deal*. I caught a glimpse of the receipt, and it was the number two, followed by a truly eye-popping number of zeros.

Two hundred thousand euros. I feel faint. I could run my business for the next two years for the amount of money Leo spent on my engagement ring. I could exhibit at Milan Fashion Week without wondering if I could afford it. I would never have to fret about the number of customers walking through my boutique door, worrying if I'd earned enough to make rent.

"Can I ask you a question?"

"You just did."

I bite my lip, not knowing how to bring up the subject. "Are you secretly rich?" Leo works for the Venetian Mafia, and he's one of their top lieutenants, but even so, that shouldn't extend to dropping two hundred grand on a diamond ring. Especially when it's an arranged marriage that he clearly doesn't want to be in.

I don't expect him to solve my curiosity, but he does. "It's not that much of a secret," he says. "I was illegitimate. My married father had an affair with my mother but cut off contact when he found out she was pregnant. My mother never talked about him, and I never met the bastard. He died when I was thirty, and there were no other heirs. I inherited all his money." He shrugs his shoulders. "There's a lot. I generally want nothing to do with it, but it's useful from time to time." He gives me an amused look. "Look happier, Rosa. You get to spend it all."

I doubt Leo will appreciate me spending his money on fabric. "Do you want a prenup?"

He rolls his eyes. "What's a prenup going to do? If you leave me, your brother dies." He opens his door. "Let's go break the happy news to your parents. Should I ask your father for your hand in marriage?"

My parents. "Hang on. If we go in and I introduce you as my boyfriend, my mother will have a thousand questions about how we met. We need to get our stories straight." Oh, crap. Earlier this evening, she asked me if I was seeing someone, and I said no. How am I going to explain this?

Leo looks impatient. "Make something up. I'll go along with it."

"And if we're separated? My dad is always rebuilding one car or the other. He's going to want to show that off to you. If he asks you a question, then what are you going to say?"

"Okay, fine. Let's just stick to a version of the truth. I met you in December, we've known each other for nine months, and yes, that's quick, but when you know, you know."

His tone is mocking. I dig my nails into my palms so I don't react. *When you know, you know.* The sentiment is perfect, and he doesn't mean a damn word. "I can't tell them you work for the Mafia."

"Tell them I work in private security," he replies. "I'll handle the follow-up questions. Anything else?"

I'm not looking forward to the next few hours. I might fudge the truth here and there about my dating life to preserve the peace, but I've never outright lied to my parents, and certainly not about something as big as this. "Umm. . ."

"You're stalling," he points out. "It'll be fine. I promise I'll survive the interrogation. I even promise not to strangle your idiot brother." He gets out, comes around my side, and opens my door. "Shall we, principessa?"

I fold my arms across my chest and glare at him. I want to throw something at him. A rotten egg, maybe, and watch the yolk drip down his elegant nose. "If you keep calling me principessa in that mocking tone, I'm going to strangle you myself."

"You?" His gaze slides over my body, slow and assessing. "I'm terrified."

A ripple of excitement flows through me like a live current at his appraisal. "You shouldn't underestimate me. I've been taking MMA classes for three years."

"Have you now?" His smile grows. "I'm intrigued. Will you show me your skills, Rosa? Are you going to pin me down on the mat?" The words could be interpreted as innocuous, but his tone is openly carnal, and a shiver of need runs through my body.

Leo *notices*. He opens his mouth to say something else, and then his expression shutters. "Come on," he says. "Let's go deal with your family."

8
LEO

Rosa's parents live in a small terracotta-roofed house on the outskirts of town, closer to the beach than to the city center. The compound is enclosed by a three-foot tall cinder-block wall, and the small front garden has a handful of flowering shrubs in it.

It's a security nightmare of a location, but that doesn't matter. I can't protect them in Lecce. It could be a fortress, and I still wouldn't be comfortable leaving them here. They're going to need to move to Venice.

We get out of the car, and Rosa straightens her shoulders. "To answer your earlier question, no. You don't have to ask my father for my hand in marriage. I'm not *property*. That's a ridiculously sexist custom."

A strand of her jet-black hair comes loose from the ponytail at the back of her neck, and she makes an impatient noise, removes the band, shakes her hair free, and then ties it back again. "Trust me, you won't get any opposition from them. They won't care who I'm marrying; they're just going to be delighted I'm doing it."

"Why?"

She opens the outside gate. "As my mother likes to remind me, she had a child when she was my age, and I've never even had a serious boyfriend."

"You've never had a serious boyfriend?"

"Nope."

Why not? I want to probe, but Rosa's opening her front door, and I'm distracted by the fact that they don't lock it. Yup, they're definitely moving to Venice as quickly as I can arrange it. Once the deal with Santini is made, I doubt he's going to want them to stick around anyway.

The door opens to a small living room. It's filled with things—two couches, a television, houseplants in blue and white pots, and another collection of red vases on the coffee table—but everything is spotlessly clean, and there's not a speck of dust anywhere.

I remember the glimpse I caught of Rosa's apartment. I don't remember much of it—my attention was on her, not her surroundings, especially when the strap of the silk slip she was wearing slid off her shoulder, offering me a tantalizing look at her small, luscious breast. But if my recollection is right, every table surface was covered in fabric, thread, and tissue paper. This place could not be a bigger contrast.

"Rosa, where did you go?" Her mother comes into the room, a harried look on her face. "I've been worried sick. Hugh still won't tell me what's going on, then you take off. Your father is fiddling with his car again, and you know that means he's going to get engine grease all over his nice shirt. Honestly, it's a shock—"

Then she notices me, and her flow of conversation abruptly cuts off. "Who is this?"

"Mẹ, this is Leo Cesari." Rosa sounds nervous. "My boyfriend. Leo, my mother, Elaine Tran."

Rosa's mother is five-foot-five and slim, her black hair cut fashionably short. She's wearing a purple dress with a flared skirt. I don't know anything about women's clothes, but even I can tell this is something special. The fabric has a subtle shimmer and drapes beautifully. I wonder if it's one of Rosa's designs.

"Boyfriend?" Her eyes narrow. "I thought you said you weren't seeing anyone."

"Leo and I had a fight." Rosa laces her fingers with mine. "I thought it was a relationship-ending one." She looks up at me, a smile in her eyes. "But then he showed up."

She really is a good actress. Everything about her performance is pitch-perfect. "To apologize," I add. "And grovel. You were right, principessa. You're always right."

"I'm going to remember you said that," she quips.

Her father walks into the room just then, wiping his hands on a rag. "You *did* work on that car with your nice shirt on," Elaine says, throwing up her hands in the air in exasperation. "But never mind about that. Ben, look. Rosa has a boyfriend."

"I'm Leo Cesari." I shake his hand. "Good to meet you, Signor Tran."

Ben Tran surveys me with narrowed eyes. No doubt he's noticing the grey hair at my temples, the lines on my face that clearly telegraph that my youth is in the past. But he doesn't say anything about my age, not yet. "Rosa has a boyfriend? Since when?"

"We've been dating since December," Rosa replies.

Her mother opens her mouth to ask another

question, but Rosa jumps in first. "I thought Leo could join us for dinner."

"Dinner?" Hugh Tran finally makes an appearance. "You sure that's a good idea?"

I give him an assessing glance. Rosa's brother looks extremely young. He's twenty-two, Valentina said, but he looks younger than that. His expression alternates between fear and bravado. "Hey," he says. "I'm Hugh."

"Leo." I shake his hand. "I'm Rosa's boyfriend."

"Boyfriend? But I thought—"

This idiot is going to ruin everything. "Yes," I say firmly. "Boyfriend. Dinner sounds excellent." I glance at my watch. "Rosa tells me your reservation is for eight-thirty. We should go, yes? I'm afraid I've already delayed Signora Tran's birthday dinner."

"Not at all. And please, call me Elaine." She gives me a long look. "After all, we're practically the same age."

It was only going to be a matter of time before the age gap between Rosa and me came up, but still. *Ouch.*

Rosa takes a seat across from me at the restaurant. Elaine is next to me, and Ben sits across from her. Hugh is at the head of the table.

The waitress fills our glasses with water and hands us menus. I grab her attention and order a couple of bottles of wine for the table. I barely have a chance to glance at the menu when the questioning begins. "Tell me, Leo," Elaine says. "How did you and Rosa meet?"

A slight smile tips the corner of Rosa's mouth. She predicted questions, and she was right. I've never had to 'meet the parents.' Patrizia was the girl next door, and I knew her mother all my life. I have no need to impress Elaine or Ben—I'm not desperately in love with their daughter, and I don't need their approval—but their scrutiny still feels discomfiting.

"We met through a mutual friend," I reply. "Valentina Linari."

"The one who just got married?" Elaine asks

Rosa. "The one who set up the website for your little business?"

She puts business in air quotes. "Yes, that's her," Rosa replies.

If she's bothered by her mother's dismissiveness, she doesn't show it. But I'm nowhere as calm as she is. I'm angry on Rosa's behalf. Fashion is a brutally difficult business, one that chews up designers and spits them out, but she has more than held her own. She has a boutique in Dorsoduro, one of the trendiest parts of Venice, and every time I walk by, it's filled with shoppers. According to Valentina, dozens of women are lined up for a custom Rosa Tran wedding gown.

"Rosa's little business, as you put it, is doing extremely well," I say, keeping my voice mild with effort. "She's so successful that she's got a waitlist for her services. I'm very proud of her."

Rosa's head snaps up in shock. Elaine gives me a rather strained smile. "So are we," she says placatingly. "What do you do, Leo? Do you also build websites?"

"No, I work in private security."

"What does that mean?"

"When celebrities come to Venice, they'll sometimes bring their own bodyguards, but most of the time, they contract out for protection." The lie falls easily from my lips. This is my standard cover story. "My firm handles the details."

"Is there a lot of demand for that kind of thing?" Ben asks skeptically.

"You'd be surprised," I say blandly. "I do okay." It's a real job, the one I'm describing. My friend Zade owns a company that does this kind of work, and he makes an extremely good living.

"And why are you dating a woman half your age?"

"Bő," Rosa protests. "Leo is our guest. I don't think—"

She's not half my age, thank fuck. That's about the only thing I can say in my defense. Still, her father's not wrong—Rosa is entirely too young for me. If it wasn't for her idiot brother, I would have never gotten involved with her.

That's not what you thought at Valentina's wedding.

"That's okay, *principessa*," I say. "Let me reply." I face her father squarely. "Rosa's twenty-five, and I'm forty-one. She's sixteen years younger than me. It's a significant difference; I'm not going to pretend otherwise." I smile at Rosa. "The first time I set eyes on her, I knew she was someone special. I tried to stay away, but—"

"I wouldn't let him," she says. Her voice is sweet, but there's a sharp edge underneath, one only I seem to be able to hear because, for some reason, Rosa's family doesn't *see* her. "Like you said, Leo, when you know, you know."

Elaine glares at her husband. "She's finally seeing someone, and you're scaring him off?" She pats my shoulder. "Don't let Ben get to you, Leo. Forty-one is nothing. You're in the prime of your life."

Somebody kill me now. Thankfully, the waitress shows up before the conversation can get more awkward. "Do you know what you'd like to eat?" she asks us, notepad at the ready. "Our specialty is lobster in a garlic butter sauce, served with the vegetable of the day. Today, it's broccoli and red peppers."

"That's what I'm having," Elaine declares immediately.

"Me too," Hugh says. He gives his sister a slyly amused look. "What about you, chi? I'm assuming you're going to spare the lobster's feelings by getting something else?"

Once again, Rosa ignores the bait. "I'll have the vegetable pasta," she says, handing the waitress her menu. "Thank you."

The waitress turns to me. "And you, Signor?"

I just met these people. I don't know what their deal is, but I don't like the way they put Rosa down. First, her mother dismisses her accomplishments, and now Hugh is mocking his sister because she's too soft-hearted to order a lobster? Given what we're doing to save his ass, you think he'd shut up and be grateful, but no.

"I'll have the pasta too."

Hugh really doesn't know when to shut up. "Oh God, Leo. Don't tell me that my sister has roped you into her ridiculous quest to save the animals."

I give him an icy glare. "Just so we're clear, my girlfriend's feelings are *never* ridiculous." Oh, what the hell? I was going to wait until after the meal but fuck that. I top up my wine glass and get to my feet. "I was going to hold on until later, but I can't wait another second." I pull the square box out of my jacket pocket. Flipping it open, I hold it out to my fake girlfriend. "Rosa Tran, there are no words to describe how I feel about you. You make my life better just by being in it. Will you marry me, principessa?"

She gives me a long look. The candles on the table make her deep brown eyes seem almost luminous. And then she smiles, wide and fake, and leaps to her feet. "Yes," she squeals. "Yes, orsacchiotto mio, yes."

I slide the ring on her delicate finger, the diamond glowing against her golden skin. I expect to feel a strong sense of wrongness, but strangely, I don't. Instead, I'm thinking, *orsacchiotto mio?* Did she just call me *her teddy bear?*

We're *really* going to have to work on that nickname.

9
ROSA

Predictably, my mother is thrilled. "My baby girl is getting married at last," she says, dabbing her eyes with a handkerchief. My news has temporarily pushed her worries about Hugh to the background, and for that, I'm thankful. It's her birthday. She should enjoy it. "I thought this day would never come. And the ring." I dutifully hold out my hand so she can admire the huge pink diamond. "So large," she coos. "And so shiny. This must have been really expensive, Leo."

She has no idea.

Leo gives me a tender smile. "There isn't a diamond in the world good enough for Rosa."

My parents beam. Hugh's eyes stay fixed on Leo. My brother isn't an idiot, and he's got to know all of this is fake. Thankfully, he's smart enough not to ask questions in front of our parents.

"Do you know if you want a long engagement or a short one?" my dad asks.

"We haven't decided," Leo responds. "But soon." He reaches across the table and takes my hand in his. "I know I don't want to wait."

He's a really good actor. Everything he's said and done in the last hour has been perfect. When my mom was dismissive of my boutique, Leo came to my defense. I didn't realize he knew I now have a waitlist for my custom-designed wedding gowns. Valentina probably mentioned it in passing, and he *remembered.* He ordered the vegetarian pasta instead of the lobster, all because I told him I couldn't bring myself to eat them.

But I have to remember that Leo is playing a part. None of this is real, and if I allow myself to forget that, I'll be in a world of hurt.

LEO KISSES my cheek in view of my parents when he drops me off after dinner. "Look excited," he murmurs. "We have an audience."

"Who?" My heartbeat quickens, and I tell myself it's because of the danger. My reaction isn't a response to his touch—how can it be? It's a quick kiss, the barest brushing of lips against skin. The kind of casual kiss I offer a thousand times a day, a gesture of greeting between acquaintances. But when Leo nears me, the smell of him fills my nostrils and sets my head spinning. He smells clean and freshly showered. There's something else, too, but it's a scent I can't put my finger on. I think it's Leo himself. There's something strong and steady about him, and it comes through to all my senses.

"One of Santini's goons, probably."

I swallow. "Already?"

"Hmm." He squeezes my hand. "They've agreed to a truce," he says into my ear. "The consequences of breaking it are severe. So wipe that expression of fear off your face, principessa."

Easier said than done. I imagine that I can feel the mafia hitman staring at the back of my head, and it freaks me out. My mother's standing in the doorway of the house, a clear target for a stray gunshot. I want to scream at her to go inside. Shut the curtains and barricade the doors as if that'll serve as a deterrent for the people determined to kill us all.

I cling to Leo for another greedy second, wishing I could absorb his strength just by hugging him. I'm trembling, and Leo can undoubtedly feel my terror. He hugs me back, his hand stroking the small of my back. "Antonio and I are meeting Rocco Santini at midnight," he says, his voice gentle. "We're going to sort this out. You'll be safe, Rosa. You have my word."

I need to pull myself together. Leo comforting me isn't part of our deal, and I don't want to ask for more than he's prepared to offer. I take a deep breath and pull away from him. "Sorry. Momentary freak-out. It won't happen again."

"You have nothing to apologize for."

He turns to leave, and I stop him with a hand on his arm. "Leo. This meeting at midnight. . . You must have done something this dangerous dozens of times, and it's probably ridiculous to tell you to be careful, but please, be careful."

A strange expression fills his face. "You're worried about me?"

What a strange question. "Of course I am."

He studies my face. "You're not lying," he says, astonished. "You really are worried. I think it's the first time anyone's been concerned for me." His big hand cups my jaw, and his ocean-blue eyes soften. "I'll be fine. Sleep well, principessa. I'll see you tomorrow morning."

I'M READING for bed when there's a knock at the door. It's Hugh. "Do you have a minute, chi?"

"Sure." He's got to have a million questions about my sham marriage, and I have just as many about what the hell he's gotten himself into. Hopefully, the lobster put him in a talkative mood.

He comes into the room and sinks onto my bed. "Who is Leo?" he asks. "And how were we safe enough to go out for dinner?"

"He's the head of security for the Venice Mafia." I tell my brother everything I know, which isn't a lot. "The truce is in effect until midnight. I'll know more tomorrow after Leo's meeting."

"You can't marry him," he bursts out. "I can't let you sacrifice your life for me."

I was afraid he'd say something like this. If Hugh thinks even for a second that I'm having any misgivings, he's going to blow up the entire deal. "Hugh," I say briskly. "Come on. Look at the guy. Being married to him isn't going to be a hardship."

He studies me carefully. "You like him, don't you?"

Sometimes, I really wish I had a poker face. "Yup, I do."

"He likes you too." His glance falls to my ring. "That's a huge diamond."

"It cost two hundred thousand euros," I reply, taking it off so my brother can take a closer look. Hugh went through a gemstone phase as a teenager. "The sales guy in the store nearly had an aneurysm when Leo whipped out his credit card."

He brings the diamond closer to his nose. "You saw the receipt?"

"I caught a glimpse of it. Why?"

"No reason." He hands the ring back to me, a small smile playing on his lips. "He likes you too, you know. You should have seen the way he looked at you at dinner. And he kept jumping to your defense." He laughs. "He nearly punched me when I teased you about the lobster. I was wondering how he'd react."

Hugh did that deliberately? My brother really has a death wish. "You're lucky he didn't punch you."

I should stop there, but a stupid, romantic part of me keeps going. "How did he look at me?"

"Like he can't quite believe he gets to be with you."

I wish. If Leo looks like he's been hit by a boulder, it's probably because he's wondering how the hell he's been roped into marriage with me. Not to mention two to three years of celibacy.

That's Future-Rosa's problem. Right now, I have my brother to worry about. I sit down on the bed next to him and lean on his shoulder. "Ten million euros, Hugh. Did you invest it in the stock market? In crypto? What happened? How did you lose that much money?"

His eyes drop away from me, and he worries the fringe on my bedspread. "It's complicated."

My stomach sinks. If Hugh's being evasive, that's not a good sign. I have a bad feeling that there's a lot more going on than he's letting on. But maybe I'm just being paranoid. After all, it's been a very difficult day. Maybe I'm imagining it.

"Leo and Antonio Moretti are negotiating with Rocco Santini *right now*. This is not the time to be cagey. If there's something they need to know—"

"There isn't." There's no certainty in his tone. "He won't... They don't know..." He gets to his feet abruptly. "None of that matters now. It's over. Everything will be okay once we leave for Venice."

I stare after his departing back. Antonio and Leo are going to negotiate with the Mafia here, and my family's problems should be over once they make a deal. But I have a very bad feeling they're just beginning.

10

LEO

The restaurant where we meet Rocco Santini screams Mafia so badly that it's almost a parody. The room is long and narrow. To the left is a bar where a handful of patrons sit, their eyes glued to the soccer match on the screen behind the counter. Lecce is playing, doing their best to avoid relegation. To the right, a couple of guys play billiards on a table that's seen better days.

The padrino and I are in enemy territory. Every single person here is a foot soldier of Spina Sacra.

Antonio and I walk in together. A man tears himself from the football long enough to pat us down. "What are you doing, you idiot?" Rocco

Santini chides from a table in the back. "What's the point of searching them for weapons? They don't need guns or knives; Cesari is the weapon."

I see that my reputation precedes me.

The foot soldier waves us through to Santini's table. The Mafia leader isn't alone. A younger man, early thirties from the look of it, sits next to him, his hand curled casually over a glass of red wine. I don't know him. It's not Lorenzo Corio, Santini's second-in-command, who is, like his boss, in his mid-sixties.

Rocco doesn't stand up to greet us. "Sit," he says shortly, indicating the chairs next to him. He performs perfunctory introductions. "Max Guerra, meet Antonio Moretti and Leonardo Cesari."

We take our seats. A cocktail waitress wearing a very short skirt shows up to take our drink orders. "I'll have whatever Signor Santini is having," Antonio says.

"Just water for me, please," I say. "Sparkling, if you have it." I've done a lot of drinking today. Prosecco for breakfast, vodka for lunch, and a couple of glasses of wine with dinner as a way to get through the proposal. Though it hadn't been as hard as I imagined to sell the lie to Rosa's parents.

"Water?" Santini gives me an exaggerated look of shock. "No, no, that won't do. Maria, bring us a bottle of wine. A good bottle, something from the cellar. We have to celebrate Cesari's engagement." His tone is jovial, but his eyes stay cold. "A very surprising engagement. Not to mention sudden."

Antonio leans back in his chair and stretches his legs out. "Surprising?" he asks, his voice unconcerned. "Why would you think that?"

"Because of what happened the last time Leo Cesari got married." Rocco surveys me thoughtfully. "It was my understanding that you swore to never repeat the experience."

Don't react. You knew they'd find out about Patrizia; this isn't a surprise.

Guerra speaks up. "Also, there have been no signs that Cesari is dating Rosa Tran." He sets his wine glass on the table. "No romantic evenings together. No candlelight dinners, no holding hands and strolling through la Piazza."

Damn it. "You can't stroll through la Piazza," I say snidely. "It's too crowded with tourists."

Guerra continues as if I hadn't spoken. "The happy couple doesn't live together. At Signor Colonna's wedding, they danced together but left separately."

To gather this information in a matter of hours. .

. I have no idea who Max Guerra is, but he makes a formidable opponent.

The waitress shows up with a bottle of Barolo. She shows the label to Rocco, who nods his approval. She must sense the tension in the air because her hand trembles as she pours the wine into our glasses. She scampers away as soon as she's done.

"I don't do my courting in public." I take a sip of the full-bodied red. "Too many prying eyes."

"That's one explanation," Santini says. The affable tone is gone; we're done celebrating my engagement. "The other explanation is that you're trying to save Tran's life by entering into this marriage, thereby forcing the obligation of a blood claim upon me."

I open my mouth to respond. Antonio gives me a discreet hand signal and sets his glass down. "It sounds like you're calling me a liar, Rocco," he says, his voice frosty. "That's an unfortunate accusation."

Santini backs down. "I'm just listing the possibilities." He knows as well as we do that if the South went to war with the North, the only people who would win are the Russians. Plus, there's enough infighting in Spina Sacra that an ambitious clan member would stab him in the back. It's not worth it, not for the life of one upstart financial adviser.

"Let's lay our cards on the table," he continues. "Ten million euros have gone missing. I can't wave away that loss. Before I can commit to anything, I need to be made whole."

Ten million euros have gone missing. That's an interesting way to phrase it. According to Rosa's hasty explanation, her brother lost the money in an investment gone wrong. But that's not what Santini is implying. Surely the boy wasn't stupid enough to steal from them?

The Mafia boss suspects something, but he doesn't have proof. If he did, not even the blood claim would keep him from exacting vengeance. Losing Spina Sacra's money might be forgiven under the right set of circumstances, but stealing? Never.

Hugh Tran is young and stupid, and Santini is a lying snake. I don't trust either of them.

Antonio nods, his face expressionless. "Leo is a valuable member of my team, and I don't want him to start his marriage on a sour note. The Trans are now family. I will be happy to cover their debt."

"Good." Santini's expression is sour. "When's the wedding?"

"We haven't set a date."

His eyes narrow. "Set one," he says coldly. "And make it soon. I want to dance at Cesari's wedding."

Guerra's lips tighten in annoyance, but he doesn't say anything to contradict his boss. "Next month, then," Antonio responds. "Is that soon enough for you?"

"Yes." Santini leans forward. "Let's talk terms."

The two of them start to haggle. I listen to the conversation, my thoughts drifting. Rosa was worried about me. It's been a long time since someone's cared enough to worry. I thought it would feel constrictive, but it didn't.

I didn't know she took MMA classes. I think about her in gym clothes, shorts gripping her round ass, sweat dripping down her body, her hands up and her legs spread in a boxer's stance, and my cock stirs. Fuck me, but I want to wrestle her into submission, lay her down on the mat, part her legs, and lick her until she comes. I want—

"Good, we have a deal." Antonio's voice jerks me from my thoughts. I replay the last couple of minutes of the conversation. I'm getting married to Rosa next month, Rocco Santini will be attending the wedding, and the Trans have to leave Lecce within the week. In exchange for ten million euros and a new trade route for smuggled goods, Spina Sacra will renounce their retribution.

Rosa's brother is going to be okay.

"We do," Santini agrees sourly. "But be warned, Moretti. Money comes and goes like rain from the sky. What separates a man from the beast is honor. Tran has besmirched mine." He gives me a long look. "But if I get the slightest sign that this is all a ruse—"

Antonio gets to his feet. "We're done here." He shakes Santini's hand. "Pleasure doing business with you."

IT'S DRIZZLING OUTSIDE. A cloudy, starless night. We walk in silence to Antonio's car. Once we're safely inside, Antonio calls Valentina. It's late, but she picks up on the first ring. "We got a deal done," he says. "Nobody dies."

She exhales in relief. "Thank you, padrino."

"Don't thank me, thank Leo." His fingers beat a restless dance on the steering wheel. "Max Guerra. I want a dossier on him as soon as possible. Drop everything else you're working on. Oh, and also, send me a copy of your wedding guest list, please."

"My wedding guest list?" Valentina asks, sounding confused.

"Yes. Someone there talked to Spina Sacra. I want to know who."

He hangs up, and we drive in silence. The wipers move back and forth, cleaning the raindrops that splatter the windshield, their movement hypnotic. "They have eyes in Venice," he says finally. His voice is level, but I know the padrino. He's furious.

"Yes."

"Venice is impossible to secure. Too many damn tourists." A muscle ticks in his cheek. "Santini's itching for a war."

"I got that sense, too. Any idea why?"

"Who knows? Maybe Tran really did steal the money, like he implied."

So Antonio caught that as well. I'm not surprised.

"Find out what happened to it, if you can," he continues. "But if I had to guess, I'd say the money is a smokescreen. Santini is looking for a fight so he can clean house in the tumult." He shakes his head. "All that talk about honor. His daughter is twenty-six,

The Fixer

and he married her off to Lorenzo Corio. A sixty-five-year-old abusive alcoholic."

I didn't know that. I try to ignore the uncomfortable parallels. Sure, I'm not abusive or an alcoholic—today's drinking spree is an exception, not the rule—but the age difference between Rosa and I is almost as bad. "Why?"

"Santini has a son, Romeo, that he's grooming to be his successor. But Corio also wants the top job. He was getting restive, so Santini sold his daughter to him to keep him happy." His lips twist. "A man like that wouldn't know what honor is if it slapped him in the face." He glances at me. "I don't want a war," he says. "For a thousand little reasons and one very big one. Lucia is pregnant."

For the first time today, my heart lightens. "She is? Padrino, my congratulations."

"Thank you. It's early. We're not telling anyone yet." His expression is very serious. "Know this, Leo. I will sacrifice Hugh Tran and Rosa's entire family before I raise my child in a war zone. Santini's itching for a fight. It's up to you to defuse the situation."

I take a deep breath, afraid of where this is going.

"As soon as the two of you get back home, move in together. Dates, romantic evenings, candlelight dinners—do them all. Have dinner with her family every week. Everyone—and I mean everyone—needs to believe this is a real marriage. Do I make myself clear?"

Fuck. I thought I had time to get used to this situation, but I don't. My window just evaporated.

"Yes, *padrino.*"

11

ROSA

It takes me until three in the morning to fall asleep. When I finally drift off, my rest is plagued by terrible dreams, all connected to my upcoming marriage. I show up at the altar, dressed in a beautiful lace wedding gown, and Leo isn't there. I show up at the altar, a veil covering my face, and when Leo lifts it and sees me there, he recoils. I show up at the altar, and Leo is there, dressed in a crumpled white shirt and faded jeans. "Your brother is dead," he says. "Why would I want to marry you now?"

At seven, my mother bangs on my door. "Rosa, wake up. There's a delivery here for you."

A delivery? I pull on my pajama bottoms, duck into the bathroom to quickly brush my teeth, and head downstairs. There's a giant bouquet of roses in a crystal vase on the dining table. These aren't huge, showy blooms with petals the color of blood. No, these look like wild roses—softer, prettier, and delicately fragrant—in colors that range from the softest blush pink to a brighter magenta hue, and there are dozens of them. *Dozens.*

My mother comes up next to me. "I counted. He sent you a hundred roses."

Oh, wow. I bury my nose in them and breathe in their aroma. Nobody has ever given me a vase overflowing with flowers, like a summer garden come to life.

"Last night," she continues, "I was a little concerned about the age difference between you two, but then this bouquet arrived, and I was reassured. He knows you well, your Leo. You wouldn't have been happy with a dozen red roses, so instead, he sends you a hundred pink ones."

I look among the blooms for a note, but there isn't one. "I'm happy anytime someone sends me flowers," I tell my mother. I'm trying to play it cool, but there's a lump in my throat, and it isn't because I haven't yet had coffee. "*Were* you concerned? I couldn't tell. You were so thrilled I'm finally getting married. After all, as you keep telling me, by the time you were my age—"

"I was married with a child." My mother lets my mild admonishment glide off her back. "You should hurry on that, by the way," she says. "Don't put off having children. You're young enough, but Leo isn't."

I stare at her in astonishment. "Mę, I just got engaged. Are you honestly pestering me about kids *already?*" Not that I have any idea how I'm going to produce kids if Leo's refusing to sleep with me. Also, Future-Rosa's problem.

My mother has the grace to look a little embarrassed. "It's a mother's job to worry," she responds. "But you're right. I will not nag you until after the wedding. Don't wait too long to get married, though. You want tea?"

I TAKE my roses upstairs while my mother sets the kettle to boil. As I'm doing that, my phone buzzes with a message from Leo.

> Have breakfast with me at nine.

He follows that message with the address of a cafe by the beach. I fight the urge to reply with snark and fail miserably.

> Yes, my lord and master. I live to obey.

> Somehow, principessa, I very much doubt it.

There's also a message from Valentina, who wants me to call her as soon as I'm awake. My friend is, like me, a night owl. Unlike me, she has a child, which means she's also forced to wake up early to do parent stuff. As a result, she has the weirdest sleep schedule of anyone I know. She sleeps between two and six in the morning, and then once Angelica has eaten breakfast and is off to school, she goes back to bed for a few more hours.

I call her. She sounds like she's in the middle of breakfast prep. "Hang on a sec," she says. "Let me turn the cooking over to Dante."

"Can he manage?" I quip. Valetina's husband has many good qualities, but cooking isn't one of them.

She laughs. "Toast is within his skill set." She puts me on mute for thirty seconds, and then she returns. "So. Yesterday was a lot. How are you doing?"

How am I doing? My head is spinning, my sleepless night catching up to me, and the tension of the last twelve hours has given me a headache. "I'm relieved Hugh is going to be alright and so grateful. Thank you for your help."

"I barely did anything," she responds. She pauses, and I get the impression she's choosing her next words carefully. "What did Leo tell you?"

"He wants a marriage in name only. We'll have to pretend in public, but that's it." I pull a rose out of the arrangement and stroke its blush-pink petals. "I can never repay Leo. He didn't have to get involved, but he did."

"Did he say why he's doing it?"

Every word Leo said to me is etched in my memory. "He said he owes you a debt, and this will help pay it off."

"I love Leo like a brother, but I want to strangle him right now," Valentina snaps. "There is no debt. There's never been a debt, and even if there had been one, Leo's paid it off already. I've said this to him a thousand times, and he refuses to listen." She exhales in a long breath. "Anyway. How are you doing?"

Valentina and I have been friends for half a dozen years now. She knows, more than most, how much I wanted someone to fall madly in love with me. She understands I'm searching for someone who would put me first, no matter what.

"You already asked me that," I point out.

"And you gave me some bullshit about your family. Forget them for a second. Tell me how *you* are. This marriage couldn't have been what you wanted—"

"It doesn't matter," I interrupt. "I'm doing this to save Hugh's life. It's worth it." I blink away the tears that appear out of nowhere. "I'm grateful Leo's being honest with me. I'd rather know the truth than hope for—" I cut myself off before I can say anything else. Valentina already knows I'm attracted to Leo, but there's no need to be pathetic about it. "We'll largely lead separate lives. We're both adults; we can make this work. And anyway, we haven't even picked a date for the wedding. Everything feels strange now, but I'll get used to the situation."

"Your brother fucks up, and you pay the price?" Her voice is sharp. "How is that fair?"

"It isn't." But it's the way it's always been. When we were kids, Hugh would be careless with his toys, and I was expected to give him mine. He would demand a large ice cream cone, and when he spilled it on the ground, I would be told to share my own. There's a reason I'm in an MMA class three times a week, taking out my frustrations in the ring. "What would you have me do instead, Valentina? Should I stand by and watch the Mafia kill my brother? My father and my mother, too?"

"Fair enough," she says with a sigh. She's silent for a long time. "Rosa, listen. I should probably just mind my own business, but you're my friend. Underneath that gruff, grumpy exterior, Leo is a good guy who always comes through for the people in his life. I don't think he agreed to marry you to pay off a debt. It's more than that. I honestly believe he didn't want you to face the pain of your family's death."

"He's chaining himself to me for the rest of his life because he doesn't want to see me sad? I thought I was the romantic here."

"All I'm saying is, he's not indifferent to you. You might not have had a choice about entering this marriage, but you do have control over how it goes. There is definite chemistry between the two of you. The first time you met, Leo couldn't take his eyes off you."

"He couldn't take his eyes off my boobs, you mean."

She chuckles. "In his defense, you were practically flashing him. In any case, you have cause for optimism. This doesn't have to be a loveless, sexless marriage."

"It's what Leo wants."

"So what?" she retorts. "Stop worrying about your family, and stop fretting about Leo. It's time to start thinking about yourself. What do *you* want, Rosa? Figure out what that is, and then go get it."

I STARE at the flowers for a long time after my phone call. Soft pink roses, not red, because I said I didn't like showy pieces, and Leo deduced that my sentiments about jewelry would extend to flowers. Vegetarian pasta, not lobster, because I couldn't bear to think about the way the creatures were cooked.

Valentina is right: I do have cause for optimism.

Leo keeps calling me principessa. And in all my favorite fairy tales, the princess doesn't wait around to be rescued. She saves herself.

I'm getting married to Leo. I don't want to cheat on him. I don't want to wait two years and then take a secret lover, and I certainly don't want him to do the same.

I want a real marriage. I want my happy ending. I don't want to give up on my dreams, not without a fight. Even if I'm risking heartbreak, I have to try. Leo might want a marriage in name only, but I'm going to do my best to change his mind.

Breakfast is at nine. That gives me an hour and a half to sew up a dress that will leave him speechless.

Operation Make Leo Cesari Fall In Love With Rosa Tran starts today.

12

LEO

Do I dream about Rosa when I finally fall asleep? Of course I do. I dream about her all night long, the images vivid and carnal because my subconscious is a dick and loves to torture me.

She's dressed in a wedding gown, all white silk and lace, a sheer veil obscuring her face. The neckline scoops low, exposing the swell of her high, round breasts. She glides down to the altar, and when she reaches me, I sink to my knees. It's not her veil I'm planning to raise—no, Dream-Me has an entirely different plan in mind. "Hold up your skirt, principessa."

She obediently hikes up her skirt. Her stockings are white and sheer, held up with garters and a belt that cinches her narrow waist. Ignoring our assembled guests, I kiss my way up her silk-clad leg until I get to her bare flesh. The brown-gold of her skin is a vibrant contrast to the white of her gown, and I lick that spot until she moans and her legs fall apart.

God, she's perfect.

The gusset of her panties is damp from her arousal. I slide my finger under the elastic, seeking her hot nub. "Leo," she moans. "Please."

"You like this, principessa?" I pull the scrap of lace down her hips and kiss her mound. Her knees buckle, and she loses her grip on her dress. It slides down, brushing my shoulders. "You like it when I pleasure you with my mouth? My tongue?"

She tastes like chocolate dotted with sea salt, like the clean tang of the ocean breeze. She's a forbidden pleasure, and I would defy the world to have her. Dream-Rosa whimpers as I circle her clit with the tip of my tongue and slide two fingers inside her tight sheath. *Mine,* I think triumphantly as her body jerks in response to my touch. They can look all they want, but that's all they can do. She's mine.

The buzzing of my phone wakes me up. My heart is pounding, and I'm drenched in sweat. Instinctive alarm shoots through me as I remember

The Fixer

every detail of my dream, and my rock-hard cock confirms an unpleasant truth.

I'm attracted to Rosa. I've been attracted to her since the first time I met her, and my feelings haven't changed in the last nine months. So far, I've kept things under control by avoiding her as much as possible.

But that's no longer an option. We're getting married, and she's going to be living with me.

And somehow, I'm going to have to keep my hands off my *wife*.

Fuck.

THE COFFEE SHOP I chose is right next to the beach. I get there a few minutes in advance and scope out the joint, but I don't have long to wait. Rosa arrives promptly at nine.

Last night, she was wearing an ankle-length dress with long slits up both sides. She looked pulled-together and sophisticated.

Today though? Today, she oozes sex appeal. She's dressed in a short turquoise skirt that stops a couple of inches above her knees and a matching turquoise crop top that reveals a sliver of her midriff every time she raises her arms. She looks like a hot fifties pin-up, and I'm not the only one who thinks that. The four businessmen at the table near the window stop discussing their portfolios and openly ogle her. A young man who doesn't look a day over eighteen gives her a blatant once-over, stopping only when I give him a threatening glare. Is he blind? Can he not see my engagement ring on Rosa's finger?

She sees me, and her face lights up. "Leo," she says with a smile. This isn't the wide and obviously fake smile she gave me last night when I asked her to marry me at the seafood restaurant. No, this one is small and a little shy, and it feels like a punch to my gut.

She comes up to me. Even with the heels, her head barely reaches my chin. It doesn't deter her. She stands on tiptoe and brushes her lips against my cheek. "Thank you for the flowers. They were lovely."

It's a light, gossamer-soft kiss that ends almost as soon as it starts, designed to convince anyone watching us that we're together. But the delicate scent of her lotion fills my nostrils, roses overlaid with jasmine, and it makes my head swim. "You're welcome."

"I have no idea how you found someone to deliver them at seven in the morning."

I threw money at a florist until they agreed to cooperate. "I can be persuasive."

"I bet you can." She looks around appreciatively at the small cafe. The large window looks out on a patio and, beyond that, the ocean. "This is a lovely view."

"Do you want to sit outside?" It's not exactly the nicest day for it. The sun is hidden behind some ominous-looking thunderclouds, and it looks like it might rain at any minute. But the interior of the cafe is busy and noisy. Plus, that kid has resumed eye-fucking Rosa, and if I sit inside, I'm going to punch his face.

"I'd love that."

I nod toward the patio tables. "Why don't you grab us a spot, and I'll get breakfast. What do you want?"

"I don't know. Some kind of breakfast pastry." She reaches into her red bag. "Hang on, I'll give you some money."

"No," I say flatly.

She opens her mouth to say something, then thinks better of it. "Okay. Thank you. I'll be outside."

I get in line, watching Rosa as I wait. She picks a table with the best view of the beach. Her skirt rides up on her thighs. The flash of skin makes my cock harden and invokes a sense of deja vu. It's from my dream, I realize after a minute of thought. I kissed up her legs and bit those soft thighs in my dreams, and judging from the stirring in my groin, my cock *remembers.*

Fuck. I'm in trouble.

I ORDER one of every pastry they have on display and take it outside. Rosa looks at my loaded tray, and her lips twitch. "Let me guess, you're really hungry."

"I wasn't sure what you wanted, so I got a little of everything. One of the tarts is corn and black bean, and the other is spinach, onion, and olive."

"Thank you. I think I'll start with the spinach tart. Want half?"

Sharing food feels like a very couple-like thing to do. "Sure."

She cuts the pastry neatly into two halves and offers me one. Blowing on her cappuccino to cool the steaming beverage, she looks up at me through her long eyelashes. "What happened last night?"

"One second." I pull one of Valentina's gadgets out of my pocket, a flat round disk that's no bigger than a coaster, and power it on. "I don't exactly understand how it works, but Valentina says it prevents drones from recording our conversation."

"Ah." Rosa's expression turns sober. "I really don't like being watched all the time. Thank heavens we go back to Venice soon."

"About that..." I clear my throat. "Rocco Santini had knowledge of our movements. He knew we danced together at Valentina and Dante's wedding but that we left separately. He knew we hadn't been spending time together. I don't know how, but he has eyes in Venice."

"Could someone in your organization be a spy?"

"I doubt that." After Angelica was kidnapped, and it turned out that one of my people, Andreas, was a traitor, Dante and I did a full investigative screening on every single member of the Venice Mafia. "Chances are, he has every one of us watched as a matter of policy." I give her a wry smile. "We do the same."

"And now they're going to be watching me too." She takes a deep breath. "It's okay. I'll get used to it."

"I'm sorry," I tell her and mean it. This is my world, and while I might be used to it, Rosa's being tossed into the deep end of the pool.

"None of this is your fault." She reaches across the table and links her fingers with mine. "It's a good thing I like acting. What else happened?"

We're holding hands because Santini undoubtedly has someone watching us. That's the only reason. I'm not marveling at how soft her skin is, such a marked contrast to my own callused hands. I'm not gliding my thumb over the small scar on her fingertip, wondering how she got it. I'm not being driven insane by the distracting sliver of midriff that shows every time she moves.

I yank my thoughts away from the dangerous quicksand they've found themselves in. "The deal is done," I tell her. "And your brother is safe. But Santini's suspicious, which complicates things. We need to move in together right away, and our wedding needs to happen next month."

Her mouth falls open. "Next month?" she asks faintly. "Sure. Why not? It's not as if this isn't spectacularly bad timing or anything. Any other surprises?"

"Your family needs to leave Lecce within the week."

Her head snaps up. "Where are they going to go? What about the house, my mom's job, my dad's garage. . ." Her voice trails off, and she pushes her plate away. "It'll be safest if they move back to Venice, won't it?"

She sounds less than thrilled. She lifts her cup to take a sip of her coffee, but she's too stressed to enjoy it. "You don't sound excited by the prospect of your family moving back."

"I love my family," she replies immediately.

"Your love for them isn't in question." I squeeze her hand. "Their love for you, on the other hand. . ."

She rushes to their defense. "They love me." She hasn't pulled her hand away. Her wrist is so slender I could snap it like a twig. "They just don't understand my choice of career. My grandparents worked long and hard to give their children a better life. My parents value stability and a steady paycheck. My dad works in an auto shop, doing oil changes and tire rotations, even though his passion is auto restoration. My mother is an extremely talented painter, but she's so busy at the bank that she rarely finds time to do her art. If it were up to them, I'd make similar choices and prioritize a steady paycheck over my passion."

"You're not the one who got into trouble with the Mafia. Shouldn't they be more critical of Hugh than you?"

"That's just the way they are."

From what I saw last night, Rosa's parents clearly favor their son over their daughter. Who stands up for her? Who praises her accomplishments? Who tells her they're proud of her? No one. And she's used to it, resigned to the way things have always been, and she loves them so much that she's sacrificing the rest of her life to keep them safe.

She deserves better.

"You said that this is spectacularly bad timing. Why?"

"I've applied for a spot in Milan Fashion Week," she says. "The application only needed me to provide sketches, but if I'm selected to participate in the next round, I'll have to sew samples of the portfolio. I'll hear back from them on Friday. Three clients are coming in for wedding dress fittings this week. Next week, Gisele, my shop assistant, is heading home to Lyon for her annual holiday, and the woman I usually hire to watch the boutique while she's away emailed me two days ago to tell me she can't do it. And in the middle of all of this, I need to find my parents a place to stay in Venice at the height of tourist season." She takes a deep breath. "Sorry. I don't know why I'm unloading my problems on you. You've already done so much more than you need to. It'll be fine. I'll figure it out."

I can't offer her love. But I can be there for her in a way that her family isn't.

"You don't have to solve this alone, principessa." I cradle her hands in mine and give them a reassuring squeeze. "We're going to be married. Your problems are my problems. I've already arranged an apartment for your parents. My friend Ander runs a garage, and he's ready to hire your father. Tomas, who handles my finances, will give Hugh a job and make sure he stays out of trouble. I also have a call scheduled with the president of your mother's bank on Monday. I'm a client of some value. I'm sure that in exchange for me agreeing to bank with them, they'll move her to whatever branch she wants to work at."

She stares at me. Her eyes are brown, but that mundane word doesn't come close to describing them. Up close, there are amber and hazel flecks in them, compelling and hypnotic. "Why are you doing this?" she says softly. "Why are you helping me?"

I'm solving her problems because the world expects me to. That's all. But those aren't the words that come out of my mouth.

"You take care of everyone," I say quietly. "Let me take care of you."

The wind gusts just then, whipping her hair in front of her face. She pulls her hand away from me to tie it back into a ponytail. Her top rides up as she raises her arms, exposing her midriff even more. Desire punches me in the gut, and I fight the urge to leap across the table and stroke that bare patch of skin. "This is a really good tart," she says, not meeting my eyes. "Do you want to split the corn one with me, too? If I eat the whole thing, I won't be able to eat the almond croissant, and that's my favorite."

I can't take my eyes off her. Echoes of my dreams run through my mind like aftershocks. "If it's your favorite, why don't you eat it first?"

"You have to eat your vegetables before you can eat dessert."

"That's very proper of you." She has a crumb at the edge of her mouth. I reach out to brush it away and glide my thumb over her lower lip. "Do you always deny yourself pleasure, principessa?"

Everything recedes. The sound of the ocean waves, the chatter of the other patrons... everything fades into the background, and only Rosa is in focus. She stares at me with her luminous eyes, and I feel like I've been hypnotized. I lean in, drinking her in, all the little details that make her who she is. Her pert little nose, the small mole on her right cheek, the fullness of her lips I can't stop touching. I need to kiss her, squeeze those lush, round breasts until she moans, and when she does, I want to slide my tongue into her mouth and devour her. I want to comb my fingers through her long tresses. I want—

My phone beeps, the noise jerking me back to reality. What the fuck am I doing? Rosa is pretty, yes. Beautiful, even. But this attraction I'm feeling—I have to put a stop to it. I loved Patrizia, and I promised her my love and loyalty. It's bad enough that I'm marrying another woman. But to touch her the way I touched my lost love? Impossible. That would be a betrayal of my vows, and I won't do it.

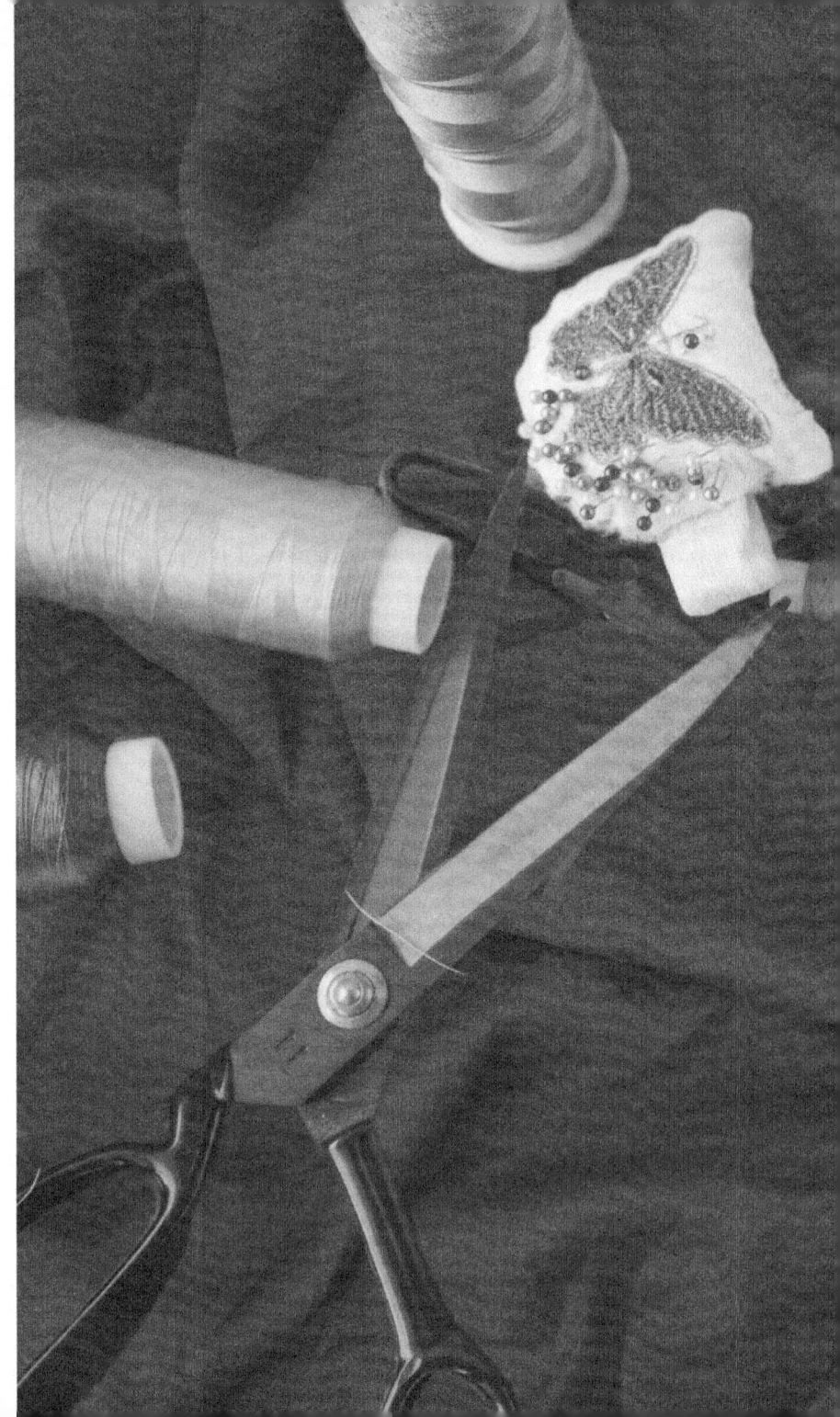

13

ROSA

Leo touches my face, and my pulse speeds up. My heart is beating so fast I'm convinced he can hear it. Every nerve ending in my body is aware of his touch. His eyes are as vividly blue as the ocean, and his expression holds me prisoner. A beat passes, and then another. Wild horses couldn't tear me away from him.

And then my phone beeps, destroying the moment. Leo's expression shutters. He drops my chin as if it scalded him and shoves the plate holding the still-uneaten almond croissant toward me. When he speaks, his voice is clipped and angry. "Eat your pastry."

"Oh." Hope, swelling inside me like a balloon, bursts into nothing. I thought for a second that Leo was going to kiss me, but he pulled away. His words echo through my mind, a cold slap of reality to my heart. *This won't be a real marriage in any sense of the word. We won't share a bed, and we won't sleep together. I'm not interested in you. There's only one reason I'm doing this, and that's to save your brother.*

I straighten my shoulders and make myself eat the croissant. It looks and smells delicious, but it tastes like ashes in my mouth.

IT'S hard to stay sad when the sun is shining and the beach is *right there.* It's hard to mope when my to-do list has a billion things on it. Well—it's hard for me to mope. Leo is brooding like a champion. By the end of the meal, I've recovered my spirits. "When are you going home?" Leo asks as we're getting up to leave.

What do you know, he still knows how to speak. "This afternoon. I'm booked on the two p.m. train."

"The train?" He frowns in disapproval. "That'll take too long. We'll fly home."

I give him my sweetest smile. "Does this usually

work for you, orsacchiotto mio?" I ask him, tilting my head to the side. "Barking orders at people?"

"I really don't like that nickname."

"Is it annoying when I keep calling you that anyway?" I raise an eyebrow. "Imagine that."

His lips twitch. "Touché, principessa. I strongly recommend we fly home. It's safer."

My heart does an uncomfortable lurch. "You think there's still danger?"

"I'm alive because I'm paranoid," he replies. "There's a two o'clock flight to Venice. I would like us to take it."

That's almost a request. Baby steps. "Okay. I can pay you—"

He rolls his eyes. "This, again. Rosa, I admire your desire to be independent, but I have an obscene amount of money, and I'm sure that Rocco Santini knows it. It would be odd if I didn't shower you with gifts." He grins, clearly pleased with his logic. "I'm afraid you're going to have to get comfortable with spending it."

"Fine," I mock-grumble. Leo's smile is sunshine personified, and it transforms his face. "Please pay for my plane ticket. You win this battle."

He gets to his feet. "I'll try not to get used to it."

Leo comes to my parents' home with me. He takes Hugh aside for a private conversation while I pack. I have no idea what they talk about, but it seems to have made an impression because Hugh knocks on my door as I'm zipping up my backpack. "Hey," he says. "Leo just filled me in on the details."

"You know you have to move?"

He nods. "I'll break the news to the parents."

"Are you sure?" I ask. "I can stick around and help with that if you want."

"No, chị. You've done enough." He forces a smile on his face. "Besides, your Leo threatened to punch me in the face if I keep involving you in my messes."

He did? Warmth blooms in my chest. Leo is being protective of me, and that's not something I'm used to. "He's not my Leo."

"Whatever you say. You're taking the roses? Will they even let you take them on the plane?"

"Absolutely. Nobody has ever given me a hundred roses before. I'm not leaving them behind for mẹ to make into potpourri." I hug my brother tightly. "I'll see you in a week," I say, blinking the tears away. "Try not to get into any more trouble."

"I'll do my best."

Something is going on with Hugh. His eyes are red, and the sadness there is unexpected and new. If I didn't know him better, I'd say he's nursing a broken heart. But every attempt to talk to him has failed—he won't tell me what's wrong.

AT THE AIRPORT, the security guards take one look at Leo's face and decide against objecting to my roses. On the plane, a smiling flight attendant takes the vase from him, promising to stow it in the coat closet. "These are so pretty," she gushes. Her name tag reads Andrea. "Don't worry, I'll take good care of them."

I've never been in love in my life. Never even been close. As a result, I've never been jealous of another woman. Worse than that, I've always judged territorial women a little. If your boyfriend strays, that's not because of the other woman; it's because he's inclined to cheat. It's his morals that are a problem.

I pay for my smug superiority now because Andrea flutters her eyelashes at Leo, and I want to scratch her eyes out. *He's mine,* I want to scream. *Get your claws away from him.*

We fly first class. A first for me. Even on this short flight to Milan, it's an entirely different experience than coach. Andrea offers us complimentary glasses of prosecco even before the plane takes off. I lean back in my seat and sip mine. "I could get used to this," I admit. "You're probably used to it, but this is nice."

"The prosecco?" he asks, his lips twitching. "I don't fly first class much. This might be my third time."

"That's it? Why?"

He shrugs. "I get the seat with extra legroom, and that usually seems good enough. Tomas keeps an eye on my money, but it mostly just sits there." He sips his wine. "This is good."

I probably should keep my questions to myself, but I'm wildly curious about everything Leo. "Why don't you spend your money? Is it because you're angry with your father for never contacting you?"

He looks amused. "I don't have any trauma about

that bastard if that's what you're asking. When I was younger, the money would have made a difference. My mother worked herself to the bone to provide for us. I would have loved to make life easier for her and then for—"

He cuts himself off abruptly. "But by the time I inherited, she was dead. Antonio had just taken over the organization, and he was someone I trusted. Someone I was happy to work for. Besides, what am I going to do with it? I'm not Antonio; I don't want to collect art. I'm not Dante; I don't need a garage filled with race cars." He smiles. "Have you ever heard Dante talk about his Ferraris? Once he gets going, he won't shut up. Your father and he are going to get along like a house on fire."

Andrea approaches us, the bottle of prosecco in her hands. "Would you like more?" she asks, bending over Leo and giving her a view of her bountiful cleavage. Irritation rises in me. I resist the urge to hiss at her like an angry cat and place my left hand over Leo's, a blatantly possessive gesture that warns the other woman to back off. Leo looks momentarily startled, and then the corners of his lips twitch. He strokes my hand, his thumb sliding over my engagement ring. Andrea, to her credit, backs off. She refills our glasses and hurries away, her cheeks red.

Leo's smile widens. "Jealous, principessa?"

"Wildly, orsacchiotto mio. I'm crazy about you, remember?"

"Of course." His smile dims, confusing me. Did Leo *like* my display of possessiveness? *Why?*

I look at our interlinked hands, and then my attention is caught by his shirt cuff. It's a little frayed. Leo follows my gaze, and he looks rueful. "I need to go shopping," he says. "I somehow never seem to find the time."

We're not that different, Leo and I. He takes care of everyone around him. He's responsible for protecting Antonio and Lucia, Dante and Valentina and Angelica, and so many more people. And now he's taken on the problems of my family. He's a big guy, tattooed and scarred. He looks invulnerable, but he's only human. *Let me take care of you,* he said in the cafe. But who takes care of him?

Me. I want the answer to be me.

"Your shirt isn't off the rack, though."

"You can tell?" He looks briefly surprised. "Of course you can. Yeah, store-bought clothes don't tend to fit well. If they fit across the shoulders, then the body is too large, and the sleeves are *always* too short. I used to get my clothes tailored, but my tailor died two years ago." He looks at my expression. "Don't look alarmed, *principessa*. He died in his sleep. Niccolo was ninety."

That wasn't what I was thinking at all. "You mean you didn't kill him because he poked you with a pin during a fitting?" I tease. "That's reassuring, *orsacchiotto mio*. You're telling me that you haven't been able to find another tailor in two years?"

"Nicolo was one of a kind. Besides, it just hasn't been a priority." He looks at the frayed cuff. "Nobody's looking at my clothes."

I am.

Well, let's be honest, I'm mostly looking at the man.

Leo Cesari, my soon-to-be *husband*.

"I apprenticed with a menswear designer in Paris for six months, long enough to know it wasn't for me. There's a lot of work that goes into a bespoke suit. Hours and hours of hand-stitching. No, thank you. I'll stick to women's clothing. But I know a handful of menswear tailors. If you like, I can make an appointment for you."

"Is that a polite way of telling me to get my act together?" A smile flashes across his face. "Thank you, *principessa*. I'd like that."

I FALL asleep on the plane and only wake up when we're touching down in Venice. To my mortification, I realize I used Leo's shoulder as a pillow. "Sorry about that," I say, my face red. "I didn't get a lot of sleep last night."

"Don't apologize." He tucks a stay tendril of hair behind my ear. "I didn't mind."

Omar, a member of Leo's team, meets us at the airport and ferries us home. He gives me several curious looks as the boat cuts through the water, his eyes darting from my engagement ring to the giant vase of flowers. I edge closer to Leo and whisper, "Does he know the details of our arrangement?"

"No. The fewer people who know, the better." He gives Omar a thoughtful glance. "We danced together at Dante's wedding, and word got around. There might have been a betting pool."

"A betting pool?"

"On us."

I start to smile. "So let me get this straight. Your

team saw us dance at the wedding and started betting on the odds of us sleeping together?"

He looks like he bit into a lemon. "Not sleeping together," he says. "Dating."

I grin widely. Looks like I'm not the only person rooting for Operation Make Leo Cesari Fall In Love With Rosa Tran. "Interesting." I move closer and clutch his muscled bicep. "Don't look so grouchy, orsacchiotto mio. Someone might be watching. Put on your best besotted impression."

He gives me a dry look. "You're having entirely too much fun at my expense, principessa." He moves closer and wraps his arm around my shoulder. I breathe him in, basking in the now-familiar scent of pine and sandalwood. "You can dish it out, but can you take it?"

My pulse skitters at his nearness. It's an act designed for anyone who might be watching, but even knowing that I feel myself respond to the suggestive note in his voice. A shiver runs through me, and my insides tighten. I imagine him slipping his hand under my top and peeling the fabric off me with a growl. Pinning me back in bed, spreading my legs, and kissing his way up them.

He knows the effect he has on me. But this isn't all one-sided. I drop my gaze to his crotch, and I can see the hard outline of his erection pressed against his trousers. "Can you?"

Speaking of his erection... It's huge. Leo is a big guy, and I figured everything would be proportional, but even so. *Gulp.* Maybe, for the sake of my vagina, I should put a halt to my efforts to seduce Leo.

Then again, no. Andrea wouldn't shy away from the challenge, and neither will I.

The boat comes to a stop. Omar clears his throat loudly, looking everywhere but at the two of us. "We're here."

I give him a sweet smile. "Thank you." I take my roses, step out of the boat, and turn back to look at my fiancé. "Coming, Leo?"

14

LEO

What the hell am I doing? First I tell Rosa I want nothing to do with her, then I almost kiss her at the cafe. I flirt with her on the plane, and now I'm practically eye-fucking her?

It's her dress. *It has to be.* Every time I catch a glimpse of her tantalizing, sun-kissed midriff, my brain short-circuits. I can't tear my eyes away from her. I want to push her against a wall like a caveman, tear her dress apart, and kiss every inch of her skin the way I did in my dream. I want to thrust into her like an animal, punishing her for the way I'm reacting to her body.

But now she's staring at me with hope in her

eyes, and I have to shut this down. No more flirting, no more almost-kisses. In public, we have a role to play, and we'll both do what's necessary. But when we're in private, I need to stay the hell away from her. Anything else is deeply unfair.

I lost my ability to love when Patrizia died, and all that's left is a husk of a man, bitter, jaded, and cynical. Rosa wants something from me that I can't give her.

I am not what she's looking for. I have nothing to offer her except my protection.

I WALK her to her apartment, hooking my arm around her waist like the besotted fiancé I'm supposed to be. She stops in the foyer to get her mail. "Sorry," she says. "My favorite fabric store, Tessuti Gelli, sends out a catalog four times a year. I've been waiting impatiently for it."

I don't know anything about fabric. "Is it in Venice?"

"Yes." She unlocks her front door and pushes it

open. I follow her inside. "They have the most beautiful fabric. Remember the dress my mother wore to dinner last night? That was from Tessuti Gelli."

"You made your mother's dress?"

She looks surprised by my question. "Of course."

"Did you make the dress you're wearing now?"

"Yes," she says. For some reason, she flushes when she says it. "I make most of my clothes. The only things I buy are jeans." She looks down at her skirt. "This isn't my best work, though. I was in a hurry when I was making it, and it's a complete mess on the inside."

"It looks great."

"Thank you." She avoids my gaze, and the feeling I'm missing something intensifies. "Can I get you something to drink?"

I want to say yes. Rosa is made of contradictions —dutiful yet driven, shy yet sassy—and I want to sit on her couch and discover all her hidden facets.

But I need to get the hell out of here while I still can.

"I can't stay. What does your schedule look like this week? We have to move in together. Does Wednesday work?"

"That soon?" she asks, dismayed.

She looks horrified, and I don't blame her. I wouldn't want to live with me either. "Yes," I bite out. "This is the price you pay for keeping your brother alive."

She blinks in confusion. "Moving in with you isn't a problem," she says. "But I need to be at my boutique both Tuesday and Wednesday. I just don't know when I'll find time to pack."

Oh. "I'll send movers. They'll pack your stuff."

She rests her small hand on my cheek. "Thank you, Leo," she says softly. "Thank you for everything." Then she stands on tiptoe and kisses me.

It's the merest brushing of lip against lip, but it catapults me back to Dante's wedding, back to that dance floor, when she blushed prettily and asked me to come back to her hotel room.

I craved her then, and I crave her now.

But nothing has changed.

I still have nothing to offer.

Rosa Tran is sweet, sinful, temptation. Before I do something I will always regret, I take a step back from her, pivot on my heel, and *flee*.

It's only when I reach home that I realize I forgot to ask her if she knows anything about her brother's missing money.

The Fixer

Tomas is waiting for me in my office on Monday morning. "I got the strangest alert this weekend," he says, leaning back in his chair and taking a sip of his coffee. "Evidently, you spent two million euros at a jewelry store in Lecce. The bank couldn't reach you, so they called me to make sure the transaction was legitimate."

Tomas manages my money and has access to all my accounts, so I guess it makes sense that the bank called him. I'm also not surprised my purchase set off some red flags—it's the first time I've ever done anything like this. "It was for an engagement ring. I'm getting married."

"I heard. Dante filled me in. I also heard I'm getting a new employee, and I should watch him closely." He lifts his coffee cup, his expression a mix of concern and amusement. "Congratulations seem to be in order."

"Thank you. You don't look thrilled."

"You told me about Patrizia once. Do you remember?"

I nod briefly. It was a long time ago, and I was very drunk. "I'm surprised you do." I wasn't the only one drowning my sorrows that night.

"It's not the sort of story you forget." He surveys me over the rim of his cup. "I'm glad you're moving on, Leo. I don't know Rosa; I've only met her at Antonio and Dante's weddings. But she seems very nice, and if she makes you happy—"

What did Dante tell Tomas? "This isn't a real marriage. It's a way to keep her brother alive."

"Interesting," he says. "If it isn't real, why did you spend so much money on the ring?" A faint look of distaste crosses his face. "Or did she insist on the fancy diamond?"

"What? No." I frown at my friend. What exactly is he implying? "Rosa doesn't expect anything from anyone, even when she should. But she liked this ring." She hadn't been able to take her eyes off it.

"So you bought it for her. If she didn't know how rich you are then, she does now. Please tell me you're at least getting a prenup."

And that's quite enough of that. "It sounds to me like you're calling my fiancée a gold-digger, Tomas," I say, keeping my voice even with effort. "We've been friends a very long time. I'd hate for that to change."

Tomas smirks into his coffee. "Not real, Leo? Are you sure?"

Oh, for fuck's sake. "Can we cut this out? If you insist on hanging out in my office and wasting my time, you can help me solve some problems."

"Leo, I love you like a brother, but I draw the line at giving you sex advice."

Everyone's a comedian. I make a rude gesture in his direction. "I need a place to live. The padrino wants us to move in together, but my apartment isn't big enough."

"Or clean enough," he quips.

He's not wrong. It's also drafty in winter, too hot in summer, and there's rarely enough hot water for a decent shower. "She does a lot of late-night sewing, so the new place needs to be large enough to accommodate that. I also need a wedding planner and movers to help Rosa pack her boxes. Oh, and an employee with fashion and retail experience."

"Anything else?" Tomas asks sarcastically. "Do you want a pony while we're at it? Or a unicorn? Well, at least you have a lot of money to throw at the problem. When are you moving in together?"

"Wednesday."

His eyebrow climbs up. "How about that apartment you own on the mainland?"

"We can't live in Marghera; it's too far for Rosa to commute every day. Besides, her parents will be staying there."

Tomas doesn't point out that most of the people who work in Venice commute from the mainland. "I'm assuming that something temporary is out?"

I don't have to spell it out for Tomas—he's one of the smartest people I know. "Unfortunately, yes. No hotels, no stopgap leases. It needs to look like we've been planning this move for a while."

"There is the obvious solution. The house you inherited from your father."

I grimace. I've only set foot in the palazzo once, shortly after I found out my father had died and I had inherited all his wealth. I went to look at where he lived in luxury with his wife while only a few streets away, my mother was struggling to feed and clothe me, trying to find a sign he knew or cared about my existence. There wasn't one.

The palazzo has been lying empty for almost ten years, and I have no idea what kind of condition it's in. The windows are probably broken, and the roof undoubtedly leaks. But it's in Santa Croce, not too far from Rosa's boutique, and even better, it's large enough that Rosa and I can stay out of each other's way.

"It's probably in terrible shape."

"It almost certainly is," Tomas agrees. "But given the timeframe, it might be your only option." He gets to his feet, his expression serious. "If you tell me this isn't a real marriage, Leo, I'll believe you. But I think you should give Rosa a chance. You might find yourself being a lot happier with her than you expected."

"I can't."

"Because of Patrizia? I didn't know her, Leo, but do you really believe she'd want you to mourn her for the rest of your life? I don't think so. If she loved you, she would want you to find happiness with someone else."

Tomas is my friend, and I've already snapped at him this morning. So I hold my tongue. But the truth is, I have no idea what Patrizia would want. She's dead. Her life was cut short. *Because of me.*

It's tempting to believe that I can be happy with Rosa, but how can I allow myself to want that? I don't deserve it.

And yet...

And yet, I assign bodyguards to watch over Rosa and arrange a team to do the same for her family once they get into Venice.

That afternoon, I find myself walking past the fabric store she loves. When I see a bolt of fabric in the window, a deep, brown cotton with flecks of green and gold woven through it, I freeze to a halt.

That fabric is the precise color of Rosa's eyes.

Pushing the door open, I go inside.

15

ROSA

I wake up on Monday morning with the sun streaming into my bedroom and the familiar sounds of the city outside my window, and for a minute, I almost wonder if the events of the weekend were a dream. Then my eyes land on my engagement ring, and everything comes rushing back.

I'm getting married to Leo early next month.

Can't dwell on that. I have a ton of work to do this week. At least I'm all set for the fitting today. Last night, after Leo's abrupt departure, I couldn't fall asleep, so I sewed up a new muslin for today's bride, Clara. It was almost three by the time I finished, but I can check it off my to-do list, so I'm calling it a win.

I head downstairs for coffee and then continue work on the wedding dress I'm making for Daniela Zaniolo, a hugely popular fashion influencer from Milan. Two years ago, I would have given my right arm to be able to design for Daniela, but today, I'm struggling to keep my attention on the dress. I keep looking at my phone, wondering if Leo is going to text me.

He doesn't. I don't end up hearing from him until Tuesday night. I'm cooking lemongrass chicken when my phone beeps.

> The movers will be at your house at ten. Be at home to let them in.

I roll my eyes. Nothing for two days, and then he texts me with *instructions*.

> Of course, my lord and master. I live to serve.

> Interesting. Tell me more, principessa.

A frisson of excitement runs through me. Damn it. A hint of suggestiveness, and I'm horny for Leo. A devilish urge seizes me.

> Where am I moving, by the way? You live in a studio, and there's only one bed. I'm delighted to share it, of course, but you're shy.

Shy???

I snicker at his outrage. I would give anything to see Leo's face right now.

> Terribly shy. So where am I moving?

A place with more than one bed. Fair warning: it's a bit of a mess, and there's not much furniture yet.

> You're being cryptic, orsacchiotto mio. Tell me more.

And ruin the surprise? You'll see for yourself tomorrow evening, principessa. I'll pick you up after work. What time do you get off?

> I have MMA class. I'll be done at eight.

Ah, yes. So you can kick my ass. I'll pick you up at eight.

THE MOVERS SHOW up exactly on time. There are three of them, all women, who introduce themselves as Marta, Paulina, and Gina. "We'll take good care of your stuff," Marta says. She's a few years older than me and beautiful, with glossy black hair, high cheekbones, and a cupid bow of a mouth. "Leo said you're a fashion designer, and you have the most beautiful clothes. Don't worry. We'll be careful with them."

Leo thinks I have beautiful clothes? I float through the day in a happy haze. My mother calls me at lunch to tell me they'll arrive in Venice Friday morning, and even that can't get me down.

Ali texts me as I'm leaving.

> Are you coming to class tonight?

> Yes. Why?

> One word. Simon.

Simon is the co-owner of the gym I train at. He's one of those guys who believes he's God's gift to women. Comes on too strong, doesn't know how to take no for an answer, and is mean and condescending to Ali. He keeps asking me out and ignores me when I turn him down. I hate him.

> Is he teaching the class? Because if he is, I'm out.

> No, I'm teaching it. But he's teaching the six o'clock class, so he'll be at the gym.

> Ugh. Thanks for the heads-up.

I show up a little later than usual, hoping to avoid him, but unfortunately for me, Simon's hanging out in the foyer when I arrive. "Rosa," he leers, his gaze locking on my cleavage. "Long time, no see."

Yup, that's deliberate. "Simon, hey."

"How've you been?"

"Good. I need to get changed. I'm late for class." I start to move past him into the changing rooms, but he plants himself in my way. "What's your hurry?" His eyes travel my body, and he puts his hands on my shoulders. "You look tense. Your muscles are so tight." He leers at me suggestively. "I can loosen them for you."

No, thank you.

My engagement ring is in my purse. I didn't want Ali to see it before class. If she did, she'd have a thousand questions for me, and I didn't feel like dealing with it. I really regret that decision now. Then again, Simon only sees and hears what he wants anyway. "I'm good," I say, pulling away from him. "Let me go."

He doesn't want to. His hands tighten instinctively, but then he realizes that the front of the gym is all window, and we're in full view of the street. He releases me with an ugly smile. "You're playing hard to get, Rosa, but that's okay. I like to chase."

My patience runs out. Simon's been pulling this bullshit for six months, and I'm done. I prefer to avoid confrontation, but he hasn't left me a choice. "I'm not playing hard to get," I say, as clear as I can make it. "I'm not interested in you. There's somebody else."

"You're seeing someone?" He looks skeptical.

I repress my urge to scream. I shouldn't have to mention a boyfriend for Simon to leave me alone, but here we are. "Yes. Now, please get out of my way so I can get to my class."

Ali is in the changing room. She takes one look at my face and sighs. "You ran into Simon in the foyer?"

"I hate that guy. Sorry."

"You don't have to apologize; he's my ex for a reason." Her face is unhappy. "I wish I could afford to buy him out."

Simon has no interest in running the studio, but he's petty as fuck. Ali wants to buy out his share, but he's asking for an insane amount of money. Meanwhile, he doesn't do a damn thing to keep the business going. That's all Ali.

"Anyway." She straightens her shoulders. "How was your mother's birthday? Did she like her dress?"

"She loved it." And then our lives all fell apart.

"As she should have. It was lovely. All your clothes are." She casts an eye over me. "Is that a new skirt?"

I look down to see what I'm wearing. Oh, my Paris skirt. I'd fallen in love with the fabric at first sight. It's blue, with little red Eiffel towers printed on it, interspersed with baguettes and bottles of wine. "No, I made this a couple of years ago."

"I've never seen it before. I love it." She slips out of her sandals and puts on her trainers. "Thank you for lending me your red dress, by the way. I'd have brought it back tonight, but I went by the dry cleaner on the way here, and it wasn't ready."

"No worries." Ali was attending an industry award ceremony but had nothing to wear. We're roughly the same size, so I told her to borrow anything she wanted from my closet. "How did it go?" Ali was up for an award. "Did you win?"

"I did."

"Congratulations!" I stare at my friend as I change into my sports bra. "Why don't you look more excited?"

"Take a guess. Go on."

"Simon was there."

"Yup. They seated us at the same table. He spent the entire evening telling anyone who'd listen that he was the one who designed the class, not me, but he let me take credit out of the goodness of his heart."

"Have I mentioned I hate Simon?"

She shuts her locker door with a bang. "Get in line, Rosa. Get in line."

The Fixer

Leo shows up halfway through my class. I feel a weight on the back of my neck, and when I turn around, he's standing outside, staring at me through the glass window, a brooding expression on his face.

My heart jumps. For a moment, I lose focus entirely and fall flat on my ass. Great. So much for my vaunted self-defense skills. I pick myself up, my cheeks flushed, and make myself pay attention to Ali as she leads us through kicks, rolls, and grappling. When the lesson is done, I change quickly, slip my ring over my finger, and head outside.

"Sorry I kept you," I say, stretching up and kissing him on the cheek.

"You didn't," he replies. "I was early. I wanted to watch you fight." He grins. "Very impressive."

Thank heavens Leo wasn't here when Simon grabbed my arm. Somehow, I don't think that would have gone well for Simon. He might be a trained MMA instructor, but my money is on my fiancé.

"I fell flat on my ass."

"Falling is an occupational hazard." He inclines his head toward me. "Want to go get dinner?"

I'm starving. Lunch seems like hours ago. "I'd love to."

"What do you feel like eating?"

"Pizza?" I ask hopefully.

"Sure."

Leo picks a small, intimate restaurant. "Best pizza in Venice," he promises. "Trust me."

The waitress brings us a carafe of red wine and takes our order. Once she's gone, I take a sip and smile at Leo. "This is delicious. Do you come here often?"

"Once a week, sometimes less." He grimaces. "When you get to my age, you'll realize your body doesn't appreciate pizza for every meal."

I give him a daringly blatant once-over. "I can't see anything wrong with your body. At all."

He chokes on his wine, and I swear he blushes a little. *Adorable.* "When you invited me to your hotel room, you couldn't even meet my eyes. You looked like you were ready to bolt. What happened to that version of Rosa?"

"I'm older now. I turned twenty-five, you know."

"Our encounter was less than two months ago."

The Fixer

He surveys me, a smile dancing in his eyes. "And you didn't turn twenty-five in June. Your birthday is in April."

"How do you know that? And when's your birthday?"

"September," he replies, ignoring my first question.

I lean forward. "It's September now. Oh God, it isn't today, is it? I don't have a present for you."

Leo gives me a puzzled glance. "It's not today, and even if it was, why would I expect you to get me anything?"

Oh, buddy, you have no idea. "Birthdays are a big deal in my family. When in September?"

"In a couple of weeks."

Getting Leo to volunteer personal information is like pulling teeth. I smile sweetly at him over my glass of wine. "What date, orsacchiotto mio?"

His lips twitch. "The twenty-first," he admits grudgingly.

I pull out my phone and mark it on my calendar. The pizza arrives as I'm tucking it away. I ordered a fig, gorgonzola, and prosciutto pizza, and Leo went old school and stuck to the Margherita, which also looks amazing. I'm trying to think of a polite way of asking him if I can steal a slice when he says, "Want to share them?"

"You are the best."

He shakes his head bemusedly. "You need to raise your standards, principessa."

I fall upon the pizza as if I haven't seen food in years. Leo wisely makes no comments about my appetite. "Have you heard from your parents?" he asks instead.

"My mother discovered texting four years ago. Ever since then, I hear from her at least three times a day whether I like it or not." God, this fig and prosciutto pizza is delicious. And so is the Margherita. Can't decide which one is my favorite. "She called this afternoon. Her transfer came through in record time, and she wanted me to thank you. And my dad said he didn't realize that your friend Ander was Ander Reinhart of Reinhart Automotive. Evidently, working there is his dream job." I reach across the table and squeeze his hand. "Thank you for doing this."

"It was nothing," he says, uncomfortable with my gratitude. "I needed to bank somewhere anyway, and Ander's always looking for good people. He'll owe me a favor for this. What about Hugh? How's he doing?"

According to my mother, Hugh hasn't left the house this week. "He spends all day in his room, and he's not eating," she told me today. "Yesterday, I made his favorite soup, and he didn't even eat a bowlful. Do you know what's going on?"

I don't. I wish he'd talk to me. I've texted him a couple of times since I got back, asking how he's doing, and both times, he's replied with just one word. Fine. But I know Hugh. He's a happy extrovert, someone who likes to be the life of the party. For him to stay in his room...

I have so many worries about my brother, but I don't want to burden Leo with them. "Hugh is Hugh," I reply. "He'll be fine once he's in Venice. Are you going to tell me about where we're moving?"

"So impatient," he says with a laugh. "You'll see it in less than an hour. Don't get your hopes up. It's a bit of a dump. Marta did her best to clean it, but it needs much more than vacuuming."

"Marta, the same hot woman who packed my stuff?"

His lips curve up. "You think she's hot?"

The wine is loosening my tongue. "Why, are you going to fantasize about the two of us making out? Naked?"

"Marta doesn't show up in my fantasies,

principessa. You, on the other hand—" He stops what he's saying abruptly and drains the rest of his wine.

And as daring as I've been tonight, I can't bring myself to ask him to finish that sentence.

16

ROSA

"This is it."

Leo stops in front of an honest-to-God palazzo, and I stop and stare at my new home. The location is fantastic—the large, squat building in Santa Croce is steps from the Grand Canal. But it's seen better days. The exterior is covered in peeling white paint, and the shutters that were once forest green are now worn and faded. Empty flower boxes hang from the windows, and more than one glass pane is broken.

"I don't know what to say."

He laughs. "You're very tactful. It's a disaster."

This is Venice. This crumbling palazzo is likely worth millions. "You own this?"

"It was my father's," he replies. "I inherited it

along with everything else. I'm going to warn you—the inside isn't much better." He unlocks the front door. "After you."

Bracing for cobwebs and mice, I step inside, but the interior is in better shape than I expected from the outside. The walls are freshly painted, and the floors are scrubbed clean. Marta's best is pretty damn good. I walk from one empty room to another, Leo following behind. "Your father lived here? It's so big."

"A mansion for two people," he says, his voice bitter. "And now it's ours."

I give him a sidelong look. "It's yours, not ours."

"Whatever you say, principessa," he responds agreeably. "Speaking of which, Daniel has some marriage-related paperwork for you."

"Daniel Rossi? The lawyer?" The paperwork had better be a prenup. I need Leo's help to save my family, but I'm not comfortable with spending his money. At all.

He nods. "Can you meet him Friday afternoon?"

"Depends on the time. My parents get in on Friday, and I have to help them unpack."

He gives me an exasperated look. "The movers will unpack for them."

"Try telling my mother that."

"I will if you'll let me," he retorts. "You cut a promising internship in Paris short because your mother had a heart attack. You took a nine-hour train ride to Lecce so you could be there for her birthday. Yet they don't see any of your accomplishments. They make fun of you about the stupid lobster, and they denigrate your choice of career. Yours is the most lop-sided relationship I've seen, and that includes my own father, who, in case you don't remember, didn't even bother to acknowledge that I exist."

I stop and stare at him. Leo's angry on my behalf. He's ready to fight my battles. He doesn't have to give a damn—this isn't a real marriage—but he does. And if I open my mouth to thank him for caring, I think I'm going to burst into tears.

"I'll share my calendar with you," I say instead, averting my face so he can't see my expression. "My schedule is on it." I link my arm with his. "Now, give me the tour."

It's not much of a tour. There are a lot of empty rooms, and the palazzo obviously needs renovation. The kitchen—the less said about it, the better. Clearly Leo's dad and his wife never cooked because it looks like it hasn't been renovated in over a hundred years. The living room has a newly bought set of couches and a big-screen TV. "I did some shopping," Leo explains. "But just enough to make the place habitable. There didn't seem much point buying a lot of furniture only to have it ruined during a renovation."

Leo hustles me past the second level and onto the third. There, I count four bedrooms. Leo's stuff is in a bedroom at the eastern end of the house, and my bed has been set up in the room the furthest away from his. There's a message here, and I would do well to remember it. Leo might be physically attracted to me, and I might hope he cares about me, but he's always been clear that he doesn't want a relationship.

I shouldn't let hope replace reality. That way lies only madness.

"Why did you hurry me past the second floor?" I give him a teasing look. "If you have a mad wife, you know it's the attic you're supposed to lock her in."

The smile wipes off his face. "Go see," he says stiffly.

What did I say? I descend the stairs, puzzling over Leo's reaction. It can't be my teasing. On the plane, I asked him if he murdered his tailor, and he'd laughed at me. So why the surly response to my Jane Eyre joke?

Then I push open the door to the right of the stairwell and stop dead in the doorway.

This is a sewing room. Tall windows on three sides promise an abundance of light during the day. Glass-fronted cabinets line the fourth. My framed Vogue pattern envelopes hang from the walls. A giant square cutting table dominates the center of the room, and my sewing machine is set up on the far side, as is my serger, ironing table, and dress form. In a corner, a comfortable stuffed chair beckons, flooded by the warm glow of lamplight. Next to it is a desk for my laptop and a small coffee station.

Everything's here. Everything's been set up *perfectly.*

I cross the floor and open the cabinets. They hold my fabric, the yardage neatly sorted the way I prefer, by fabric type and then color. Leo watches me carefully. "I wasn't sure if you wanted to set up this space yourself, but you said you were busy this week, so I thought I'd take the chance. Valentina said you sew when you're stressed, and there's going to be plenty of that in the future." He hesitates at my continuing silence. "Everything can be undone. And if you don't like the furniture—"

"I love it." *You said you were busy this week. Valentina said you sew when you're stressed.* He might not want to get involved with me, but in all my life, nobody's seen me the way Leo does. Nobody has paid attention to my wants and needs the way he has. I blink away tears before they can spill down my cheeks. "I love everything."

Then I notice the large gift-wrapped box on the cutting table.

"What is this?"

His eyes sparkle with laughter. He's regained his good humor. "It's a housewarming gift, principessa. The usual protocol is to tear open the paper and see what's inside."

"But I didn't get you anything."

"And you don't need to," he replies. He nods toward the parcel. "Go on, open it."

It's fabric. Not just any fabric. Tessuti Gelli has an online store, and this package contains every piece of fabric I've added to my shopping cart this year. More Leo magic. "How?" I ask helplessly.

"It was easy," he says, a touch of smugness in his tone. "Haven't you ever got an abandoned cart email from a retailer? You must know they store all that data, principessa. I went in there and told them I wanted to get you a gift, and they were extremely helpful."

I bet they were. Tessuti Gelli isn't cheap, and I

add fabric to my shopping cart with abandon. This is thousands and thousands of euros of fabric. Silk and wool, cotton and lace. Hours of inspiration in one square box.

I lift each of the pieces out reverently. In the bottom is a brown cotton I don't remember. "This wasn't on my list, was it?"

"You kept track?" He shakes his head in disbelief. "Why am I not surprised? No, this was me. I saw it and couldn't resist."

"Why?" I stroke the cloth. It's a deep brown cotton, with strands of green and gold woven through it. It's lovely—at first unassuming, but when you look closer, you see the subtle shimmer that makes it special. "I didn't have you pegged as a cotton connoisseur."

"I'm not. It's just that this particular shade..." He comes closer and cups my cheek in his callused palm. His ocean-blue eyes lock onto mine, and I feel like I'm on a surfboard. Struggling for balance, knowing that I can be thrown off at any time, but loving the ride. "It's the precise color of your eyes."

I don't stop to think about whether this is a good idea. Instead, I wrap my hand around the back of his neck and tug his head down.

And then I kiss him.

Leo doesn't respond for a moment, and I'm wondering if I fucked up, but then... *he does.* With a growl, his mouth closes on mine, and he takes control. One hand strokes my neck, his fingers gripping my hair, while the other rests possessively at the small of my back. His lips coax mine open, and his tongue slides in.

My entire body comes alive.

This isn't a casual peck or a light brushing of lip against lip. No, this is the kind of kiss they write poems about. The taste of him floods my senses. I slide my hands up his arms as I kiss him back, feeling his hard muscles flex under my touch. Heat sizzles all over my body. Oh God. This is so good. He lifts me onto the cutting table, and I spread my thighs open, inviting him to occupy the space between my legs. He squeezes my breast over my T-shirt. "You drive me mad," he growls. "For months, I've wanted to do this."

Do it now. My pulse skitters wildly. I close my eyes and breathe in his scent. I wrap my arms around his waist, tugging his shirt from his waistband and touching his warm skin. My skirt rides up my legs, exposing my thighs to his hot gaze. He steps back and looks at me, his eyes glazed with lust, and I thrill at his blatantly male appraisal. "Take off your shirt."

"You're barking orders at me again." I should tell him to go to hell on principle, but principles don't get you off, and I'm hoping Leo will. I tug my T-shirt over my head, and my nipples ache, pebbling with need. Underneath, I'm wearing a white satin bra. Nothing special, though I wouldn't know that from the look on Leo's face. He makes an appreciative male noise, and then he bends his head, pushes the cups down, and sucks my nipple into his mouth.

I'm sitting on fabric that costs hundreds of euros a meter. The beaded silk will be crumpled beyond repair, and I can't bring myself to care. Leo trails a line of kisses down my shoulders and neck, and my skin burns where he touches me. I only had a glass of wine at dinner, but I feel drunk. Dizzy. I grip his waist, anchoring myself to him. "Leo," I moan. "Please." His tongue claims mine, and his teeth nip my lower lip, and I'm drowning and flying all at once. I'm ready for more. All my life, this is what I've been searching for. This feeling of overwhelming intensity. And now I've found it, and I'm ready for *everything*. "I want... I need...."

Leo's phone rings, its shrill sound slicing through my lust.

17

LEO

"What?" I bark into the phone.

"Sorry to interrupt, Leo," Goran, my right-hand man, says. "But we have a situation here. Max Guerra just walked into our headquarters. He wants to talk to you."

I grow cold. What the hell is one of Spina Sacra's lieutenants doing here? "I'll be right there." I hang up and look at Rosa. Her face is flushed, her lips swollen. She's never looked more beautiful to me. "I have to go."

"Trouble?"

"I don't know," I answer. "I hope not." I tuck my shirt back inside my waistband. "Don't open the door, don't let anyone in."

She licks her lips nervously. "Okay."

I go downstairs, jump into my boat, and speed toward headquarters. Fear has me in a vicious grip. I couldn't protect Patrizia. People who get close to me get hurt. And now, less than a week after the deal with the Lecce mob, Max Guerra is in Venice.

Goran has put Guerra in an interrogation room. He follows me inside. Max looks up, and a smile touches his face. "Cesari," he says. "Good to see you."

"I'm not in the mood for pleasantries." I sit across from him. Goran positions himself behind me. "What the fuck are you doing in my city?"

His eyebrow creeps up. "Your city? I wonder what Antonio Moretti would think of your claim."

"Do you see the padrino here? No, you don't." Both Antonio and Dante are away from Venice, something Max undoubtedly knows. Antonio and Lucia are in Paris, stealing a painting from a private collector, and Dante, Valentina, and Angelica are camping near Lake Como. "You waited until he was away to sneak into Venice." I put some menace into my voice. "Tell me why."

Guerra laughs in my face. "Come on, Leo. If I wanted to sneak into Venice, why would I visit your headquarters? I need to talk to you." He looks at Goran. "Alone."

"No."

His expression turns frustrated. "Why the fuck not?"

"Because I have no reason to trust you or anyone else from Spina Sacra."

"Ah." He rests his hands on the steel table. "Then you'll be delighted to hear I don't work for them." He undoes his cuffs, rolls up his sleeves, and holds his forearms out so I can see his markings. No Spina Sacra tattoos. Not that it means anything. Guerra is a spy of some kind. He wouldn't be stupid enough to cover himself in identifiable tattoos.

"Who do you work for?"

I don't expect him to answer, but he does. "Ciro Del Barba."

I bite off a curse. Behind me, Goran stiffens. If the Kingmaker is involved, things are going to get very messy, very quickly.

I get to my feet. "Check him for the mark," I tell Goran. "I need to make a call."

"Leo Cesari," Del Barba says. "I thought I'd be hearing from you. Yes, Guerra works for me."

I massage my temples. "What the fuck is going on, Ciro?"

"It's complicated."

"Simplify it for me."

"Guerra needs to talk to Hugh Tran."

"No," I say flatly. "No, he doesn't. Rosa Tran is my fiancée. Nobody touches her family. Not even you."

"You owe me a favor."

I open my mouth and shut it. When Angelica was kidnapped this past January, her abductor used an aerosol sedative to put her under. I needed its chemical composition analyzed in a hurry, and it was Ciro's lab that did the work.

Del Barba is a fucking spider who sits in his web in Milan, spinning plots and collecting favors until his prey lands in front of him.

"Guerra isn't there to bust your fake marriage," Del Barba continues. "And he isn't there to hurt Hugh Tran. He just wants to talk to him."

"About what?"

"I can't tell you."

"Goddamn it, Ciro."

There's a long moment of silence. "This isn't about the ten million that Hugh Tran stole," he says finally. "I don't care about that. Guerra is looking for someone, and Tran is the key to finding them. He won't hurt Tran or the family. You have my word. I will personally guarantee their safety."

"You're sure Hugh stole from Spina Sacra?"

"Yes."

My heart sinks. Del Barba has the best information network in the country. If he's sure, then there isn't any doubt that Hugh took the money. I don't care about the ten million euros—I'll pay Antonio back, but why did he do it? Only an idiot would steal from the Mafia. Rosa's brother might be reckless, but he didn't strike me as stupid.

"The padrino is going to have some questions."

"I'll talk to Antonio," Del Barba replies. "Dante, too. Do we have a deal?"

Valentina's daughter is alive because of Del Barba. The Kingmaker is ruthless, but when he gives his word, he keeps it.

"I won't throw Guerra out of Venice," I reply. "Anything beyond that, he's on his own. But hear this, Ciro. If any harm comes to *any* of the Tran family, our arrangement is off."

"Deal," he says promptly. "Thank you for your cooperation, Cesari. You're sure you don't want to work for me?"

Come into my parlor, said the spider to the fly. "I'm happy in Venice," I say lightly. "Why would I work for the Kingmaker when I can work for the King?"

Ciro laughs, amused. "It's not the person on the throne that wields the power, Leo. It's the person behind it. You'll realize that one day."

I TURN Max loose and head back to Santa Croce. My thoughts are bleak. Events are moving around me, and I feel like a pawn on a chessboard. But more than that, I feel like I'm watching a train wreck in slow motion, helpless to do anything to avert it.

Had Goran not called when he did, I would have slept with Rosa tonight. I was ready to fuck her on her cutting table; I was ready to take her to my bed.

But I can't. *I shouldn't.*

This isn't just about sex. I haven't been a monk

since Patrizia died. I've fucked plenty of other women and spent a reasonable amount of time at Casanova, Venice's fanciest sex club. If my desire for Rosa was purely carnal, I could deal with it. But it isn't. I like Rosa. I find myself thinking about her at odd times of the day. Her nickname for me makes me laugh. And tonight, when one of the guys in her class tossed her on the floor in a practice exercise, it took all my willpower to keep from punching him in the face.

And that affection toward her, combined with the intense, all-consuming chemistry. . . If I'm not careful, I could very easily find myself falling in love with Rosa Tran.

Twenty years ago, my wife was collateral damage in a war that had nothing to do with her. Patrizia wasn't part of the Mafia; it was her association with me that cost her life.

And now Rosa is tied to me. If she marries me, she's at risk, always in danger because she's my wife. If she doesn't marry me, her brother dies. Talk about a fucking Catch-22.

I don't know how to fix this. But I need to stay the hell away from her. Because if I were to fall in love with Rosa and something were to happen to her, I wouldn't be able to survive it.

It's almost one in the morning, but the light is on in one of the front windows, and when I let myself in, Rosa is sitting on the couch in the living room. "You're still awake."

"I tried to sleep but couldn't, so I gave up." She gives me a small, tentative smile. "I was worried."

"About me?" My heart flutters, and I squash the reaction. Fuck. It would be so easy to give in to this. She's offering me her warmth and her love, and it would be so easy to take it. So easy *and so wrong*. "I've already told you, principessa. You don't need to be." My voice is harsh, vicious, and cold. "Nobody is watching us here, so there's no need for you to pretend. This isn't a real marriage, and we'll both do well remembering that."

Her expression turns stricken. Hot guilt slices through me. *I'm sorry,* I want to say. *I'm a wounded animal, lashing out at you because you're a convenient target. I didn't mean to hurt you.*

But I don't say any of that. Instead, I go to bed.

Alone.

18

ROSA

I'm done with Leo. He was all in until he went to his meeting, and when he got back home, he rejected me? Done. Totally, *absolutely* done with his mixed messages.

Or, a logical voice points out, *something at that meeting freaked him out.*

Hmm. Okay, that could be a reasonable explanation. Or maybe it's not, and I'm just fooling myself. Either way, I need to be careful with my heart.

Because Leo Cesari could break it without even trying.

I don't sleep well. At six, I give up the struggle and get out of bed. Leo is nowhere to be seen. I wander down to the kitchen and open the refrigerator, not expecting very much, but to my surprise, I find food there: eggs, cheddar, tomatoes, basil, and more. More of Marta's magic.

I make myself a cup of coffee and start chopping onions.

Leo comes downstairs half an hour later. From the dark circles around his eyes, he hasn't slept either, and I feel a surge of sympathy for him. Last week, he was just living his life. Six days later, everything has been turned completely upside down. At least I'm getting something out of this deal. My brother doesn't get killed by the mob. I still don't see what Leo gets.

I pour him a cup of coffee. "Do you want breakfast? I made plenty for both of us."

"Does the stove even work?"

"Barely. Eggs?"

"You don't have to cook for me."

Somebody grant me patience. "Okay, orsacchiotto mio. I won't tomorrow. But right now, I have enough food for two people. If you don't eat the eggs, they're going to end up in the trash."

His lips twitch. "You're cranky in the mornings," he says. "Good to know. Yes, I'll have some breakfast. Thank you."

The Fixer

We eat in silence. When he's almost done with his meal, he looks up. "You made eggs," he says.

"Umm, yes? Why do you sound surprised?"

"I thought you'd eat something more Vietnamese."

"Ah. I'm a second-generation immigrant, Leo. My parents were born in Italy. Some days, I eat eggs, sometimes it's French toast, and sometimes it's bánh mì or bún. Why? Do you not like Vietnamese food? I don't have to cook it when—"

"I love it," he cuts in. "Valentina and Dante were over for dinner on Saturday, and Valentina brought a Vietnamese feast. She said they were your recipes. If we hire a chef, I want to make sure they know how to cook the food you enjoy."

"You want to hire a chef? For the two of us? That's ridiculous. I can cook."

"We have the money."

"*You* have the money," I correct. "Cooking relaxes me. But if you want to hire someone to clean this place, I'm not going to protest."

"I've got Marta scheduled every Thursday morning." His blue eyes lock onto mine. "Don't ever change what you eat because of me, Rosa. Don't ever change anything about yourself. You're perfect exactly the way you are."

Then he washes both our plates, puts them in the drying rack, and leaves. And I'm left staring after him with an open mouth.

19

LEO

Tomas intercepts me when I get to work.

"What now?" I ask wearily. "Let me guess. It isn't enough that Max Guerra is in Venice, so Rocco Santini decided to join him. You're here to tell me there's a war waging in the streets."

"No." He enters my office and sits down. "This is something else. Goran and I tossed a coin to see who got to tell you about it."

"You're being very mysterious, Tomas."

"Not for long." He hands me a USB key. "Play this."

"There isn't a virus on it, is there?" I ask suspiciously. Valentina, our resident hacker, constantly warns us not to plug strange USB keys into our laptops. According to her, it's one of the easiest ways to hack into a computer. If she were here, she'd have a fit.

"It's clean." Tomas pauses, Valentina's admonishment undoubtedly ringing in his ears as well. "I think." He gets up with a roll of his eyes. "Damn it, she got in my head. Hang on. Let me find a spare laptop."

He returns in a minute with a brand-new computer. "Not connected to our network or the Internet," he announces. "Okay, let's try this again." He boots up the laptop, skips past the various customization prompts, and inserts the USB key. "This is a recording from a security camera in Rosa's MMA gym yesterday."

I come to attention. "What happened?"

Tomas takes his time getting to the point. "Ignazio was on duty and had eyes on her," he says. "He saw this interaction. He was just getting ready to intervene when—"

"Tomas," I grind out between clenched teeth. "What the fuck happened?"

In reply, he plays the video.

Rosa enters the gym, and a man immediately accosts her in the foyer, blocking her way to the changing room. He says something, and she responds, her body language screaming discomfort.

Then he puts his hands on my fiancée's shoulders and starts to massage them.

I see red.

Rosa tries to pull away, and his grip on her tightens.

I dig my nails into my palm. "Who is he?"

"His name is Simon Groff," Tomas says. "He co-owns the gym along with Alina Zuccaro. The two of them dated for three months two years ago, shortly after her mother died. Groff somehow convinced Alina to invest her life savings plus her inheritance into the purchase of this gym. He's not interested in running it. He leads two sparsely attended classes a week while she runs twenty, but it's his name on the storefront." Tomas sounds disgusted. "According to Valentina, Alina's been trying to buy Groff out, but he wants more than a million euros for his share, and it's not even worth half that."

"Let me guess: he likes to use the gym as a way to prey on women."

"Looks that way. Last year, one of his students complained about him. Two days later, a video of her having sex with her boyfriend ended up on the Internet. It was a mess. The boyfriend was a married high school principal. He accused his girlfriend of leaking the video to ruin his marriage, she got fired from her job and had a nervous breakdown, and in the tumult, Simon Groff was conveniently forgotten."

I've heard enough. "Where is he right now?"

"He finishes with a class in twenty minutes."

I get to my feet and roll up my sleeves. "Good. I think I'll pay him a visit."

My rage builds as I walk to the gym, that video playing over and over in my head. Rosa's acute discomfort as Groff encroached into her personal space, her flinch when he put his hands on her.

He touched my fiancée without permission.

He made her uncomfortable in a space that brings her joy.

He is going to regret it.

The class is over by the time I get to Dorsoduro, but a handful of guys linger, surrounding Groff and laughing at something on his phone. I slam the door shut behind me, and their heads snap up. "I want to talk to Groff," I say flatly. "Everyone else—get out."

They're all wannabe MMA fighters, but they

must hear the danger in my voice or see it in my face because, after a short moment of hesitation, they flee.

"What the—?" Groff begins. "Who are—"

That's all he manages before I cross the room, grab him by the jacket, and slam him into the wall. I jam my forearm against his throat to shut him up. "I'm going to do the talking," I say conversationally, "and you are going to listen. You harassed my fiancée, Rosa. And, from what I hear, she's not the first one."

He tries to twist out of my grip, and I let go of his neck and hammer a vicious punch into his gut. The breath whooshes out of him, and he collapses on the floor. "I'm going to say this just once, so listen carefully. You speak one word to Rosa, and I will cut out your tongue. You look at her covetously, and I'll gouge your eyes out. You lay your hands on her again, and that'll be the last thing you ever do." I snap a kick into his side, think about it for a second, and break both his wrists for good measure. "Is that clear?"

20

ROSA

I don't see Leo for the rest of Thursday. I do hear from Daniel Rossi, though. The lawyer calls me shortly after lunch. "Leo told me you were busy tomorrow," he says. "I'm in your neighborhood now. Do you have a few minutes?"

The boutique isn't busy. "Sure," I reply. "Come on by."

He shows up ten minutes later. "Congratulations on your upcoming marriage." He opens his briefcase and pulls out a thick folder. "These are for you."

That's a lot of paperwork. "Should I get my own lawyer to look through the prenup?" I joke. A few years ago, my landlord was jerking me around, and Valentina asked Daniel to help out. By the time he was done, my landlord was ready to offer me anything as long as it got my lawyer off his case. "After all, I know how you feel about your clients signing anything before you've had a chance to review it."

"I'm always going to advise you to get your own counsel," he replies. "But in this case, there's nothing to sign. There's no prenup."

I gape at him. "What do you mean, there isn't one? Leo needs to get one to protect his interests."

"Not according to him, he doesn't." He opens the folder and starts handing me documents. "Bank account details," he says. "You've been added as a joint holder on his account. Life insurance policy, Leo's updated will, listing you as the sole beneficiary... Oh, and this."

This being a black credit card, similar to the one Leo whipped out at the jewelry store. I stare at it blankly, struggling to make sense of what's happening. "What's the limit on this thing?" I splutter.

Daniel looks like he's trying not to laugh at me. "There isn't one." He shuts his briefcase and prepares to leave. "Have a nice afternoon, Rosa."

Leo is nowhere to be seen Friday morning either, so I can't yell at him about Daniel's visit. I eat breakfast alone, drink a couple of cups of coffee, then shower, get dressed, and walk to work. The streets are packed with tourists, and I have to struggle to get through the throngs. I get bumped more than once, the last time hard enough that I drop my phone on the ground. Whoever hit me doesn't even bother to apologize. Muttering a curse, I grab my phone and hurry into my boutique.

Gisele is already there. "What's wrong?" she asks.

"Oh, some idiot just bumped into me. I dropped my phone. I'm lucky the screen didn't shatter." I shake my head. "Is it too much to ask that people look where they're going?"

"Tourists are good for business," Gisele points out practically. "Speaking of which, how's the search going?"

I make a face. Gisele is about to be on vacation for the next two weeks, and I've been looking for someone temporary to take her place. But so far, I've had no luck finding help, and I can't see the situation changing. I'm looking for someone with prior experience working in a small boutique, but the pay isn't great, and I need them to start on Tuesday. It's just not going to happen. "Let's talk about something else."

She frowns. "How are you going to manage? You have three wedding dresses to make, a calendar filled with fittings, and samples to sew for Milan."

"I haven't heard from Milan yet. They might not pick me."

"They'll pick you," Gisele replies. "You're swamped. Do you want me to postpone my trip?"

"No!" It's incredibly kind of her to offer, but this isn't her problem to solve. Plus, she's been looking forward to visiting her family. "No, of course not. I'll manage. You just worry about having a good time."

"You're sure?"

"I'm positive."

Gisele switches back to her favorite topic of conversation, my surprise engagement. On Tuesday, she admired the ring and asked me a thousand questions about Leo. Wednesday, she found out that we were planning on moving in together but that I didn't know where I'd be living. "I don't have time to handle the details, so Leo is," I said, hoping that would be the end of it, but of course it wasn't. Gisele is astonished that I don't want to have a say in my new home. Which is, to be fair, a pretty valid thing to be shocked about. "How did the move go? Where do you and your new fiancé live now? Was the apartment he found adequate?"

"It was more than adequate." I hand her my phone. "Look at my new sewing room."

She swipes through the photos. "Wow," she says. "You have so much space." She zooms in on the cabinets. "Glass doors, nice. And look, you have empty shelves. You can buy more fabric."

"I think it's safe to say I don't need any more fabric." I unpack a box from my manufacturer and sigh. No matter how carefully Daria packs them, stuff always gets crumpled in transit. I pull out the ironing table and start to press the dresses, Gisele hanging them up as I finish. Then it's time to open.

GISELE LEAVES at noon for lunch. I check my phone —again—but the only message is from my mother asking me what time I'm going to get to their house.

Nothing from the Milan committee. I let out a long exhale. As much as I tell myself that it's too early to give up hope, it's hard not to get discouraged. I thought my portfolio was strong, and I hoped I'd be one of the front-runners. But maybe I'm fooling myself? Maybe I'm not ready for the big leagues yet.

"Hello? Are you Rosa Tran?"

I look up. The woman speaking is in her late fifties or her early sixties. She's dressed in a white cotton shirt and a narrow pencil skirt, her auburn hair pulled back in a bun. The clothes are nothing fancy, but everything is of the highest quality, and she looks effortlessly elegant.

"I am. Can I help you?"

"I understand you have an opening for a salesperson," she replies. "I would like to apply."

I blink in confusion. I put up a sign in the window out of desperation when I got back from Lecce—did she see it? "Do you have any sales experience, Signora...?"

"My name is Annalisa Bartolo," she says. "And yes, I do. I worked for Moda Nono for fourteen years and for Saratoria Strambelli for another four." She holds out a piece of paper. "My resume and references."

The Fixer

Somebody pinch me, I'm dreaming. Moda Nono is one of the oldest clothing boutiques in Venice. Maya Strambelli, who owns Saratoria Strambelli, opened her store a couple of years before me. If Signora Bartolo is telling the truth, I could not have dreamed up a more perfect candidate for the position.

After weeks of searching, this feels like a miracle. I want to pinch myself. "How did you hear about the vacancy?"

"Leo called me."

What?

"He said his fiancée needed help and asked if I could come out of retirement for a couple of weeks." She gives me a warm smile. "Naturally, I had so many questions. He's kept very quiet about you, and I'm quite annoyed with him. But, of course, I was ready to help. Leo is like family, and I'm so happy that he's finally found someone." She gives me a searching look. "He hasn't mentioned me either, has he?"

"Umm..."

"My father Niccolo was his tailor."

Ah. "Leo said he was one of a kind."

"He was that and more." A shadow falls over Signora Bartoli's face, and then she straightens her shoulders. "I'm sure you want to contact my references—"

"No!" I blurt out. I will do my due diligence, but honestly, Leo's recommendation is good enough. "That's not necessary, Signora Bartoli. Can you start on Tuesday?"

"Yes," she replies. "And call me Annalisa, Rosa. After all, you're going to be family, too."

I mentioned Gisele's departure to Leo *once*. A throwaway comment about how much work I had, nothing more than that. But he *heard* me, he called Annalisa, and he asked her to come out of retirement to help me.

He might have bitten my head off last night, but once again, he's solved my problems.

I pull out my phone to text him my thanks, but just as I do, I get a message from Leo.

> What time are you headed to your parents?

He remembered they were coming into town today. My heart warms. Leo never misses the details.

> Three-ish. Thank you for sending Annalisa my way.

> It was nothing. I'll come with you to their apartment. Pick you up at your boutique at three.

My lips twitch. Leo's telling me what to do again instead of asking me, and it should annoy me. But it's impossible to be angry at someone who makes all my problems go away.

> Okay, I'll wait for you.

I stare at my phone for a long time after that. Leo took away one of the largest sources of stress in my life. *Again.* Every time I have a problem, Leo makes it go away.

I keep thanking him, but my words feel so inadequate. I need to *do* something. Something meaningful. But what?

And then I think about the fabric from last night, and it comes to me. The thing I can do. I don't really like sewing menswear, and I haven't made a shirt in ages. I'm sure my skills are incredibly rusty. But for Leo, I'm going to make the effort.

His birthday is in a week. I have just enough time.

I'M PACKING up my stuff to leave when my phone rings.

No, not my phone. My ringtone is different.

The noise is coming from my bag.

I rummage through the contents and find a small black phone. This isn't mine; I've never seen it before. Where did it come from, and why is it here? Frowning, I pick it up.

"Rosa Tran," a male voice says. "Your brother stole ten million euros from me. I want it back. Tell him that if he doesn't stop ignoring my calls, he's in for a world of pain."

Shock renders me almost speechless. "Who are you?"

The man on the other end ignores my question. "Oh, and if I were you, I wouldn't tell anyone except Hugh about this call. If you talk to Cesari or anyone else, I will kill your family."

The phone goes dead.

21

LEO

Something is wrong with Rosa. She smiles at me when I get to her boutique, but the smile doesn't reach her eyes. She introduces me to her shop assistant Gisele, and we make conversation, but she is not as animated as she usually is. And when we step outside, she reaches into her bag, pulls out a pair of sunglasses, and puts them on, hiding her eyes from me.

"What's wrong?" I ask her as we walk to my boat. It can't be about Groff; I'm having him watched.

She swallows. "Nothing."

"Have you heard from Milan? You were going to hear from them today, right?"

"You remembered?"

"Why wouldn't I? It's important to you."

She takes a deep breath. "You can't say things like that to me," she blurts out. "I wish you'd stop."

I'm a little lost. "Stop what?"

"Pretending I matter." Her hands clench into fists. "Doing nice things for me, like setting up a sewing room or reaching out to Annalisa. Adding me to your bank account, making me the sole beneficiary in your will, or giving me a credit card without a limit. I have no idea where I stand with you. You do a thousand thoughtful things for me, but when I wait up for you because I'm freaking out and worried, you bite my head off."

The wind blows her hair in her face, and she violently pulls it back into a ponytail. "You keep telling me we're not in a real relationship, but you constantly blur the line, and I don't know what to do anymore."

She is not wrong to be confused. I am a walking, talking study in contradiction. I'm drawn to Rosa. Even now, I'm struggling to hold back the urge to pull her into my arms. Something has upset her, and I want to make it better. Two nights ago, I had my mouth on her nipples. I want that again and more, and I want it with painful intensity.

And yet I keep holding back, and I keep pulling

away, and the reasons for doing that are becoming increasingly unclear.

Why wouldn't she be confused? I'm confusing the fuck out of myself.

It's not about Patrizia anymore. I loved her, and she will always have a place in my heart, but Tomas was right. She wouldn't want me to mourn her forever. She would want me to *live,* not just go through the motions. She would want me to have a life filled with laughter and love.

It's not her memory that's holding me back.

It's fear.

I'm afraid to fall in love again, afraid of how vulnerable it makes me.

"Can't friends do nice things for each other?" *Liar,* a voice inside me screams. *You want much more than her friendship. You want everything.*

"Yes."

"So, we're friends, then."

I wait for her to point out that friends don't almost fuck each other on a cutting table, but she doesn't. She's oddly subdued today, her usual effervescence absent. Maybe it's because of the mixed signals I've been giving her?

But Rosa's never let me faze her before. She always has a snappy comeback for me. What's wrong today? Is it because she hasn't heard from Milan? Is it because her parents are in town, and she has to deal with their favoritism up close? Or is it something else entirely?

She regards me for a long time, but her damn sunglasses keep me from seeing her expression. "Okay," she says. "Friends. And since you're my friend, I'm going to give you a word of advice: leave now and save yourself from my mother's cleaning spree."

"I'll manage. Besides, Marta has cleaned the apartment from top to bottom."

"It doesn't matter," she predicts. "My mother will still find something to do."

DESPITE ROSA'S FEARS, her mother is pleased with the apartment. "It's lovely, Leo," she says after our initial hugs of greeting. "And such a convenient location. It's so close to work for both Ben and me."

"I'm glad you like it."

Her father shakes my hand. "Ander Reinhart," he

says, looking bemused. "Reinhart Automotive. I still can't believe they wanted to hire me."

"Believe it," Rosa replies. "They're lucky to have you. Were the movers fine?"

"Of course," Elaine beams. "They were perfect. When Hugh told us we had to move, I wasn't sure what we'd do, but everything was so easy." She pats me on my hand. "All thanks to Leo."

Rosa's parents are displaying epic levels of denial about their son's activities. I glance at Rosa, expecting her to be rolling her eyes at the praise being thrown in my direction, but instead, she looks stressed. "Where is Hugh?"

"Oh, he went out as soon as we got here," her mother replies with fond exasperation. "You know how he is. He'll be back in time for dinner; you'll see him then. You're staying for dinner, aren't you?"

"Actually," I interject, "We just came by to see how you were settling in. But if there's nothing we can do to help, then we have an appointment with the wedding planner."

Rosa looks at me in surprise. "We do?"

"Violette had a last-minute availability on her schedule. I told her we'd try to make it if we could."

"Yes, yes," Elaine says, making shooing motions at us. "Go meet her. Have you set a date yet?"

I exchange a glance with Rosa. "Next month," she responds after a beat.

"Next month?" Her mother's mouth falls open. "Rosa, are you preg—"

"No," my fiancée cuts her off, her voice harsh. "I'm not. We just didn't want to wait, that's all."

Oh. For the first time, it occurs to me to wonder if Rosa wants children. If she does, that's another thing she's giving up by marrying me. I feel awful. Fuck. It's a testament to her inherent sweetness that she doesn't hate me.

"But the details," Elaine says, her hands fluttering. I'm her soon-to-be son-in-law, and she's too polite to tell me that this idea is insane, but her unhappiness at the rush is obvious. "The planning. How will we even find a venue in time? What about a dress? Invitations have to be sent out, a caterer found... You can't do all of that in a month."

"Violette is very good at her job," I say calmly, getting to my feet and holding out my hand to Rosa. "She'll handle all the details. All you'll need to do is be there."

Rosa laces her finger in mine. "Tell Hugh to call me tonight," she says, her expression stressed. "I need to talk to him."

The Fixer

WHILE ROSA IS SAYING goodbye to her parents, I head outside and call Ciro Del Barba. As usual, he picks up on the first ring. The man must spend his life glued to his phone. He picks it up in the middle of sex, for all I know. "Cesari," he says. "I didn't expect to hear from you. It can't be something Guerra did. He's heading back to Lecce for the next couple of weeks."

He is? "This isn't about Guerra. I need a favor."

Come into my parlor. . . "Of course," Ciro says smoothly. "What can I do for you?"

"Rosa applied to show at Milan Fashion Week," I reply. "She hasn't heard back from the committee yet, but if she's not on the shortlist—"

"You want me to make it happen. Okay."

"What will it cost me?"

"The usual. You'll owe me a favor in the future."

"Nothing that will compromise my loyalty to the Padrino."

"Agreed." His voice turns amused. "You seem very protective of your wife, Leo. I'm not surprised. I saw you dance at Dante's wedding, and it was obvious how you felt about her."

Not Del Barba, too. Next, I'll find out he's participating in the office pool. And knowing Del Barba, he'll win it. I hang up on him without comment just as Rosa comes out. "Where are we meeting the wedding planner?"

She still looks stressed. Hopefully, hearing about Milan will take some of that away. "Lido."

"Lido? We're going to the beach?"

"There're other reasons to go to Lido, principessa," I tease. "But yes, we're going to the beach. We'll meet Violette, and then I thought we could spend the rest of the afternoon soaking up the sun. And don't tell me you don't have time; I know you cleared your schedule so that you could help your mother clean."

"But—"

"I'll take you back home if that's what you really want. But when was the last time you went to the beach?"

"In Venice? It's been years. It's so close by, and yet somehow there's never time." I can see her struggle with temptation. "I don't have a swimsuit."

"Buy one there." I picture Rosa in a dressing room, trying on bikini after bikini, twirling in front of me and asking me which one is my favorite, and my cock hardens. *Fuck.* I must love to torture myself.

"There *are* a couple of boutiques in Lido that I want to visit..."

"Spying on the competition? I like it." I help her into my boat. "Come on, principessa. Take the afternoon off. You know you want to."

She bites her lip thoughtfully, and then she makes up her mind. "Okay," she says, giving me a heart-stoppingly wide smile. "Let's do it."

VIOLETTE MAES CAME to Venice fifteen years ago on vacation, fell in love with the city, and never left. Her father is Belgian, her mother is American, she speaks seven languages fluently, and she's the most well-connected woman in Venice. If she ever decided to use her powers for evil, she could give Ciro Del Barba a run for his money.

We meet her in the lobby of the Excelsior. Violette greets Rosa with kisses on both cheeks. "Rosa, I haven't seen you since Valentina's wedding. When Leo told me the two of you were getting married, you could have knocked me down with a feather."

"Me too," Rosa says with a laugh. "Hello, Violette."

The wedding planner quickly figures out Rosa loves the ocean and suggests a beach wedding. "We could have it here," she says. "The wedding department manager at the Excelsior owes me a favor."

Rosa's eyes shine. "A beach wedding?" She glances at me. "Could we do that? I know you wanted to get married in church—"

Fuck, no. That's the last thing I want to do. Too many bad memories, too many ghosts from the past. "I'm good with the beach."

"Perfect. I'll check with Giacomo to see what dates are available in October, and I'll get back to you on Monday. Rosa, I'm assuming you'll be making your dress?"

Violette is the best in the business for a reason. In thirty minutes, we hammer out the details. Well, the two of them sort out the details, and I wisely keep my mouth shut, offering my opinion only when asked. Rosa is beaming by the time we're done. "Smart move hiring Violette," she says, linking her arm with mine. "She was great at Valentina's wedding. Really great."

"Another thing off your to-do list."

She laughs. "It's a never-ending list," she says. "But I can safely check this one off. Beach?"

ROSA VISITS TWO BOUTIQUES, spending ten minutes at each. She buys a plain black bikini at the second, and then we head back to the Excelsior, change into our swimsuits, and claim a pair of beach chairs with umbrellas. A white-clad waiter brings us towels and drinks. "This is nice," Rosa sighs as she takes a sip of her Aperol spritz. "I should do this more often."

I can't take my eyes off her. "Why don't you?"

"Have I mentioned the never-ending to-do list?" she asks wryly. "There's always something when you run your own business. When was the last time you were here?"

"I don't remember," I tell her honestly. The sight of her in her bikini is making the blood rush from my brain to pool much lower. Warm brown skin, round breasts, curved hips, legs that go on for days. . . My cock aches for her.

Get yourself under control, for fuck's sake.

I adjust myself discreetly. I need a boner-killing topic of conversation, and I need it now. "Do you want children?"

She gives me a sideways glance. "Do you?"

A little girl with Rosa's luminous eyes. "I've never thought about it," I lie. "And you're avoiding answering my question."

"I want children at some point, yes," she replies. She's wearing those damn sunglasses again, and I can't see her expression. "But not for a few years yet." Her gaze lingers on me. "In three or four years, maybe one of those lovers I'll take will do the deed."

I *hate* the thought of another man touching her the way I did. *Hate* that another man might hear her moans, glide his coarse hands over her delicate skin, part her soft thighs, and—

Fuck.

I clench my hand into a fist. *This is your choice,* an unwelcome inner voice points out. *You can have a relationship with Rosa. You just won't let yourself.*

I LAPSE INTO A BROODING SILENCE. Ten minutes later, I get a text from Del Barba.

> She's in.

> Thank you.

> No thanks are necessary; I didn't do anything. She was already on the shortlist.

But, of course, I'll still owe him a favor. Deal with the spider, get trapped in his web. I regret nothing.

> When are they going to tell her?

> She should be getting an email any minute now.

Just as he says that Rosa's phone buzzes. She makes a face and reaches for it. "It could be Gisele," she says. "I better check." She picks it up, then her face breaks out into a smile. "I got an email from the Milan Fashion Week committee," she says happily. "I'm in."

"That's fantastic. Want another drink to celebrate?"

She looks up at the sky. Sometime in the last ten minutes, ominous-looking rainclouds have rolled in.

"I don't think we have time," she says as a bolt of lightning flashes across the sky. "In fact, I think we better run."

It's still raining when we pull up at the dock. "Let's make a run for it," I suggest as I help her out of the boat. "We only have a couple of blocks to go."

"I can't," Rosa replies regretfully. "Wrong shoes. I'll slip on the cobblestones and break my neck. You go ahead, though. There's no need for both of us to get soaked."

I roll my eyes and scoop her up into my arms. She squeals in surprise. "Leo," she laughs. "Put me down. This is ridiculous."

"Not as ridiculous as your shoes."

"I'll have you know that my sandals are works of art," she says loftily. "And if you wanted me to wear sensible shoes, orsacchiotto mio, you should have warned me we were going to the beach."

"Touché."

We're both drenched and laughing by the time we

get home. I unlock the front door, but when I set her down inside, her laughter dies away. "I think I'll make an early night of it," she says, not meeting my eyes. "I'm going to take a hot shower and head to bed."

"You haven't eaten."

"I'm not hungry." She kisses my cheek. "Good night, Leo."

I make myself a sandwich and eat it in front of the TV. A movie about a jewelry heist looks interesting, but once it starts playing, I can't focus. With Rosa not here, the silence feels oppressive. I stare balefully at the walls of my father's cavernous palazzo and brood. I don't want her taking another lover in three years. Rosa's going to be *my wife*. Mine. And I don't share. I don't want a mistress either, damn it. I just want Rosa.

It takes me a very long time to fall asleep.

A SCREAM SPLITS THE AIR. I jerk awake, my heart pounding. Bad dream? Then Rosa shrieks again, and fear twists my insides. I jump out of bed, grab my gun, and run full speed toward her bedroom, skidding to a halt as I throw open her door.

Then I blink.

Rosa's standing next to her bed, her cream nightgown soaking wet. Water has turned the fabric transparent, and I can see every curve of her body. The deep brown of her nipples, the dark triangle between her legs, everything.

Why is she wet? "What happened?"

In reply, she points upward.

I look up. Water is running down through the ceiling.

It's not a trickle.

It's a downpour.

22

ROSA

Rain is pouring from the ceiling in a deluge. I'm soaked, my mattress is ruined, and puddles are starting to form on the floor. My bedroom is uninhabitable. But when Leo comes running in, I forget all my discomfort.

Because he's naked.

My brain short-circuits. Leo is gorgeous all the time to me, with his sharp cheekbones, the scar angled across the left side of his face, and his ocean-blue eyes. But I've never seen him naked before. Hell, I've never even seen him shirtless before.

And I can't stop staring.

His body is firm, muscled, and scarred. A priceless sculpture vandalized by graffiti. Except the scars are an integral part of Leo, the story of his life, written on his skin.

Then there's his cock. As hard as I try to keep my gaze averted, my eyes keep returning to it. Already impressively long and thick, it starts to engorge as he stands there until it juts out, hard, eager, and ready.

"You're very bi—" I shut my mouth before I can finish that thought, though, from the dark flash in Leo's eyes, he knows what I stopped myself from blurting out. "Naked. You're naked. And you have a gun."

"You cried out."

I look closer at his face and notice the sweat beading on his forehead. Leo bolted out of his bedroom without bothering with clothes because *he was afraid for me.*

My cheeks feel hot. *Stop looking at his cock,* I scold myself. *Stop wondering what touching it would feel like.*

"I'm not in danger. The roof, on the other hand. . ."

I'm not the only one having difficulty keeping my eyes to myself. Leo's gaze moves over my body slowly and appreciatively. I'm sure I look like a drenched rat, but he must not think so because when he looks at me, something intense flares in his eyes.

There's a tingling in the pit of my stomach. My

heart jolts, and my pulse pounds. Desire keeps me rooted in place, a strong, crippling longing that only Leo can satisfy.

Just stop.

I make myself move. Grabbing the robe hanging on the back of the door, I toss it to him. He catches it, his expression puzzled, then appears to register his nakedness and puts it on. It's ridiculously short on him. It barely covers his ass, his erect cock tents the front, and it does nothing to quench the flame burning inside me.

He looks at me as if he wants to devour me, and I want him to. I want him to consume me.

"The gun is real?" What a dumb question. Leo works for the *Mafia*. Of course the gun is real.

"Yes." He clicks the safety back on and runs his hand over his face. When he looks at me again, the moment is over, and he's back to his calm, collected self. "You're shivering," he says. "You can't sleep here. Take a hot shower, and I'll make you something to drink."

It's not because I'm cold—I haven't even registered the temperature. I'm shivering because of his nearness.

And it doesn't matter. It doesn't matter how much Leo wants me because he's not going to let himself do anything about it. I've banged my head against this wall often enough that I've given myself a concussion, and it's time I stopped.

"You're snapping orders at me again, orsacchiotto mio," I say through gritted teeth.

He exhales slowly. "You're shivering," he repeats. "I don't want you to catch a cold. You can either take a shower of your own accord, or I will pick you up and put you there myself. You *will* be safe under my watch. Is that clear, principessa?"

My forehead furrows. His voice is level, but a wild storm rages in his eyes. *You will be safe under my watch.* This isn't about a leaky roof, and this isn't about my soaking wet nightdress. This is about something else entirely.

I'm missing something important.

Without another word, I turn and head to the bathroom. My lord and master has ordered a hot shower. I live to obey.

LEO IS in the kitchen when I emerge from the shower wearing black silk pajamas and a matching tank top, and his eyes rest on me an instant too long before he drags his gaze away.

"Cocoa," he says, handing me a mug. He's fully dressed in a faded pair of jeans and a T-shirt that clings to the taut muscles of his chest and abs. "My mother used to make me cocoa when I got caught in the rain."

I cherish the freely volunteered snippet of personal information. "Thank you."

"I checked the bedrooms. Your room took the brunt of the storm. I'm afraid your mattress is ruined." His lips twitch. "Before you ask, your sewing room is dry, and your fabric is safe. The water damage seems to have confined itself to that floor."

I hadn't thought about my fabric at all. "That's good." The cocoa is hot, rich, and creamy. I tend to default to tea when I need a warm beverage during the day, but hot chocolate is coming in strong as a contender.

"I'll find contractors in the morning. As for the rest of tonight, you can sleep in my bedroom."

"Okay."

I finish my cocoa and follow Leo back upstairs. Three of the empty bedrooms have buckets in them to catch the leaks. No buckets in my bedroom—

there's no point as my mattress is acting as a giant sponge—but towels cover the floor, soaking up the puddles. "You've been busy."

He grunts in reply. I trail after him to his bedroom, which miraculously has remained completely dry. He waves me toward the king-size bed. "I'll sleep in one of the other bedrooms."

"Seriously?" This is ridiculous. "On what mattress?"

"The floor is fine."

If I strangle him right now, there's not a judge or jury in the city that will find me guilty. "Leo, half the bedrooms have leaks," I say, clinging to my rapidly dwindling patience with both hands. "This is the only dry room on this floor, and you have a king-size mattress. There's plenty of room for both of us."

It's not just my patience that's eroding. It's also my optimism. Leo's attracted to me, and yet he persists in pushing me away. His many rejections have worn me down, and I'm struggling not to burst into tears. The rest of my life stretches in front of me, a wasteland devoid of love, warmth, *touch.* I've never slept with anyone; I was waiting for fireworks and animal magnetism. Had I known my future would be a dry, sexless desert, I would have fucked the first guy I kissed.

He edges toward the door. "That's a bad idea, Rosa."

"Why? Because you're attracted to me?"

"I'm not—"

That's it. My optimism gauge hits empty. First I get that mysterious phone call, then my brother gives me the run-around, and now this from Leo? I have officially run out of fucks. "Liar," I snarl, a wounded animal fighting for its life. "Stop giving me that bullshit. I bet you a hundred euros that you are hard for me *right now.*"

He stares at me for a long moment, then he takes his wallet out, extracts a crisp hundred-euro note from it, and tosses it on the bed between us.

"So, what?" I give him a look of disbelief. "You're just going to throw the money down and walk away? Just like that?"

"Yes." He rakes his fingers through his hair. "It's for the best. I told you once I was no good for you. That hasn't changed, principessa."

His damn nickname for me is what does it. It's the last straw. "Fine!" I half-scream, half-sob. He's walking to the door, his back to me, and it feels like he's walking out of my life. "Make your excuses and run away. I'll just stay here, fall asleep on your bed, and stay a fucking virgin for the rest of my life."

He freezes. "What did you say?"

"Make your excuses and run away."

"Not that part." He sounds strained. "The other thing."

"That I've never had sex before? I thought you knew."

He turns around slowly. "No, principessa. I *definitely* did not know. That's not the kind of thing a man forgets." His eyes are dark and unfathomable. "You've never slept with anyone? Why?"

Oh, for fuck's sake. "Trust a man to make a big deal out of this."

"Why?" he repeats insistently.

Men. "Because I was never attracted enough to anyone to want to do it," I say in exasperation. "I didn't want to sleep with someone just to check it off a list."

He swallows convulsively. "And you invited me to your hotel room because—"

It's perfectly obvious why, but Leo seems to need me to say the words. "I want you."

"Still?"

Always. "Yes. But it's okay," I continue unwisely, goading him with every word. "I can wait. In three years, I'll find someone else. Someone who will fuck me on the floor and against the wall." I have no trouble remembering his words. They are permanently engraved into my memory. "Someone who will fuck me in the shower stall. He'll push my legs apart and lick my pretty clit until I come." I lift my chin and glare at Leo defiantly. "And when I come, it won't be your name I'll scream. It'll be his."

Leo *moves*. In two steps, he's next to me, looming over me like a prince of darkness. "You want me to fuck you, principessa?" He pushes me against the wall and cages me in with the hard press of his body. "You want me to shove my cock into your hot, tight pussy?"

If he's trying to frighten me away, it's not working. "Yes."

His eyes blaze. He lifts my wrists above my head and pins them in place with one hand. "Be careful what you wish for, tesoro." His voice is low and dangerous. He drags his lips down my neck, his breath hot against my skin. "Walk away while you still can."

"You think I'm scared of you?" I push against his grip, and he lets me go, taking a step back. "I'm not." I whip my tank top over my head. "I'm not going to walk away. And if I run, it'll only be because I want you to chase me."

I didn't put a bra on after my shower, and Leo's

eyes lock onto my breasts. I feel his need like a shock on my skin, a restless, aching current in my bloodstream. He doesn't move, not even an inch. Anticipation is a storm raging around us, and for a moment, we're perfectly still, caught in the eye of the hurricane.

Then his lips crash into mine.

I was overwhelmed by Leo's kisses Wednesday night. I thought I had finally discovered what passion feels like. But now, as he *plunders* my mouth, I realize how much he was holding back.

He's not holding back now. *He's all in.* He wraps his hand around the back of my neck and coaxes my lips open. His tongue slides into my mouth, teasing, dancing, claiming. One ravishing, intoxicating kiss follows another, and desire explodes inside me.

I arch my head, stand on tiptoe, and return each hungry kiss with one of my own. His hands travel down my body, his palms closing on my naked breasts, and my nipples throb against his callused fingers. "How many men have touched you here?" he growls into my neck.

"This is a ridiculous discussion," I gasp. God, the feel of him. Before, he kissed me through my bra, and I thought I died of pleasure, but today, skin on skin, I am *ablaze.* Need rages in my blood, a thirst that only Leo can quench. "I'm not going to tell you."

He plucks my nipple between his thumb and forefinger, and I gasp at the sharp, raw pleasure. "How many?" he growls.

Do that again, please, dear God, I need it. . . "One," I say, throwing my head back in utter abandon. "You."

He makes a low noise in his throat, and I can't tell if he's pleased with my answer or unhappy. "Why?" he demands, cupping my breasts with both hands and squeezing them together as if he can't get enough of them. He kisses my throbbing nipples and sucks hard, trapping them between his teeth. "Tell me."

What is it about my virginity that has him so fascinated? Everyone's a virgin at some point in their lives. It's honestly not that interesting. "It's none of your business, *orsacchiotto mio*," I say sweetly. "Besides, I already told you why. I was never attracted to anyone."

"To sleep with them, yes. But to do this?" He scratches his nails gently over the swollen tips, and the rush of pleasure leaves me momentarily speechless. "You never wanted a man to do that to you?"

Don't stop.

"I wanted to feel. . . passion. Raw desire. An all-consuming thirst." I inhale sharply as his hands move lower, slipping inside my waistband. He's just inches away from my pussy, and I want. . . *more. Everything.* "I never found it." I look into his eyes, those ocean-blue eyes whose depths I want to drown in. "Until now."

His hand stops its slow progress toward my clit, and he bites off a swear. "What the fuck am I doing?" he grinds out. "You're so fucking *young*. I lost my virginity before you were born, for fuck's sake. I fell in love before you took your first steps. Now you're stuck with me, and I'm the worst kind of asshole there is. Because I'm going to take everything you're offering and more."

Leo was in love? With whom? "You can't take it from me if I give it to you first," I pant into his skin. He smells like musk and sandalwood, soap and sweat. My heart is pounding, my body feels feverish. I lace my fingers into his hair and tug him close. "And I do."

He swears out loud, and his grip on my breasts tightens. "Please," I gasp. It was all worth it: the endless uninspired first dates, the long wait for passion, the nights where I lay awake in the dark and wondered if I was holding out for something that didn't exist. "Please, I need..."

"Tell me, principessa," he says. "Tell me what you need, and I will give it to you."

I need his fingers and his mouth on my nipples, and I need them on my clit, and I need them now. "Don't stop," I beg. "Just don't stop."

He lavishes attention on my breasts until they're heavy and aching. "I wanted to suck this nipple into my mouth the first time I saw you," he says harshly. His hand grabs my ass. "At the beach today, I wanted to sink my teeth right here. The entire world could have been watching, and I wouldn't have cared."

I wouldn't have cared either.

He tugs me closer so I can feel the hard throb of his erection against my hip. He kisses me again, a slow, lingering kiss that leaves me breathless. "You're wearing too many clothes," he says into my mouth.

I want to feel him everywhere. "You too." My fingers curl into his shirt, fabric bunching in my palms. "Take this off."

He complies, and I drink him in. His broad chest is sprinkled with a smattering of chest hair. His taut stomach, corded with muscle. And the scars, so many scars. They tell the story of a lifetime of blood and violence, and I want to kiss each and every one of them.

I run my hands all over, graze my thumbs over his nipples, and trace his scars with my fingertips. One mark on his side, fresher than the others, is still an angry red and looks as if his flesh was gouged out by a blunt object. "Where did you get this one?" I ask, stroking it gently.

"It's nothing."

"And you're avoiding answering my question." I can't stop touching him. His skin is warm, almost hot, and his muscles flex in response to my touch. "Tell me."

He trails his hand down the curve of my breast. "When Angelica got kidnapped, we figured out where she was being held. We headed over there in a hurry, and I wasn't paying as much attention as I should have. I ran into a bullet." He shrugs. "It was a graze. Nothing serious."

He's clearly fine. Joking about it, even. But my heart still jumps in my throat. Leo got shot. It could happen again. He's the security head of the Venice Mafia, and he's in danger more often than not. "Valentina didn't tell me you got hurt."

"I asked her not to." He picks up my hand and brings it to his lips. He kisses my palm and then sucks a finger into his mouth. A live current of desire jolts through me. "I don't want you to worry about me. *Ever.*" His lips curl into a wickedly sexy smile. "I took off my shirt," he points out. "I think it's only fair that you reciprocate." He slides his hand into my waistband and cups my mound, and all my thoughts and worries evaporate. "Take off your pajamas."

I slide them down my hips. Leo's fingers hook in the waistband of my panties, and he tugs them down. I step out of the pool of fabric, and he kicks them away.

Then this man, who can snap a man into half with his bare hands, kneels in front of me. He looks up, an anticipatory hunger in his eyes, his entire focus on me. "Spread your legs, principessa."

I obey.

Leo puts his hands on my thighs and pushes them apart. He kisses me everywhere—hungry, possessive kisses on my stomach and my hips—and desire stabs me so hard I almost buckle. "I've been dreaming about this moment for months," he growls, biting my inner thigh. "From the day that fucking strap slipped down your shoulder, and I first set eyes on your perfect, round breast..."

His fingers part my folds. I take an instinctive step back, clenching my eyes shut with pleasure, and my ass hits the wall. He exhales a breath on my clit, and a shiver runs through me. "So wet," he hisses. "So fucking wet." I open my eyes to see him looking at me, his expression hot and glazed with lust. "Have you touched yourself here, Rosa?"

Have I— "Leo," I say crossly. "I'm a virgin; I'm not clueless. Of course, I've touched myself. I'm an expert at getting myself off."

"Excellent." His smile widens with satisfaction. "Show me."

Oh. *Oh.* I flush as his suggestion sinks in. "I can't."

"Like you said, you're the expert here," he says, the big jerk. His hand closes around my wrist, and he moves my hand between my legs. "Get to work, principessa. Show me how you like it."

I rub my finger slowly over my clit. Leo follows it with his tongue, and I have to grit my teeth to keep from screaming. I do it again, and he licks me once more. He repeats my movements, and it's so hot. His tongue shouldn't feel that different from my fingers, but it does, *my God, it really does.* It makes all the difference in the world. His touch lights me on fire.

He continues to follow my lead, his tongue dancing over me with a vengeance, circling my swollen clit repeatedly until I'm a quivering, shaking mess. I dig my nails into my palm and surrender to the sensations that flow through me. "Leo," I groan. "Please..."

"Please what, principessa? Please make you come?" He laughs as he sucks my throbbing clit between his lips. "Not so fast."

He brings me to the edge over and over, backing off just before I fall into orgasm. I've never done this, never teased myself this way. I hate it, I love it, and I never want him to stop. He thrusts a finger inside me, and I whimper. He starts to move it in and out, his thumb pressing on my clit, and I rock my hips against his hand. It all blurs into an intense, overwhelming pleasure.

Relentless pressure builds up inside me. "Please. . ." I beg. Every time Leo's tongue flicks my clit, I unravel a little bit. I gasp and plead and writhe, helpless to resist his skillful lips and fingers. He's feasting on me, and when he looks up at me with glazed eyes, I can see that his chin is glistening with my juices. And there's something so intensely erotic about the sight that I can't hold on. Fireworks explode behind my eyes, and I come, sobbing out his name as I do.

I shudder and shiver as wave after wave of glorious pleasure crests over me. Leo stays with me until the last tremors have died away, and then he gets to his feet, wiping his mouth with the back of his hand, a look of satisfaction on his face. "Tell me, principessa. How do I stack up against your fingers?"

He knows perfectly well how he did. "Hmm," I say, trying to bite back my smile and failing. "I'm not sure. I'll have to do another test. Or three. But first. . ." I reach for his erection. It's a thick bulge straining against his jeans, and I want it. I want Leo's cock. "It's my turn. Show me how you like to be touched?"

23

LEO

Show me how you like to be touched.

She looks at me, those big brown eyes shining with anticipation, her tongue swiping over her oh-so-kissable lips. Fuck. I can't resist. All my intentions of taking it slow, of bringing her to pleasure over and over again, vanish at the thought of her soft hands wrapped around my cock, her sweet, sassy mouth taking my length.

"Come here," I growl. Need rages in my blood, a bone-deep ache that won't be denied. I get naked in a hurry, like a randy teenager, and she moves closer, swiping her tongue over her lower lip. I grab her, wrap my arm around her hips and hold her soft, sweet body against my scarred one.

"Close your fingers around my cock."

Her right hand steals down my stomach. She curves her fingers over my throbbing erection and strokes me, once, twice, a light, exploratory touch. "Like this?" she asks, never taking her eyes off my length. "Or harder?"

"Harder," I hiss, and her grip tightens. *God.* Rosa's intent on her task and eager to please, and it's so fucking erotic. The sight of her pink-gold fingernails wrapped around my cock... So unbearably sexy. At this rate, I'm going to come before she pumps a half-dozen times.

"Show me," she says. "Show me exactly how you like it."

Oh fuck yes. I put my hand over hers and stroke up and down, hard and fast. Her hand feels like warm silk, and I can't get enough. I suck air into my lungs and keep stroking, steady and even. "Like that." My eyes fall on her left hand, and it gives me an idea. "But use your other hand."

She obligingly switches hands and resumes driving me insane. "Why?"

I can't tear my gaze away. "I want to see my ring on your finger as you jerk me off," I choke out. Something about the gemstone on her delicate finger fills me with hot, possessive pleasure. *Mine. My soon-to-be wife.* "Feels good."

Good is the biggest understatement in the world. It feels amazing. The gold band of her engagement ring abrades my engorged head, and I jerk, blood rushing from my brain and going straight to my cock. I can feel my orgasm build. The grip of her fingers and the sweet torture of the ring are pushing me over the edge, but I don't want—I jerk away before I explode.

"I'm going to come undone if I can't fuck you," I say, a growl and a plea worked into one. I pick her up and toss her on my bed. "I'll be slow. Gentle. But I need—"

Her legs fall open for me. "Yes," she says. "Yes, please."

I tried to do the right thing. I tried so fucking hard to stay away from her. But she's lying on my bed, her sweet pussy wet for me, and it's not within my power to walk away. If I were a good man, I would get the hell out of here before I take something from her that I have no right to.

But I've never been that good, and Rosa's impossible to resist.

I grope for a condom, tear the packet open with shaking hands, and roll it over my length. I position myself between her legs. "Are you sure?" I ask, holding myself above her hips, trembling with the effort of staying still. "Are you absolutely sure?"

"Leo," she says. "I've been sure since the first time we met. Shut up and fuck me."

That sassy mouth of hers. I kiss her with hungry urgency. The way she's looking at me—sweet and trusting—I don't deserve it, but I'm going to do everything in my power to make this good for her. I kiss her mouth and neck and shoulders, shuddering as her hips arch in response.

"Rosa," I whisper. "You have no idea how much I want you." I feel like I'm in the grip of an all-consuming fever. I squeeze her breasts and suck her swollen nipples into my mouth, desire twisting in my gut. *Mine.* I'm greedy for her. I want to ravage her, and I never want to let go, and that thought terrifies the crap out of me.

"Leo," she pants against my skin. She whimpers and arches up, offering herself up to my touch. She's flushed and sweaty and glistening, her hair disheveled, her eyes glazed. "I can't wait. . ."

Me neither, principessa. *Me neither.*

I shift my attention lower, moving my hand between her legs. She's drenched, and it's such a fucking aphrodisiac. "You set the pace," I tell her, stroking and teasing her clit until she's gasping and shivering, her skin exploding into goosebumps. "Okay? You tell me when you want more."

"I want more now."

My heart is racing as I part her knees. I'm trembling with the strain of holding on to my control. I push forward, the tip of my cock entering her pussy. Oh fuck yes. The feel of her, tight, wet, and slick, is indescribable. It's as close as I'm ever going to get to heaven.

"More," she breathes.

I rock forward another inch. "Keep going," she orders. My sweet principessa. I laugh between gritted teeth, need clawing through me like a wild animal, and push a little more.

"Just do it," she urges, her hands clutching my biceps. "Do it now."

I push in, burying myself to the hilt. She gasps, and I freeze. "I hurt you," I say, my voice strangled. I push her hair out of her face and look deep into her eyes. "I'm so sorry. I can stop."

"Don't you dare," she responds. "I just need a minute." Her pained expression is clearing. She moves her hips tentatively, and I clench my hands into fists and fight to hold still. The velvety softness of her, the way she's clamped around my cock, gripping me like a vice. . . I'm not going to be able to hold on. I'm going to come with embarrassing speed.

She exhales in a long breath. "I'm good now. More, please."

I begin to move slowly and carefully. She holds my hips with both hands and yanks me closer. Her body is a temple I defile with my touch, but she doesn't seem to care because she's sending me a message right now, and it's one I'm incapable of resisting. More. Faster. Deeper. "So good," I groan. "It's so good with you."

I move faster, my fingers finding her clit, and she throws her head back, her muscles spasming around me. "Yes," she breathes. "God, yes. Had I known how good this would be, I would have taken a hammer to the roof myself."

I laugh into her neck. My thrusts speed up, turning jerky and uneven as my control unravels. She writhes underneath me and digs her nails into my back. Her muscles clench and quiver, and she cries out my name as she comes, and that's all it takes. My balls tighten, and I explode.

WE SNUGGLE TOGETHER, her back against my chest and her ass pressed into my crotch, and I know I'm going to be semi-erect all night long. I want to fuck her all over again, but this was her first time, and she'll be sore.

I kiss the curve of her shoulder. I haven't fallen asleep with a woman in my arms since Patrizia. I haven't been a monk. But intimacy is something I haven't permitted myself.

Until Rosa entered my life.

From the moment I saw her in her green dress, a little bit of spring in the depths of winter, I knew she would be trouble. I had a premonition that she would turn my life upside down. Demolish the walls I put around my heart to protect myself and force me to live again.

To love again.

We're quiet, both of us, but this isn't a silence we need to break. This feels peaceful. It feels like togetherness.

"I wouldn't have done it," she whispers.

Does she have regrets about how tonight turned out? My throat goes dry. "Done what?"

"Taken another lover." Her voice is so quiet I can barely hear her over the noise of the rain. "In two or three years, or whenever Spina Sacra stopped watching us." She takes a deep breath. "I just wanted you to know."

I trail a fingertip over her arm. "Why not?"

"We're going to be married next month," she replies. "We're going to promise to love and cherish each other. When I say those words, I'll mean them. I take my promises seriously."

A fist squeezes around my heart. She's offering me her love. *Just like that.* As if it weren't the most precious gift in the universe. *I'll mean them, too,* I want to reply, but I can't make my mouth form the words. When I close my eyes, I only see blood. I see the people I failed to protect.

"Are you rolling your eyes at me? You didn't know how much of a romantic I was, did you?"

"I think I had a pretty good idea." Rosa reminds me of a daffodil or a snowdrop, one of the flowers that poke their head up in the depths of winter and herald the arrival of spring. I should tell her that, but once again, the words freeze on my tongue. "People have open marriages. Do you think they're breaking their promises?"

"No," she replies immediately. "Not at all. I'm not judging. As long as everything is consensual, I don't care. It wouldn't work for me, that's all. I don't want to sleep with anyone else, and I don't want you to sleep with someone, either." She exhales in a long breath. "So now you know."

Now I know. Fuck me, but she is *so brave*. Her parents play favorites, and she goes on loving them anyway. Her brother is the child who can do no wrong, and she's willing to marry a stranger to save his life.

Unlike me, Rosa isn't clinging to her fear. Maybe she's afraid of getting her heart broken, but she puts it out there anyway. I could lie to myself and pretend it's because she's young and naive, but neither is true. It takes courage to be an optimist, *and Rosa Tran is the bravest person I know.*

"If you want to run—"

Run? Me? I close my eyes, and she's there, her jasmine scent, her luminous eyes, and her relentlessly optimistic smile. She maddens me during the day and tantalizes me in my dreams. "I'm not going anywhere," I reply, lacing my fingers in hers. "If you're trying to scare me, you'll have to work harder at it."

"You want to hear a litany of my flaws? Do you have all night?" She laughs ruefully. "I recently discovered that I have a jealous streak, and I don't like it. I wanted to claw Andrea's eyes out. It was an extremely disconcerting feeling."

"Who's Andrea?"

"The flight attendant."

"Who?"

"On our flight back from Lecce, remember? The woman who kept eye-fucking you?"

"I have no idea who you're talking about."

"Oh, come on. How do you not remember Andrea? She had truly impressive breasts."

This, at least, is easy. "When you're around, I only have eyes for you."

"And when I'm not around?" she asks teasingly. "What then?"

"You've taken center stage in my fantasies, principessa. It's just you."

She squeezes my hand. We lapse back into silence. *Tell her,* my conscience orders. *She's giving you something infinitely precious. If you can't match her bravery, at least offer her the truth. Tell her about Patrizia.*

"Tomorrow, I'll get contractors to fix the roof." I trace a circle over her hip with my fingertip. "I'll vet them, of course, but there are no guarantees that Santini hasn't paid one of them to spy on us. Until they finish their work, we should share a bedroom."

Santini is probably still a threat, but not a big one. From all accounts, he's busy dealing with his own problems. There have been at least two serious attempts on his life in the last week. He thought he bought himself some time by selling off his daughter to his second-in-command, but Lorenzo Corio seems to have run out of patience. He's trying to kill his boss, his boss is trying to kill him, and all of Puglia is a powder keg waiting to blow. Given everything happening right now, I doubt very much if he cares about whether Rosa and I are sharing a bedroom.

But now that I have her in my arms, I don't want to let her go.

"That's a good idea," Rosa replies, nuzzling into me. "Besides, we haven't fucked in the shower, and I want to see if it lives up to the hype." She kisses my palm. "Good night, Leo."

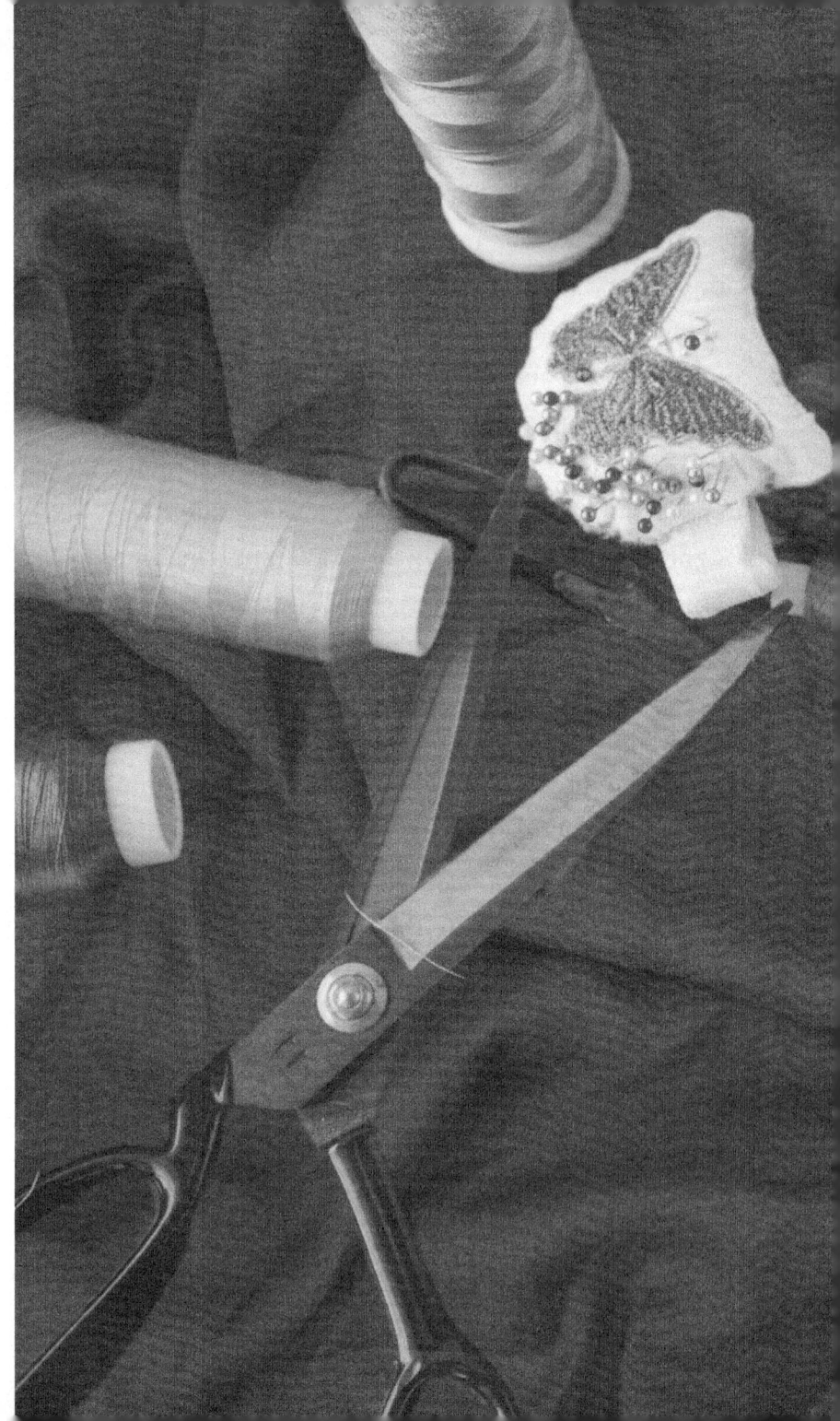

24

ROSA

Leo's still asleep when I wake up on Saturday. I sneak out of his bed and head to my room to survey the damage. Last night, I wasn't thinking of water damage to my clothes, but today I am, and I'm dreading opening my closet.

It's empty.

All my clothes—the entire contents of my closet—have been moved to my sewing room.

I swallow a lump in my throat. I sew my own clothes. I was bracing for hundreds and thousands of hours of work to be ruined, but Leo rescued them for me.

Franco, the last guy I dated, thought that fashion was frivolous. "With the world in the state it is, I think people should focus on something more important," he announced pompously. I told him about the glow on a customer's face when they tried on one of my dresses and it fit them perfectly, and Franco dismissed it as meaningless. To him, working in a hedge fund and playing financial games with the lives of working-class people was serious work, and making pretty clothes was a pointless waste of time. Franco proudly labeled himself a feminist, but he had a lot of hidden sexism that he never examined.

Leo, on the other hand? He'd probably roll his eyes if I asked him if he's a feminist. But he's never, *ever* dismissed my work as unimportant.

I climb down another flight of stairs to the kitchen and get the coffee maker going. Leo comes downstairs an hour later. "I slept in," he says, looking bewildered. "I didn't wake up when you got out of bed."

"I know." I hand him a cup of coffee. "You were out like a light. So what?"

"I don't sleep well," he replies with a frown. "I haven't slept through the night in *years*."

I fell in love before you took your first steps, he said last night. He would have been seventeen, falling in love for the first time. I'm dying to know more about the girl he fell in love with and why it didn't work out, but I hold my tongue. Leo clings tight to his secrets, and hopefully, we're taking baby steps toward a relationship. I don't want to undermine my progress by probing.

He drains his coffee and pours himself another cup, topping mine off in passing. "Are you sore from last night?" he asks. "Did I hurt you?"

I feel *great*. "No. You don't have to worry about me, Leo. I'm not breakable."

He chuckles. "Grouchy in the mornings."

I roll my eyes. "Why are guys so preoccupied with the whole virgin thing anyway? Last night, I thought you were going to beat your chest in triumph like a caveman." I replay yesterday's events, my cheeks flushing. "Either that or curse a lot."

"Mmm."

"You're not answering my question."

He grins. "I'm not risking provoking the beast. Not until you've had another cup of coffee." I glare at him, and he laughs out loud and lifts his hands in mock surrender. "I'll admit, there's a caveman part of me that did like being your first. I'm not necessarily proud of it." His expression turns serious. "But mostly, I wish you had more experience."

My heart sinks. "It wasn't good for you."

His head snaps up. "What? No, it wasn't just good. It was fucking amazing." He sighs. "Your options have been taken away from you. You were forced into this marriage with a man only a few years younger than your father. I wish things were different."

"That's what you're worrying about? Leo, I was ready to sleep with you the first time we met. At Valentina's wedding, I invited you to my hotel room. Remember that? Circumstances might have pushed us into this marriage, but I've wanted you from the very beginning. Now, what do you want for breakfast? We have eggs, cheese, and bread."

"I already told you—"

"Yes, yes, I know. I don't have to cook for you. I hang on to every word you say with bated breath, orsacchiotto mio. French toast or scrambled eggs?"

He grins at my grouchy tone. "I haven't had French toast in years."

"French toast it is."

I grab the eggs out of the refrigerator while Leo slices the bread. "What are you doing today?" he asks. "Are you going into your boutique?"

"No, Gisele's there. I'm going to focus on Milan. I have a notebook of sketches, but I need to narrow them down into an eight-piece collection and then sew up samples."

"How long do you have?"

"A month."

It doesn't seem like nearly enough time. "What can I do to help? Do you want me to find someone who can sew up samples?"

Aww. I put down my whisk and hug Leo. "You've already helped," I tell him. "It's because of you that I have time to sew at all. You asked Annalisa to work in my store, arranged for movers so I wouldn't have to spend hours cramming my possessions into boxes, and set up a sewing room so I could start working immediately. Not to mention finding an apartment for my parents, jobs for my family, and everything else."

Predictably, my gratitude makes him uncomfortable, so I change the topic. "What about you?" I dip a slice of bread into the batter and put it on the skillet. "What are you doing today?"

"I've got to get a crew on the roof." He frowns. "It'll be noisy. Is that going to be a problem?"

"Not for me," I assure him, adding another battered slice to the pan. "I put my earbuds in and listen to music while I work."

The pan is hot, and the toast is ready in no time

at all. I plate them up, slice up strawberries for a topping, then drench everything in syrup. When I'm done, we take our seats at the kitchen table.

"This is delicious," Leo says, digging in with relish. "Thank you for making it for me."

I'm not particularly domestic, but I like watching him eat the food I make. It's a very primal feeling. "You're welcome."

He proceeds to demolish his plate. When he's done, he asks, "Are you going to the gym this evening?"

"No. Why? Do you want to sexy wrestle with me?"

He starts to laugh so hard I think he's going to choke. "There's nobody like you, Rosa," he says fondly when he has himself under control again. "I have to go to work for a bit, but I thought we could grab dinner together."

"I'd like that."

His eyes rest on me. "I was going to suggest either shower sex or wrestling for dessert," he says, his raspy voice sending arousal skittering over my entire body. "But you told me you weren't sore." His thumb glides over my lower lip. "So we're going to do both."

I've almost forgotten about the anonymous

caller. *Almost.* But the moment Leo leaves, all my fears come rushing back.

HUGH FINALLY TEXTS me on Sunday evening.

> Me said you were looking for me.

> I need to talk to you.

> Sure. I'm hanging out at a bacaro with Javier and Pedro. Remember them?

I exhale in a long breath. Hugh's not stupid. This is just another attempt to avoid me, but this time, I'm not going to let him off the hook. I've been hauling that damn phone in my bag for the last forty-eight hours, staring at it when Leo's not looking like it's a bomb about to go off, wondering if the man is going to call again and threaten me.

> Hugh, this is urgent. Get to my house in thirty minutes.

His reply comes after a long pause.

> Okay. I'll be there.

I GIVE my brother a quick tour of the palazzo, and then we settle in the living room with giant mugs of steaming jasmine tea. "Where's Leo?" Hugh asks. "I thought he'd be here."

My cheeks heat as I think about Leo and last night's marathon session. The moment we got back from dinner, Leo pounced on me. He opened the front door and pushed me against the nearest wall. "Pretend I'm your captor," he growled into my ear. "Try to get free."

Let's just say that there was a lot of sexy wrestling. I tried to knee him in the groin, but he moved out of the way, laughing at me. I used all my training and managed to get out of his grip, but then he caught me again and lowered me to the floor, pinning me down with his body and kissing me. We had sex right there on the floor and then followed it by sex on the stairs, in the bedroom, and in the bathtub. And we still weren't done. When Leo jerked awake at five because of a nightmare, we made slow, lazy love in the last hours of darkness before the morning dawn.

"He's hunting down some terracotta tiles," I reply. "The contractor didn't buy enough. He'll be a couple of hours. Which is good. I need answers, Hugh, and I need them now. What really happened in Lecce?"

His gaze slides away from me. "You already know what happened. I lost some Mafia money—"

"Hugh," I cut in. "Tell me the truth. Did you lose ten million euros, or did you steal it?"

His head jerks up. "Did Cesari tell you that?" he asks. "What exactly did he say?"

"It wasn't Leo." I pull the phone out of my bag. "Someone bumped into me on my way to work and planted this phone in my bag. Then a man called me Friday afternoon. He claimed that you stole ten million euros from him, and he wanted it back." His threat is etched in my memory. "He said that if you don't stop ignoring his calls, you're in for a world of pain." I take a deep breath. "And that if I talked to Leo about his phone call, he would kill my family."

"Romeo," Hugh spits out. "It's not enough that the bastard tried to kill me?" He grabs the phone from me and dials a number. "You fucking asshole," he screams into the receiver. "How dare you threaten my sister?"

I sit up, reeling. Hugh knows this guy. He knows him well enough *to know his phone number off the top of his head.* I have two phone numbers memorized. The first was our home phone number growing up, a line that's no longer in service, and the second is Leo's number. Everyone else, even people I'm close to—Valentina, Gisele, Ali—are contacts on my phone, and if I lost it, I'd be screwed.

The man on the other end says something. "Fuck you," Hugh snarls. "You blew up my car, and now you're giving me some kind of bullshit explanation as if that's going to make it better?"

What the hell is going on here?

Hugh listens for a minute and then shakes his head violently. "Stop trying to apologize. I don't care that Max was getting close, and I don't care that you panicked. You tried to kill me. We're done. I owe you nothing. Whatever we had is over."

Whoa.

Once again, the other man tries to make his case, but Hugh's not having it. "I don't trust a goddamn word that comes out of your mouth. Forget about the money; you're not getting it back. And if you contact my sister again, or if you come near anyone in my family, I'll go to Guerra myself, and I will tell him everything. And trust me, Romeo, I have proof."

Then he hangs up.

I stare at him for a long moment. Finally, I ask, "What did I just hear?"

"It doesn't matter. It's all sorted now."

"Nope," I say sharply. "Absolutely not. Stop avoiding this conversation. Who is Romeo?"

Hugh leans back against the couch and shuts his eyes. "Rocco Santini's son."

"Mệt vãi." I throw up my hands in the air in despair. My brother is an idiot. "The son of Lecce's mafia boss tried to kill you."

"He says he panicked."

I cannot with Hugh. I just *cannot*. "Who is Guerra?"

"Max Guerra. He called himself a consultant, whatever that meant. He started working for Rocco Santini six months ago. I don't know what Santini hired him to do, but Guerra is smart. Really smart. Somehow, he found out about the missing money. Nobody was even supposed to notice it was gone."

The pieces are slowly coming together. "Romeo Santini wanted to steal ten million euros from his father?"

Hugh nods.

"Why?"

"He didn't want to tell me." His face twists. "He said that if I knew why, I'd be in danger."

And my brother trusted him. "Guerra found out? He was going to expose you."

"Exactly. But Rocco wouldn't have killed me right away. He would have tortured me first to find out who else was involved."

"Romeo didn't want his role discovered, so he blew up your car." Why the hell did my brother get involved in this sordid mess? Telenovelas are less convoluted than Hugh's life. "Why did you steal the money for him?"

He doesn't reply, but he doesn't have to. His hurt expression, his palpable air of sadness—it all makes sense now. "You were involved romantically with him, weren't you?"

"Not anymore."

"I thought you liked girls." It's an admittedly dumb thing to say, but it's got to be better than grabbing him by the shoulder and shaking some sense into him. Stealing from the Mafia, *my God*. What a stupid thing to do.

He rolls his eyes. "I do like girls. *And guys.* I'm bisexual. If you're not okay with that—"

I give him an exasperated look. "Hugh, I don't

care about that. What I do care about is that you're involved with someone *who tried to kill you.*" My voice rises to a screech on that last bit. I take a deep breath and make myself calm down. Thank heavens Leo isn't home.

"I already told you. I'm not involved with him anymore."

"Okay. Good." He's hurting. Romeo was clearly much more than a casual hook-up. Hugh's in love with him, and right now, he doesn't need a lecture from me about the man's obvious unsuitability. "Come on," I tell him. "I'll make a fresh pot of tea."

In the kitchen, I fill the kettle with water and turn it on. I find a packet of cookies and place a half-dozen of them on a plate in front of my brother. "Here's the part I don't understand. Why don't you give Romeo the money you stole for him? Then you're out of it, once and for all."

"Because I don't trust him," Hugh replies immediately, his eyes hard. "I've been thinking about this, chi. When Antonio Moretti struck that deal with Rocco Santini, it took the pressure off Romeo. Spina Sacra won't kill me, and Guerra can't torture me. For the moment, Romeo is safe from exposure."

"Okay..."

"But I'm still a threat. That hasn't changed. If I talk, Romeo is in serious trouble."

"But you're not going to talk."

"No, I'm not, but he doesn't know that." His voice turns bitter. "He doesn't trust me, but he also really wants the money. As long as he's trying to find it, he's not going to hurt anyone. If he comes near our family, I'll talk to Guerra. If I disappear unexpectedly, I've arranged for him to receive an email implicating Romeo. See? It's a stalemate. Everything's fine."

"Everything is not fine. Everything is the exact opposite of fine." I massage my temples and reach for a cookie. Maybe the sugar will help me think. "Hang on. Romeo's bound by the same deal as the rest of Spina Sacra. He can't hurt you anymore, whether you talk to Guerra or not."

"You would think that, but Romeo is a wildcard," Hugh replies. "He feels threatened, and his back is against the wall, which makes him erratic." He dunks his cookie into his jasmine tea like a weirdo. "Those ten million euros are the only thing keeping me alive."

"What's the plan? We do nothing? How long will your stalemate last?" I don't think he's thought this through. "We should talk to Leo. He'll know what to do."

"No."

"Hugh! How long do you think we can keep this up? We're out of our league here. This is Leo's world. We've got to ask him for help."

My brother relents. "Fine, but only after the wedding. Right now, you're Cesari's fiancée, not his wife. Romeo could argue that we're not yet family." I open my mouth to protest, and he holds up his hand. "Once you're married, we're formally under the protection of the Venice Mafia. At that point, even Romeo is not stupid enough to risk hurting me."

"And then you'll give back the money."

"And then, I'll give back the money," Hugh agrees.

I don't like this plan. At all. I have all kinds of misgivings about keeping secrets from Leo. But Romeo explicitly said that if I told Leo about him, he'd kill my family. And my brother believes, with one-hundred-percent certainty, that this isn't an idle threat.

I can't risk doing anything that would put my family in danger.

"Okay," I say reluctantly. "Let's do it your way."

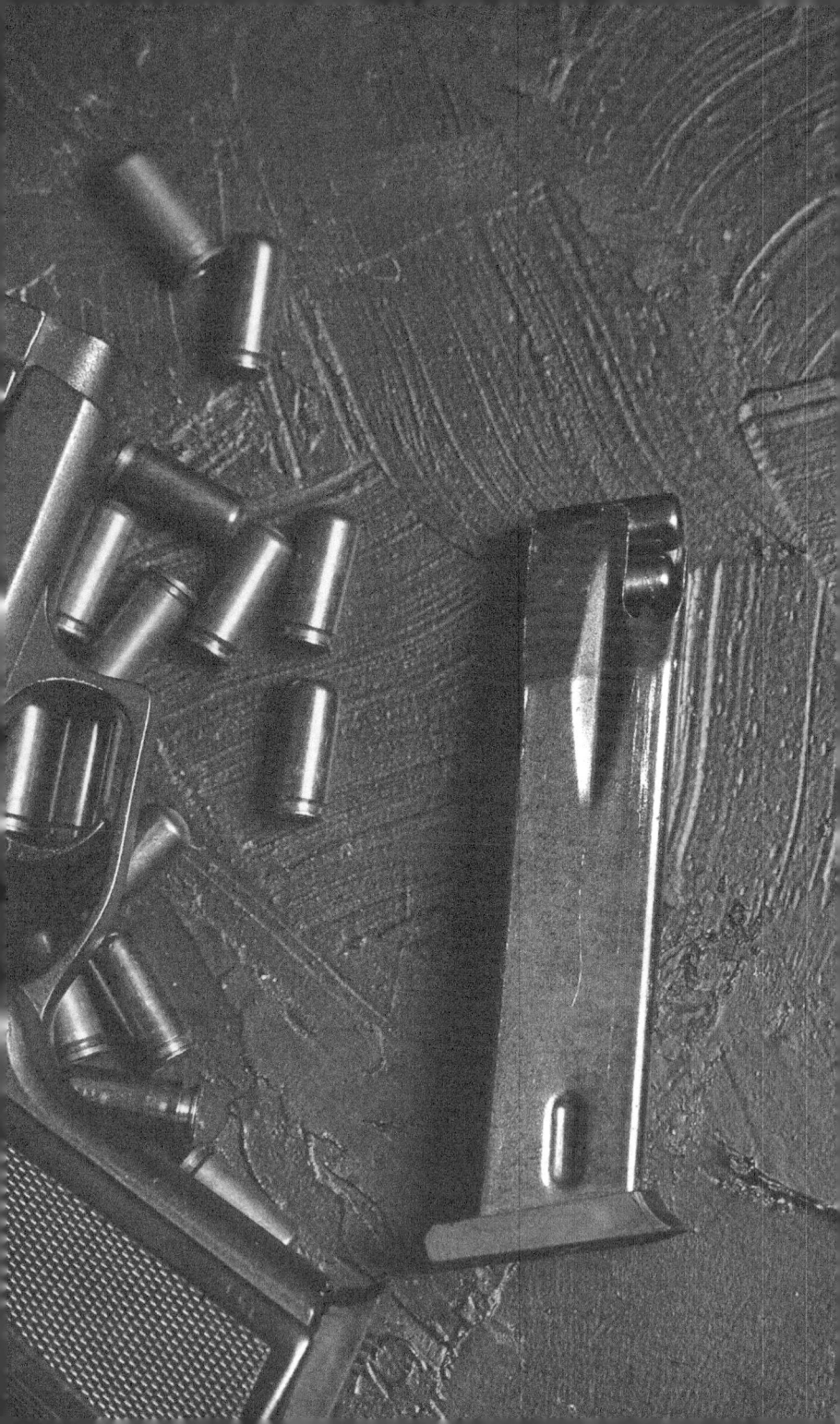

25

LEO

As promised, Violette texts Rosa and me on Monday morning.

> Great news! The Excelsior has a vacancy on Saturday, October 6.

I pull out my phone and open my calendar. That's in three weeks.

> I know it's soon, but I'm confident that we can make this happen. What do you think?

I pick up my phone and call Rosa. "Did you get Violette's text?"

"Yeah, just now. October 6."

"What do you think?"

"I don't know," she replies, a note of stress in her voice. "It's less than a month away."

That was the same thought I had, but when Rosa says it, I'm suddenly nervous. My grip on the phone tightens. "Yes," I say, keeping my voice level with effort. "It is."

"I mean, you wouldn't think it from the amount of fabric I own, but I don't have the right silk for my wedding dress. I need to go shopping, and if I can't find it in Venice, I'll have to head to Milan."

"Fabric," I repeat like an idiot. Of course. Rosa is a fashion designer. She wants to sew her own wedding dress, but there's not a lot of time, and she's already incredibly busy. That's why she's hesitating.

"The design itself is simple," she continues. "There's not a lot of lace and no finicky hand sewing, but still. . ." Her voice trails off thoughtfully. "Yep. I can do it. As long as Violette handles everything else, I can make the dress happen in three weeks."

"Let's call her."

We conference call Violette. "Let me guess," she says when she appears on the screen. "You're freaking out. Before you ask, I'm positive we have enough time."

"You are a mind-reader," Rosa laughs. "Either

that, or we're really predictable. Nice dress, by the way."

Violette grins. "Thank you. The designer first came on my radar when she dressed Lucia Moretti. I'm a huge fan. I think I own five of her dresses."

"Do you?" Rosa looks pleased. "I didn't know that."

Ah, this is one of my soon-to-be wife's designs. I know nothing about fashion, but it's a blue dress and looks good on Violette. I lean forward. "*Can* we make it work?" I don't know anything about weddings, but the last time I did this, it took Patrizia, her mother, and her sister a year to do the planning. There was at least one three-ring binder involved, dozens of wedding magazines, and lots of details I didn't care about or remember.

"You said you wanted a small wedding," Violette replies. "Less than fifty people. Is that still true?"

"Yes."

"Anyone traveling from out of town?"

"Just one on my end," I reply, thinking of Rocco Santini and his insistence that he dance at our wedding. "Rosa, what about you?"

"Everyone I want to attend lives in Venice," she replies.

Violette nods. "Then, yes, it's definitely doable.

We'll need to send out wedding invitations right away. Why don't I draft one up in the next couple of hours, and if you okay it, I can get them printed and in the mail this evening."

Events are speeding along faster than I can keep up. I look at Rosa. "It's up to you, principessa." Today, she's wearing a simple white tank top and a bright orange skirt, big golden hoops in her ears, the merest hint of lip gloss on her lips, and her lustrous hair pulled back in a ponytail. She looks like sunshine personified, and I wish I were home, lifting her up on her sewing table, spreading her legs, and feasting on her. My cock stirs in interest at the idea, and I grit my teeth and try to calm down.

We pretty much fucked in every room in the house this weekend. I couldn't keep my hands off her. There had been a small part of me that hoped that sleeping with her once would get her out of my system, but that myth has been thoroughly debunked over the last three days. The craving has only grown stronger.

Rosa bites her lower lip in a now-familiar gesture. "Let's do it."

The Fixer

TOMAS WANDERS into my office a few minutes later. "Did you have to break *both* his wrists?" he asks with a roll of his eyes.

It takes me a minute to figure out what he's talking about. *Groff.* Was that only four days ago? It feels like an eon. "Yes," I reply. "I absolutely did. How did you find out about that?"

"I went to see him on Saturday."

I tilt my head. "What did you do, Tomas?"

He shrugs. "What I always do. I offered a stick and a carrot. I told him if he stepped foot in Venice again, I would have him killed, and then I bought out his share in the gym."

"You paid his asking price? A million euros for a half-share in a small gym?" It's not unusual for Tomas to throw money at a problem, but buying a share of a business is extremely unusual. "Why?"

"A million two," he corrects. "I don't like rapists." Almost as an aside, he adds, "Interesting woman."

"Who is?"

"Alina Zuccaro." He takes a sip of his coffee. "You're looking a little shell-shocked, by the way."

He bought the gym for a woman. *Interesting.* I'd give him a hard time about it, but Tomas is deeply private and never discusses his personal life. In all the years I've known him, he's talked about a woman *once,* and that was only when we were both very drunk.

"Rosa and I have set a wedding date. October sixth. Clear your schedule."

He jots down the date on his phone. "That's coming up quick," he says. "How are you feeling?"

I don't know. "I never thought I'd get married again."

He surveys me thoughtfully. "You don't look broken up," he says. "You look content. Congratulations, Leo. I'm happy for you. Truly happy." His expression turned serious. "Have you told Francesca? You don't want her to be blindsided by this news."

Oh fuck. Francesca. If Violette is mailing invitations tonight, I can't afford to put this off. I get to my feet, not looking forward to the next few hours. "I better go see her now."

The Fixer

FRANCESCA LIVES in Murano in a red stucco house with gray shutters. I knock at her front door, and she opens it, her expression neutral as she surveys me. "Leo."

"Can I come in?"

She steps aside, and I enter, ducking my head under the doorjamb. She waves me to the couch, but I don't sit. I don't want to be here. Looking at Francesca's face is painful. There was only a year between the sisters, and this is what Patrizia would have looked like if she'd lived. Her black hair would have had a few strands of silver woven through it, the way Francesca's does. Her body would have softened into womanhood, her hips comfortably wide, and there would have been laughter lines around her eyes.

I haven't seen Francesca in three years. Maybe four. I used to see her more often but after that last time. . . She had a fight with her husband, drank a few too many glasses of wine, knocked on my door, and made a clumsy, drunken pass at me.

I never get involved with married women. I tell myself it's because getting between a couple is messy and complicated because maybe I am, like Rosa, a little bit of an idealist about marriage. But Francesca caught me at a bad time. It was the anniversary of my wedding, I was grieving, and she looked so much like her sister. . .

So when she kissed me, I kissed her back.

But it wasn't Francesca I wanted; it was her long-dead sister.

I regained my senses before we slept together, but it was close. Ever since then, I've given her a wide berth, and she's done the same.

"How are Alphonso and Beatrice?" I ask politely. "Beatrice is what, twelve?"

"Thirteen," she replies. "She's a teenager now, as she enjoys pointing out. They're both well." She crosses her arms over her chest. "I was just going out."

"I won't keep you." I take a deep breath. "I'm getting married next month. I wanted you to find out from me."

"You're getting married," she repeats. Her mouth twists, and tears well up in her eyes. "Well, isn't that fantastic? My sister is dead, and if that's not enough, you're trampling all over her memory."

Her words slice deep, cutting open a scar that's never completely healed. "It's been twenty years, Francesca," I say quietly.

"So what?" she demands bitterly. "Patti is dead. Does the passage of time change that?" She picks up a cushion and sets it down again. "Our mother begged her not to get involved with you, and I pleaded with her to walk away. We all knew that marrying you was signing her death sentence, but Patti wouldn't listen. She never did."

Her comment kicks me in the gut. "Silvia didn't want me to marry Patrizia?"

"What did you expect, Leo? You're Mafia. Your world is too bloody, too violent. So many times, I warned Patti that if she married you, it would end in tears. And it did, didn't it? The moment you put a ring on my sister's finger, she was a dead woman."

She covers her face in her hands and sinks onto the couch. I stay frozen where I am, my head reeling. My mother and I lived next door to Silvia and her two daughters. The three of us grew up together. I ate dinner with them every single Sunday. Silvia would make plump gnocchi because it was my favorite. I loved her as much as I loved my own mother.

And it turned out that the entire time I thought

they were family, *they were warning Patrizia to stay away from me.*

Francesca takes a deep breath. "I'm sorry," she says, her voice stiff. "I shouldn't have said anything. It was rude of me. As you said, Patti died a long time ago."

It's an apology that's notable not because of what she's saying but because of what she isn't. The words she doesn't say? I wish you well. I don't blame you for Patricia's death. You deserve to be happy.

Then again, why should she? She's not wrong. I was responsible for her sister's death. The moment I asked Patrizia to marry me, I marked her.

And I'm doing it again.

Once upon a time, the woman I loved died, and it wrecked me. Yet here I am, setting another wedding date. What the fuck is wrong with me? I'm putting a ring on Rosa's finger, and I'm drawing a target on her back.

And if something were to happen to her...

I will not be able to survive it.

26

ROSA

I make sure to wear my ring when I go to the gym on Monday evening, hoping to avoid another Simon incident, but he isn't there. Phew. Relieved that I've missed him, I head to the women's changing room, where Ali is lacing her shoes. "Hey, Rosa," she chirps. "I have your dress, so don't let me forget to give it to you." She bounces to her feet. "What happened to you Wednesday? I was going to ask you if you wanted to grab a drink after class, but you tore out of here."

I move my hand behind my back so she can't see my ring. It's a dumb thing to do, and I don't know why I'm feeling so weird about announcing my engagement. Things are going really well with Leo, and I'm significantly more hopeful about my marriage than I was this time last week. But Ali knows about my crush on Leo. She knows I invited him to my hotel room after Valentina's wedding and that he turned me down. When she sees the ring, Ali will have a thousand questions about how and when we got together, and unlike my mother, she won't be easy to fool.

"I had dinner plans," I mumble, bracing myself. She's bound to ask me who I had dinner plans with and whether it was a date, and then I'm going to have to tell her everything.

But she doesn't seem to register my words. "You'll never guess what happened this weekend," she bursts out. "It's the most unbelievable thing."

Ali has a positively gleeful expression on her face. I don't think I've ever seen her look this thrilled. "What happened?"

"Simon didn't show up to teach his class on Friday. I called him, and he didn't even pick up his phone."

"There's nothing unbelievable about that. Why do you look excited?"

"Because of the next part. On Saturday, he finally called me back. Guess what he said?"

She looks thrilled. I can't think of a single thing that Simon would say to put that look on her face. "I have no idea. Just tell me." Ali is one of my favorite people, but she takes forever to get to the point. Her stories are a road trip, detouring at every scenic attraction on the way.

"Well, first, he gave me some bullshit excuse about why he didn't show up to teach his class, but that's not the most important thing. He's *out*."

Hang on, is she saying what I think she is? "He's left the gym? He finally sold his share to you?" I hope Ali didn't have to go into even more debt to buy him out, but she probably did. Still, she looks delighted. So am I. Simon was awful. The gym will be a nicer place without him and much safer for the women who attend.

"Not just the gym. He's leaving Venice and moving back to London."

"No way." I freeze in the act of pulling on my shorts, suddenly suspicious. This can't be Leo's doing, can it? I'm pretty sure I haven't mentioned Simon to him. "Did he say why?"

"Nope, nothing. But to answer your earlier question, he didn't sell his share of the business to me. He sold it to somebody else."

"Wait, he can do that? Can he just sell his half to a stranger? How does that even work?"

"Exactly," Ali says emphatically. "That was my

initial reaction. I was furious. I didn't even think it was legal for him to sell to anybody but me, but unfortunately, it is. The buyer's lawyer, Daniel, pointed out the section in my contract that allowed him to do it."

Daniel. My suspicions deepen. "But you look happy now, so. . .?"

"Right! Well, this morning, I met with the guy who bought Simon's share. He came here with his lawyer to sign all the documents. The moment I set eyes on him, I knew it wasn't going to work out. He's not a fighter."

I might as well sit down; this is going to take a while. Ali settles next to me, taking a long drink out of her water bottle. "I was a little hostile," she says. "No, scratch that—I was *extremely* hostile. I asked him who the hell was going to teach Simon's share of the classes? Because it obviously wasn't him."

Okay, phew. It can't be Leo she's talking about. My future husband looks like he could break people with his bare hands. Nobody in their right mind is ever going to take a look at him and conclude that he's not a fighter.

"Then this guy looks at me with his cool gray eyes and says that he thinks fighting is a waste of time, but he'll sign a new contract with me." Ali's voice rises in pitch. "Get this. He's only going to take twenty percent of the profits."

Simon took half of the proceeds and did none of the work. No wonder Ali is excited.

"Even better, he's injecting some money into the business. You know all the repairs I haven't been able to afford to do? The broken tile in the women's showers, the gross urinals, the uneven floor in the gym? He's going to take care of it."

I don't like this. "Ali," I say gently. "Are you sure this guy is on the up-and-up? Doesn't this all seem a little too good to be true?"

She nods. "Trust me, I was absolutely sure it was a scam. But then I checked my bank account, and the money was there. He said he'd budget two hundred thousand euros for renovations, and it's already in my checking account. *Two hundred thousand euros.* And after lunch, I took the draft copy of the contract to the free legal clinic, and they said everything looks okay."

Curiouser and curiouser. "Does this mystery benefactor have a name?"

"Tomas," she replies. "Tomas Aguilar. And the lawyer's name was Daniel Rossi."

Leo strikes again. Tomas is one of his friends, a fellow member of the Venice Mafia. I met him at

Valentina's wedding. We didn't talk much, but from what I remember, he was tall, lean, and very quiet. And Daniel is, of course, the Mafia lawyer.

"You said Simon gave you a bullshit story for missing class. What was it?"

Ali rolls her eyes. "Oh, he said he broke both his wrists in an accident and couldn't teach."

Leo did what? I massage my temples, not sure if I want to laugh or cry. A conversation with my future husband is definitely in order.

My friend catches sight of my ring. "Rosa," she shrieks, grabbing my hand and examining the massive pink diamond, her eyes wide. "Are you engaged? Oh my God, forget Simon and the gym; who cares about that? Tell me everything. Who's the guy? Do I know him? When's the wedding? Have you set a date yet?"

I start to laugh. "It's Leo, of course. And you'll meet him soon enough. We're getting married in three weeks. Clear your calendar."

Her mouth falls open. For what surely has to be the first time in her life, Ali is at a complete loss for words. "Wow," she says finally. "You know, if you're pregnant, you shouldn't be taking this particular class."

"I'm not pregnant, just impatient. And when you see Leo, you'll understand why."

"I love it," Ali declares. "I love everything about it. No doubts, no second-guessing, nothing. Sometimes, I wish I were more like you."

If only she knew. Marrying Leo is the only thing I'm sure about. Everything else? Not so much. I keep staring at the black phone, waiting for it to ring. Hugh's plan makes me nervous, and I have serious reservations about keeping secrets from Leo.

I might look pulled together, but inside, I'm a mess.

JUST LIKE HE did on Wednesday, Leo picks me up after class, and we stop for pizza on our way back home. Once we've placed our orders, I fix him with a stern look. "Do you want to tell me why your friend Tomas is buying the gym I work out at?"

Leo grins lazily. "I think it's because he likes your friend Alina."

"He does?" I lean forward, intrigued. "They didn't exactly get off on the right foot. She told him he wasn't a fighter, and he said he thought fighting was a waste of time."

He laughs out loud. "She said that to his face? That's hilarious."

"Why?"

"He's an underground cage fighter in his spare time. Italy's reigning champion."

"Tomas? But he's so quiet."

"Don't tell anyone," he warns. "Tomas is very private."

"I won't," I promise. "But I would give almost anything to be a fly on the wall when Alina finds out."

Our pizza arrives. This time, I got spinach and ricotta while Leo ordered the mushrooms, black olives, and pepperoni. Before I can ask, he cuts his pizza down the middle and puts half of it on my plate. I beam like an idiot, and he quirks an eyebrow. "What? You wanted to share, didn't you?"

"I did, thank you. Did Tomas beat up Simon, or was that you?"

"That was me."

And he's completely unfazed by it. I tilt my head and survey my future husband. "Anything you want to share with me?"

"Not really."

I put half my pizza on his plate. "Leo."

He sighs. "Okay, fine. One of your guards saw Simon accost you at the gym, so I did what I needed to do to discourage his behavior."

One of my guards. What? I make a mental note to come back to that. *Guards?* "By breaking both his wrists? Doesn't that seem rather excessive?"

"Not at all. Excessive would have been me chopping off his hands with a machete for daring to touch you and then tossing that useless excuse of a human being into shark-infested waters." He takes a bite of my pizza. "This is really good."

"So you're going to beat up anyone who comes near me? That's a crazy level of possessiveness."

He puts his slice down. "I'm not crazy," he says. "There are two guys in your class, Salim and Matteo. Their hands are all over your body when you're grappling. I don't like it, but I understand that you're in an MMA class, and you can't fight without touching someone." He fixes me with a look. "That's not what Groff did. He touched you without your consent, and he made you uncomfortable. So I took care of it."

There's some logic here. Twisted logic, but Leo's not wrong. Also, who am I kidding? I'm delighted I'll never run into Simon again. "You know the names of the guys in my class?"

"I have a file on everyone there."

And that's not crazy at all. "Next time you're going to beat up someone I know, can you run it by me first?"

He smiles as if I said something very funny. "Check in with my wife before I hit someone. Okay, my sweet *principessa*. But you do realize that inflicting violence is more or less my job description?"

I'm aware, yes, but I don't like it. Leo's profession is dangerous, and the thought of him getting hurt makes my insides twist. I don't know how Lucia and Valentina live with the danger. Valentina at least works for the Mafia. Lucia, like me, is an outsider.

Speaking of danger... "Why *did* you put guards on me? Am I not safe in Venice? Is someone going to hurt me?"

He doesn't meet my eyes. "No, it's just a precaution."

"Are you sure?" Hugh's words come back to me. *Right now, you're Cesari's fiancée, not his wife. Romeo could argue that we're not yet family.* "Should I be afraid? I thought you made a deal with Spina Sacra, but if—"

"There isn't a threat. There is no need for you to be afraid."

"Do you think they might renege on the deal?"

Leo looks puzzled. "No, why would they do that?"

"I don't know. But they can, right? As long as we're not married, Spina Sacra could kill Hugh."

"No," he says. "You wear my ring on your finger. They made a deal. They can't touch your family."

"But I'm not part of the Mafia until we're married."

"That's irrelevant."

"Are you sure?" I probe.

He reaches across the table and takes my hand in his. "I'm not a lawyer," he says. "Daniel could probably tell you a hundred ways they could break the agreement. But I was there when the deal was made. Santini got his ten million euros back, along with an extremely valuable trade route that he can brag about. He gave a good talk about honor, but the truth is, he's not going to do anything to jeopardize the agreement. If we lived separately, he might be compelled to act to save face, but we live together, and we're getting married in three weeks. You're fine. You're safe."

"So why the guards then? Valentina doesn't have bodyguards following her around, does she?"

"She does not," he admits reluctantly, still avoiding my gaze. "I'm just being paranoid, that's all."

The hair at the back of my neck stands up. Leo was perfectly forthcoming when I asked him about Simon, but he's being oddly evasive about the bodyguards.

Leo's keeping something from me, and I don't know what it is. And as much as I want to push, I don't. Because he's not the only one with secrets. I have one, too, and I hate it.

27

LEO

I used to get nightmares for years after Patrizia died. Over and over again, I saw her getting shot. I would sit on the floor in a pool of her blood, put her head on my lap, and rage helplessly as the love of my life died from a bullet meant for me.

The nightmares restart as soon as Rosa and I set a date for the wedding. The first time it happens, I sit up, my heart racing in fear, drenched with sweat. Rosa stirs next to me and opens her eyes. "Hey," she says sleepily. "What happened?"

"Bad dream. Go back to sleep."

She pushes herself up and leans her head on my shoulder. "Want to talk about it?"

"No." God, no. My voice comes out harsher than I intended. I get out of bed, the images still vivid and disturbing. "I'm just going to get some tea."

She gives me a concerned look. "I'll come with you."

"No need, principessa. I can manage tea."

"Can you now?" she quips, swinging out of bed. "That's good to know. You can make me some."

But they don't stop. Every night, I have the same fucking nightmare. I fall asleep with dread in my heart, and like clockwork, my dreams show up to haunt me.

They're always the same. I'm in church, standing at the altar in front of family and friends. But this time, it's not Patrizia's family sitting in the front row next to my mother. It's Rosa's parents, beaming with joy. It's Hugh Tran fidgeting with his bowtie and Angelica sitting straight, looking around with wide, solemn eyes. The old padrino of Venice, Domenico Cartozzi, is missing. Antonio Moretti sits in his place, Dante and Tomas flanking him.

The music swells. Everyone rises to their feet and turns to face the back of the church, where a woman stands, clad in white from head to toe, a giant bouquet of roses in every shade of pink clasped in her hands, a lace veil obscuring her face.

My bride.

I turn around, my throat tight with emotion, and watch her walk down the aisle toward me, slow and sure. She's barely halfway when a guest throws herself in her path. "No!" Francesca screams, grabbing onto the hem of her dress. "Don't do it, Patti. He will ruin your life."

My bride pushes her aside in dismissal, but Francesca doesn't relinquish her grip on the lace. It rips, the noise heard above the orchestra. The guests gasp in horror, but my bride is undaunted. Her wedding dress hangs in tatters, but she continues her serene glide toward me.

The priest, in his red and gold vestments, performs the ceremony. "Do you, Leonardo Cesari, take this woman to be your wife," he intones. "In sickness and in health, for better or worse, until death do you part."

"I do," I vow.

"You may now kiss the bride."

But before I can reach for her, there's a disturbance. A tuxedo-clad man marches down the aisle, his face obscured. He lifts up his gun and aims it at the woman by my side, but his gaze is firmly fixed on me. "You should have known that this was a mistake," he says. "You should have known better."

Then he shoots her.

I lift the veil, but I already know what I'm going to see. Rosa, blood bubbling between her lips, clutches the gaping hole in her stomach and stares at me, life leeching out of those beautiful brown eyes.

And when we stop the gunman, it isn't Max Guerra. It isn't Rocco Santini. It's never any of them.

No. The gunman is always me.

THE NIGHTMARES ARE HELL. Every night, they wake me up and leave me a sweaty, terrified mess. But as the days go by, something magical happens.

Rosa always wakes up, no matter how hard I try not to disturb her. She always asks me if I want to talk about it and never gets annoyed when I refuse to tell her. She insists on coming downstairs with me to the kitchen, where we drink tea, eat Vietnamese snacks, and talk about everything under the sun. When we get back upstairs, we make love, then lie side by side in a sated heap and talk some more. And as our wedding nears, this quiet, liminal time becomes my favorite part of the day.

It becomes the thing that keeps me sane.

28

ROSA

The next few days are pretty great. I don't hear from Romeo Santini again, and slowly, the incident fades into the background. The days are busy, and the nights busier. Leo and I have a lot of sex, but it's not just that. We're growing closer—I'm sure of it. The roofers have come and gone, but Leo hasn't suggested I go back to my own room.

We're still sleeping in the same bedroom. We eat breakfast together and cook dinners in that awful kitchen, both of us swearing at the temperamental stove. We go shopping and buy some more furniture for the palazzo. We hit the antique market with Antonio and Lucia one Saturday, and the two of them help us pick art for the bare walls. "Trust me,"

Lucia says with a wink. "I have a very good eye for paintings. That's how I met Antonio, you know."

Antonio starts to laugh. "Well, that's one way of describing it."

But it's not all perfect. Leo starts to have nightmares. Bad ones, ones that cause shadows in his eyes and haunt him so badly that he doesn't want to fall back asleep.

And he won't talk about them.

Relationships, even fledging ones like ours, aren't just about the good times. They're about the hard times, too. Leo's been there for me when I needed him more than once, but when it comes to letting me help him? Nothing. He refuses to share what he's going through. He might have let me into his bed, but he won't let me into his life.

It'll come with time. Stop trying to rush it.

I can't even talk to my friends about Leo. I can't discuss my troubles with Ali because she's convinced I've manifested a life as romantic as the fairy tales I love, and I can't tell her the real reason Leo and I are getting married. As for Valentina, she's not just my friend. She's also friends with Leo, plus the two of them are co-workers. I don't want to complain about Leo and force her to take sides.

Enough whining. The truth is, I have nothing to

complain about. Leo is gorgeous, interesting, charming, and thoughtful. Bitching about him would be like winning the lottery and being grumpy because they gave you your winnings in the form of a giant check instead of directly depositing it into your bank account. It's just ungrateful.

"How do you feel about a birthday party?"

It's two in the morning. Leo had another nightmare, and we're in the kitchen, drinking tea and eating cookies. Well, I'm eating the cookies, and he's brooding.

"What?"

"A birthday party. There's usually cake, you blow out a bunch of candles, people sing—"

"Whose birthday is it?"

"Yours," I say patiently. "Your birthday is this weekend. How do you feel about us throwing a party?"

He looks puzzled. "Why? It's just another day."

I put down my tea so I don't *accidentally* spill it on his shirt. "Birthdays are a very big deal in my family.

I thought about throwing you a surprise party, but I didn't want you to be ambushed." I give him a persuasive look. "It won't be anything complicated. Some cocktails, appetizers, and cake, of course."

He fixes me with a bemused look. "And you want to do this? But you're really busy. When you're not at the boutique, you're in your sewing room. Why add another item to the to-do list?"

"Because I like parties. I want to get dressed up, wear hideously uncomfortable shoes, and celebrate."

He laughs. "Principessa, from what I can tell, all your shoes are hideously uncomfortable. You don't need a party for that." I'm bracing for him to say no, but to my surprise, he nods. "We could have some people over," he concedes. "Who were you thinking of inviting?"

"Your friends, my friends, my family. . . Let's see." I count off on my fingers. "Valentina and Dante, Lucia and Antonio, Tomas, Joao, Daniel, my parents, Hugh, Ali, Violette, Annalisa. . . Who am I forgetting?"

"That's fifteen people if you count us," he points out. "That's a lot."

"It's just appetizers and wine."

He gives me a fondly exasperated look. "If you

want to throw a party for my birthday, I have conditions. We cater the food, and we hire a bartender for the evening. And we'll get Marta to come in the next day to clean up the mess." He tilts his head to the side. "Aren't you concerned about Ali and Tomas being in the same room?"

I grin gleefully. "Can I confess something? I'm looking forward to the fireworks."

I'm on board with getting the food catered, but I'm determined to make Leo's birthday cake myself. After consulting with Annalisa, I decide on a flourless chocolate cake topped with chocolate ganache and fresh raspberries and make it on Friday after he leaves for work.

It's not nearly as complicated to make as his shirt. God, what a project that's been. Leo's noticed the number of hours I've been spending in my sewing room, but thankfully, he has no idea what I've been working on, and I've always had a decoy project around just in case he came in.

Menswear. Ugh. I haven't sewn a shirt in ages,

and my skills are seriously rusty. I had to make three practice shirts before I felt confident enough to cut into the cotton Leo bought me.

The fabric he bought because it was the precise color of my eyes.

Still, it's almost done now, and it looks great. On the day before the party, I hand-sew the buttons, give the shirt a final pressing, and pack it into a gift box.

I'll give it to him after the party. It doesn't matter whether Leo is willing to share his secrets with me or not—I'm falling in love with him. And if he doesn't know that already, he's going to find out when he sees the shirt I sewed for him.

But I don't want that to happen in front of everyone. I want it to be a moment just between the two of us.

EVEN THOUGH THIS was a bit of a last-minute idea, all our guests accept our invitation and show up promptly at eight. "I'm shocked everyone made it," I tell Valentina once the party is underway. Leo not only hired a bartender but a couple of waiters, too.

They circulate among the guests with platters of delicious appetizers, making this the easiest party I've ever hosted.

"Of course everyone came. You and Leo are our favorite topic of conversation." She gives me a sly smile. "You look like you're getting along well."

I cross my fingers behind my back. "We are."

She laughs. "That's obvious. You're positively glowing. Tomas won the bet. Of course, he had inside information, so it's not exactly fair. I'm quite annoyed with him."

I pretend I've never heard about the office pool. "Bet? Inside information? What are you talking about?"

"We all bet on when you two were going to hook up," she says. "Tomas won."

"You bet on when I was going to hook up with Leo?" I scold, trying to hold back my laughter.

"Of course," she replies, completely unrepentant. "It's summer, and work is slow. What else are we going to do? If it makes you feel better, they did this for Dante and me too. We're a gossipy bunch."

"What kind of inside information did Tomas have?"

"He's Leo's financial advisor," Valentina replies. "He gets notified when he makes big purchases. So when Leo bought a two million euro engagement ring—"

I nearly drop my glass. "What do you mean, two million euros? No, no, my ring cost two hundred thousand euros, not two million."

Valentina studies me with amused eyes. "Did Leo tell you that?"

"No." I stare at the ring on my finger as if it's going to turn into a snake and bite me. "I caught a glimpse of the receipt. There was the number two, followed by a lot of zeros."

"Yes, six of them. Rosa, this is a three-carat pink diamond. This is serious bling."

Hugh wanders by and overhears that last bit. He knows Valentina quite well from when my family lived in Venice. The two of them hug each other and exchange greetings. Then Hugh says with a grin, "You told her? I was wondering how long it would take Rosa to figure out."

I stare at my brother, outraged. "You knew? Wait, that's why you wanted to take a close look at my ring?" I punch his arm. "When were you planning on telling me?"

He laughs, and so does Valentina. "I don't know why you're freaking out," my friend says through her giggles. "It's a beautiful ring, and Leo can afford it."

I look around the room for my soon-to-be husband. He's in conversation with Joao. I excuse myself, cross the room, and join them, wrapping my arm around his waist. "Sorry, Joao. I need to borrow Leo for a bit."

The other man grins. "Of course."

I drag Leo out of the party and into a side room. "What's the matter?" he asks.

I thrust my ring under his nose. "Valentina just told me my engagement ring cost *two million euros*."

He quirks an eyebrow. "Okay?"

"Is she right?"

"Yes," he says, as calm as ever. "Why?"

I don't even know what to say. "Two million euros," I hiss. "For a piece of jewelry. Explain."

He lifts my left hand and presses a kiss into my palm. "It looks good on you," he says. "But more importantly, you really liked it. And when it comes to your happiness, principessa, two million is nothing. I would do far, far more. I would do *anything*."

There are too many people around for me to say the words in my heart. And if I say them, I might end up crying. Instead, I shut the door and pull him closer. Leo's eyes flare with heat as I unbuckle his belt and unzip his pants. "That was a very nice thing to say," I say, tugging them down his hips and sinking to my knees.

"We have a houseful of guests."

I trail my fingers over his rapidly growing shaft and look up at him through my eyelashes. "Are you really turning down a blowjob?"

"You're right," he says, a delicious growl in his voice. "I'm an idiot."

I laugh and lick his head, then open my mouth wide and take him as deep as I can. His head falls back against the door, his face clenching with desire. "Fuck, this is nice," he says. "Best birthday present ever."

"This isn't your birthday present," I mumble. I twist my tongue around his head before taking his cock between my lips and sucking him again. His fingers tighten in my hair, and my insides twist with need. I'm giving Leo a blowjob, and it's turning me on.

I moan deep in my throat, my fingers gripping his thighs as I bob my head on his length. "God, you're beautiful," Leo says, staring down at me. His voice—ragged, raw, uncontrolled—sends a fresh surge of heat through me. He's close; I can see it in his eyes and feel it in the jerk of his hips. This is such a high. Leo is huge, all broad shoulders and bulging muscles, and he's unraveling because of me. I feel powerful.

His cock hits the back of my throat, and I gulp down instinctively, taking him deeper. He groans. "I'm going to come," he grunts. "If you don't want to swallow—"

I suck him deeper. He tightens his grip on my hair and comes, and I swallow every drop. Then I get to my feet, wiping my mouth with the back of my hand and finger-combing my hair back into some semblance of order.

"Where are you going?" Leo protests, a glazed look in his eyes. "I need to get my mouth on that sweet pussy of yours."

"Later." I link my arm through his. "As someone pointed out to me, we have a houseful of guests. Let's go eat cake, orsacchiotto mio."

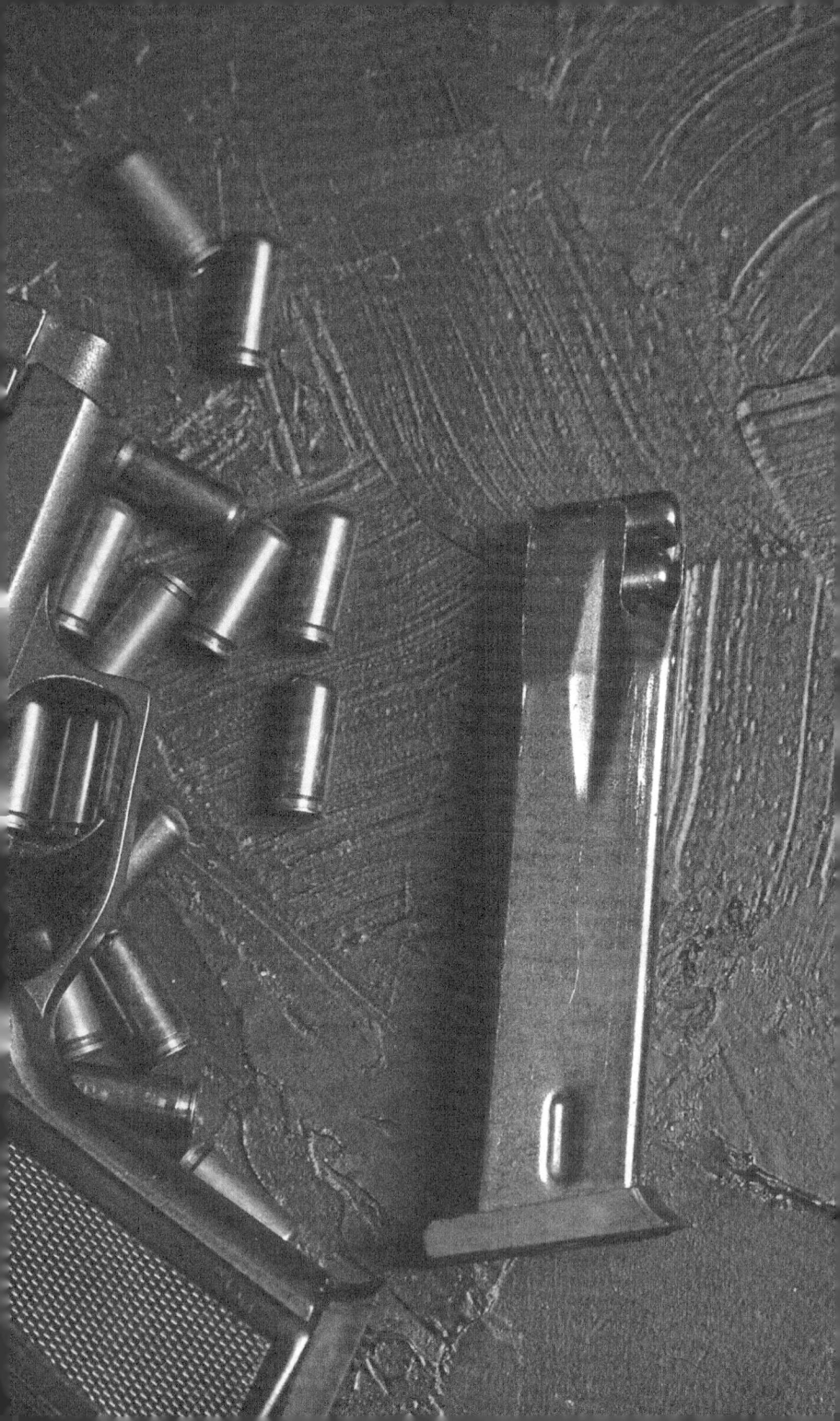

29

LEO

Rosa slips upstairs to reapply her lipstick, and I rejoin the party, grinning like an idiot. A blowjob. Fuck me, that was hot. And *unexpected*. Then again, Rosa's always been able to surprise me. I tell her she has to marry me in order to save her brother's life, and instead of freaking out, she replies that it's no hardship because I'm easy on the eyes. I nickname her principessa to annoy her, and she retorts by calling me her teddy bear.

I'm a lucky, lucky man.

My smile fades when I see Hugh Tran. Rosa's brother has been avoiding me since he arrived in Venice. I got him a job working for Tomas, but as soon as Hugh got here, he sent Tomas a message saying he'd found something else. That's fine; I'm not going to force Hugh to work for the Mafia against his will. I've been trying to meet him to get a straight answer about the missing Spina Sacra money, but he refuses to take my calls, and he's never around when I show up at his apartment.

And my hands are tied. Hugh is Rosa's brother. I can't snatch him off the street, throw him into an interrogation room, and beat him until he talks. I have to rely on my powers of persuasion, except I don't have any. This is Dante's area of expertise, not mine.

It's not about the money. I just hate not knowing what's going on, and I loathe being left in the dark. This situation is too similar to the one that led to Patrizia's death, and I have a bad feeling about it. A premonition of doom.

Hugh's talking to Valentina. I make my way toward them, determined to have this conversation with him *today*. He spots me and tries to inch away, but it's too late. "Hello, Hugh," I say calmly. "We need to talk."

"Leo," he says heartily. "Happy birthday, man." He claps me on my back. "Valentina and I were just talking about what a great house this is. So great." He drains his bottle of beer and holds it up. "What do you know, I'm empty. You two talk. I'll get a refill and be right back."

I don't think so. I pluck the empty bottle from his hand and lift it in the air. A waiter immediately materializes at my side. "Please get Hugh another beer," I tell him. "Now that's settled, let's talk. Valentina, will you excuse us?"

"I was already leaving," she replies. "Hugh, let's get lunch and catch up. Sometime next week? I'll text you."

She drifts away. I fix my future brother-in-law with a hard look. "You've been avoiding me. What the fuck have you gotten yourself involved in, Hugh?"

His eyes slide away from me. "I'm not avoiding you, man. It's my new job. Long hours, you know? It doesn't leave much time for anything else. Ask my parents. I've barely been home."

"You know Elaine and Ben will cover up for you, no matter what," I bite out. "Do me the courtesy of assuming I'm not an idiot, and I'll do the same. Why was Max Guerra in Venice, insisting he needed to talk to you?"

Hugh's eyes widen with alarm. "Guerra is here? In Venice?"

"He was. He's back in Lecce now." I take a deep breath and soften my voice. "Hugh, listen to me. I can't protect you if you refuse to cooperate." *And I can't protect Rosa.* "Talk to me. Tell me the truth about the money."

He barely registers my words. "I already told you," he says on auto-pilot. "Some of my investments didn't pan out. What did Guerra say to you?"

"Just that he wants to talk to you." I still don't know how and where Guerra fits into this puzzle. I talked to the padrino when he got back from Paris, and he had no idea either. Valentina tried to put together a file on the man, but she's been able to uncover remarkably little. Nobody connected to Guerra will talk. All we can find is that the Consultant has a fearsome reputation, and it's unwise to get on his bad side. That's not useful intelligence; I could say the same thing about half the people in this room.

"He can't." Hugh's voice is low and urgent. "Listen to me, Leo. You have power and influence. *Use it.* Guerra cannot be in Venice, and I cannot talk to him."

"Why not?"

He looks tormented. "I can't tell you." He clutches my arm. "Don't ask me questions I can't answer. *Please.* All I can say is this. For Rosa's sake, keep Guerra away from me."

Turning on his heels, he hurries away. He almost collides with Rosa, who's carrying a candlelit cake in her hands, twists out of her way and heads in the direction of the front door. Rosa gives him a briefly puzzled look and then beams at me. "It's time for cake," she announces. "Happy birthday, Leo."

The room bursts into song. My soon-to-be wife wraps her arm around my waist and smiles up at me, her eyes dancing with laughter. She's radiantly beautiful, and the cake she's made is delicious. With a shrug, I abandon the idea of chasing after my future brother-in-law and blow out my candles.

If Hugh had stuck around, I would have assuaged his concerns by telling him that Guerra doesn't work for Santini. I would have assured him that he wasn't here to discover what happened to the missing ten million euros, and I would have told him that Ciro Del Barba personally guaranteed that Guerra wouldn't hurt his family.

But he's twenty, impulsive, and prone to drama.

He freaked out and took off before I could tell him anything.

This problem can wait. Right now, Rosa is offering me a slice of chocolate cake, a cake she *baked* with her own two hands. There's food and wine and a roomful of family and friends. We'll make love tonight, and she'll fall asleep in my arms. The house is bright, the nightmares can't intrude when I'm awake, and I'm going to enjoy the fuck out of this moment.

"Nice party," Antonio says. "I saw your skirmish with Tran before he practically ran out of here. What's up?"

I summarize our conversation. "This is a mess," I finish. "On the one hand, we've got Guerra insisting that he needs to talk to Hugh. Then there's Hugh, who wants nothing to do with him."

The padrino shrugs. "Max Guerra is not our problem," he says. "All we promised Del Barba is that we wouldn't kick him out of Venice. It's not our job to make his life easier. If Tran doesn't want to talk to Guerra, that's between the two of them. We're not obligated to ensure he cooperates. And if Ciro bitches, I'll handle him."

"You're being very calm about this."

"Lucia's in her first trimester. She throws up every time she smells pasta sauce, so basically, every day. There's a small handful of things she can eat that don't make her sick." He looks at the plate he's holding, which contains a massive slice of chocolate cake and nothing else. "Cake is on the good list. She's lost three kilos in the last two months. Her doctor is unconcerned, but I'm freaking out and want her to get a second opinion." His eyes track his wife as she talks to Alina, Rosa's friend from the gym. "I have better things to worry about than Del Barba. Ciro likes the maneuvering, the deal-making, the endless machinations. I've been there; I've done that. But here I am, at a party with my wife, surrounded by friends, and eating delicious cake. This is my reward, Leo, and I'm going to enjoy it." He fixes me with a serious look. "Have you told Rosa?"

"Told her what?"

His eyes narrow. "Don't play the idiot with me. Have you told her about your first marriage?"

I take a deep breath. "No," I confess.

"Why not?"

I wish I knew. "I've been having nightmares. Every night. I dream that Rosa dies. That, once again, I couldn't protect the people I care about."

"Tell her," he urges. "There's no room for secrets in a marriage, Leo. This might have started out as a way to save Rosa's family, but anyone can see that it's much more than that now. Rosa threw you a birthday party. She baked you a cake and invited all your friends. She deserves to know what happened with Patrizia, and you'll feel better once you tell her."

He's right. I can't explain why I'm hiding my first marriage from Rosa. There's no reason to. She's not going to judge me for my failures—that isn't who she is. She's not going to turn away from me—Rosa is far too good a person to do that.

Fear holds my tongue captive, but if you asked me what I was afraid of, I couldn't tell you. I'm clinging onto old traumas and deep wounds, and I can't seem to let them go.

THE PARTY WINDS down at one in the morning. The caterers are leaving when I get a text from Goran.

> Max Guerra's private plane just touched down at Marco Polo.

There's really never a dull moment, is there? Fuck.

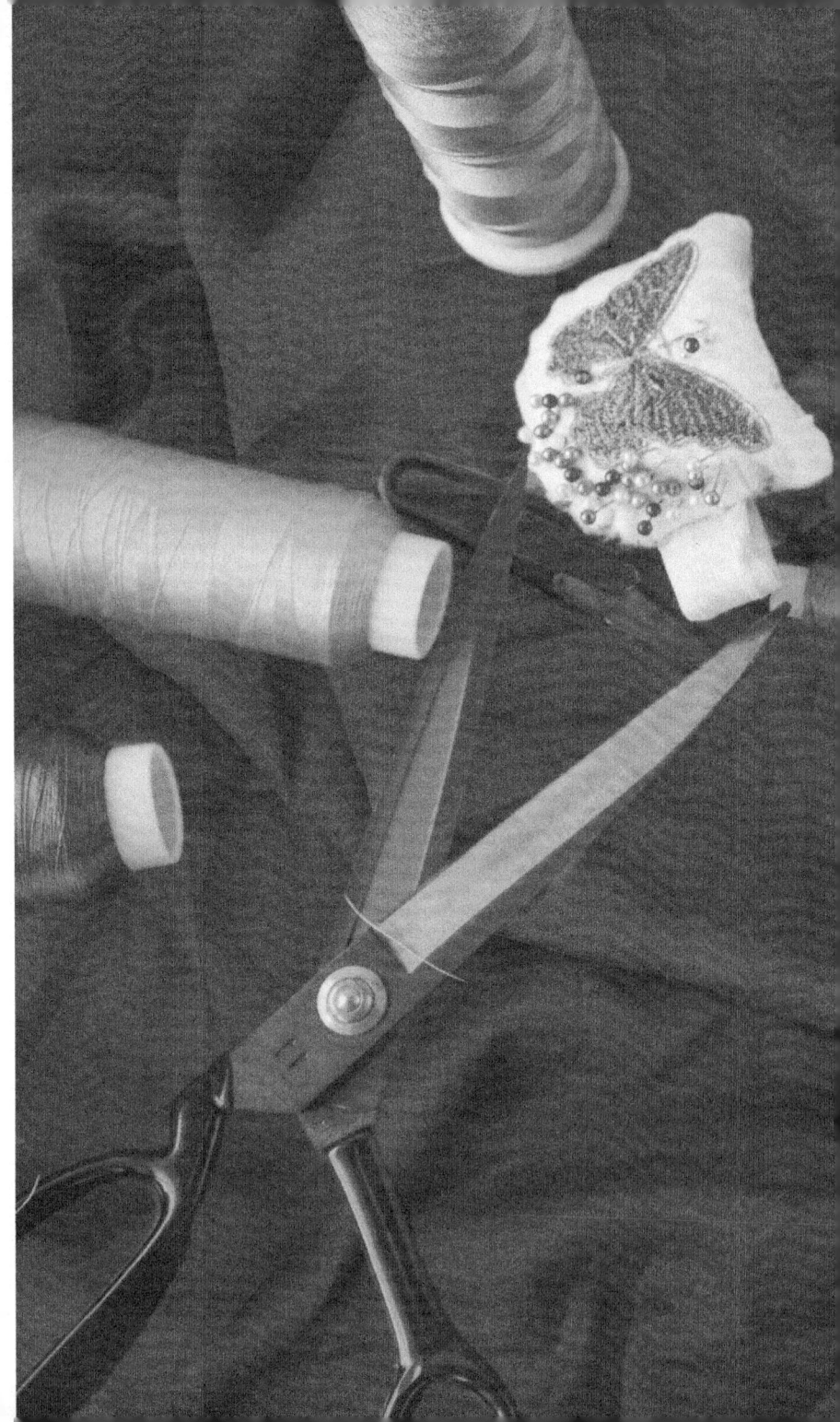

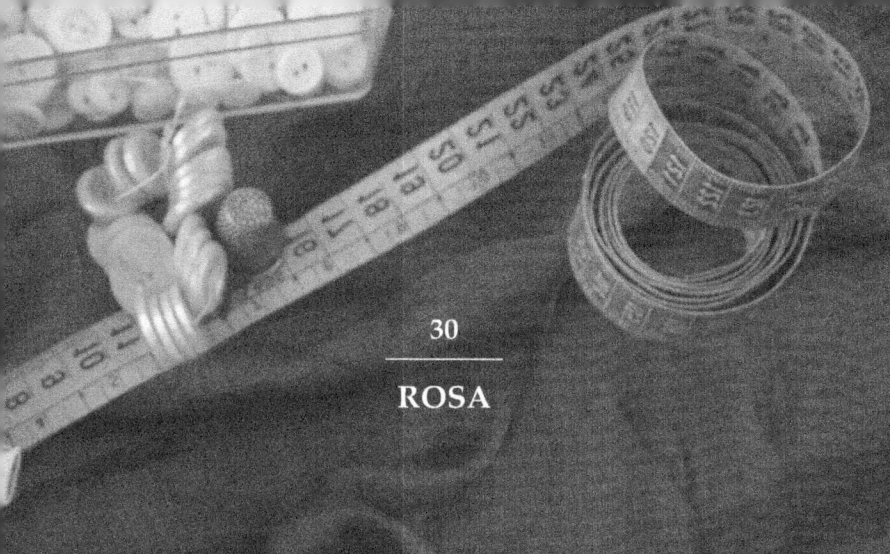

30

ROSA

It's late when everyone leaves, and I'm more than a little tipsy when I hand Leo his present. "Happy birthday."

"It's past midnight. It isn't technically my birthday any longer." He takes the box from me. "You didn't have to get me anything."

"Yes, yes, and I don't have to cook for you either. Open it."

There are two kinds of people—those who open packages carefully, sliding their finger under the tape so as not to ruin the wrapping paper, and those who are the rippers. Leo belongs to the latter category. He tears the paper apart and lifts the lid of the shirt box.

For a long minute, he just stares at the brown cotton shirt. Then he looks up. "Is this—"

"The fabric you liked? Yes."

His expression is one of total disbelief. "You made this shirt for me?" He swallows convulsively. "Why?"

Because I love you. "I couldn't think of what to buy you," I say lightly. "What do you get someone who thinks nothing of spending two million euros on an engagement ring? I'm still processing that, by the way. I haven't decided how I feel about it."

He ignores my blabbering. "You *made* this," he repeats. He lifts the shirt out of the box slowly, *reverently*. "Should I—"

"Try it on? Yes, please. I based the pattern off one of your existing shirts, so it should fit, but you never know for sure."

I drag him into my sewing room and position him in front of the full-length mirror there. Leo lifts his T-shirt over his head and tosses it aside. His fingers are careful as he undoes the buttons on the shirt I made him. "These are nice."

Finding the right buttons took four hours in my favorite button store. Four hours of holding every button against the brown fabric to see which ones looked the best. "Thank you."

He undoes the cuffs and slips the shirt over his shoulders. "It fits great."

I roll my eyes. "You don't know that until you button it up."

"*You* might not know until you button it up, principessa. *I,* on the other hand, can see it fits perfectly over my shoulders. And the sleeves are exactly the right length."

"One of us is an expert on clothing, orsacchiotto mio." I do up his buttons, my fingers lingering over his muscled chest. "The other is you." I finish and take a step back. "What do you think?"

"It's. . ." Words appear to fail him. "You said you don't like sewing menswear. On the plane ride back from Lecce, you told me you apprenticed with a menswear designer in Paris, and it was long enough to know you didn't enjoy it."

"You remember that, but you don't remember Andrea?"

He frowns. "Who's Andrea?"

I start to laugh. "Never mind. My opinion about menswear hasn't changed." I pick a stray thread from his sleeve that I've somehow missed, even after multiple rounds of ironing. "This was a very complicated project."

He stares at his reflection, his eyes shocked. "How long did it take you to make?"

Including the practice muslins, forty-three hours. "I don't know," I lie. "I didn't keep track. Do you like it?"

"I love it." He pulls me against him so my back hits his chest, and his eyes hold mine through the mirror. "If you don't like sewing shirts, why did you do it?"

"Because you're worth the effort." I twist out of his grasp and turn around. Standing on tiptoe, I brush my lips over his. "Happy birthday, Leo."

His hand cups the back of my neck, and he deepens the kiss. He drags his lips down my throat, kissing the side of my shoulder, the pulse beating at the base of my neck. "Thank you, tesoro," he says, his voice so quiet that I have to strain to hear him. "This is the most precious gift I've ever received."

He takes a step back and starts to unbutton it. "That didn't last long," I tease. "Already tired of your new shirt?"

He looks at me, a spark lighting in his eyes. "I believe I owe you an orgasm," he says. "And I honor my commitments. But clothes have a habit of tearing when we make love, principessa. My fiancée made this shirt for me, and if you think I'm going to risk doing anything that might rip it, you're very, *very* mistaken."

Leo's nightmares don't go away as we get closer to the wedding. If anything, they get worse. A lot worse. He gets to the point where he barely averages four hours of sleep a night. He seems to be able to survive on that, but I'm finding it a lot more difficult.

I could prioritize rest by sleeping in a different bedroom. But I love falling asleep in Leo's arms, and I can't give that up. I don't want to.

He still won't tell me what's haunting him. He won't tell me anything, and I'm not going to lie—it *hurts*. I have to keep reminding myself that while I might have had a crush on Leo for *months*, we're in the very early stages of a relationship, one he was forced to embark on. I just need to be patient, and he'll eventually confide in me.

But as the days go on, fear sets in. Leo likes me, I know that. He is physically attracted to me and enjoys my company. But maybe that's as much as I'm ever going to get. Maybe he'll always keep me at a distance. Maybe he's never going to let me in.

Ten days before the wedding, I crawl into the boutique at eleven. I only got three hours of sleep last night, and it's not nearly enough. My eyes are burning, I feel light-headed and dizzy, and I look like something the cat dragged in. Makeup can camouflage a lot, but it isn't magic.

Annalisa is already at the boutique, unpacking the shipments and checking their contents against the manifest. Gisele has returned from her vacation, but when Annalisa said she'd be willing to stay longer, I jumped on the opportunity to move my French shop assistant to the wedding side of my business. It's a win for everyone. Annalisa genuinely enjoys working with customers, and Gisele sews beautifully.

"Oh dear," Annalisa says when she sees me, biting back her smile. "You didn't get much sleep last night, did you? Ah, young love. I remember the days."

I give her a baleful stare. "I didn't sleep because Leo had bad dreams all night long. He's been having them for *days*. Forget last night; I can't remember the last time I got eight hours of sleep."

"Ah." She pats my hand consolingly. "That's not really surprising with your wedding coming close, is it? After what happened at the first one, I don't blame him." She pours me a cup of coffee. "You must be patient with him, my dear. He was badly traumatized by what happened, and I don't think he's ever fully recovered. All those old feelings will be coming to the foreground in the run up to your wedding, but once the big day is over and everything goes off without a hitch, I'm sure he'll settle down."

After what happened at the first one.

I freeze, ice trickling down my spine. Leo was married before? He's never mentioned it to me. That's a pretty pertinent piece of information. Business arrangement or not, he should have told me.

Why didn't he? Why did he hide this marriage from me?

And if he was capable of keeping this secret, what else is he concealing from me?

I force myself to smile at Annalisa and pretend

like everything's okay. I make myself take a sip of the coffee in my hand. "You're right," I say lightly. "Wedding jitters. It'll pass." I move toward the back on wooden feet. "It's almost time to open. Why don't you manage the front while I iron the new stock?"

That night, when Leo wakes up with a muffled scream and swings out of bed, I join him in the kitchen, as usual. I make a pot of jasmine tea while Leo rummages in the refrigerator for a snack. Our usual routine. "Lemongrass beef and rice?" he asks, holding up our dinner leftovers. "Or do you want a biscotti instead?"

"I'm not hungry," I say quietly. "Do you want to talk about your dream?" I cross my fingers under the table, a silent plea in my heart. *Please let me in, Leo. Please tell me what's going on with you. Please let me help.*

His gaze slides away from me. "Oh, it was nothing important. I was being attacked by zombies." He smiles ruefully. "I'm wrecking your sleep, aren't I? I'm sorry, principessa. I should have known better than to watch that movie before bed." He puts a biscotti in front of me. "It's lemon pistachio," he says. "Your favorite kind."

He just lied to me. It hits hard. I bury my head in my cup so he can't see the tears in my eyes. He won't

The Fixer

tell me he's been married before. I don't know why his marriage ended, but from what Annalisa implied, it was traumatic and the reason for his nightmares. But I'm only guessing because Leo won't tell me anything that matters.

And I'm supposed to sit here and pretend that everything is okay.

I can't do it. Not tonight. I fake a yawn. "I think I'm going to bed." I get up and brush a kiss over his cheek. His familiar scent of sandalwood and pine drifts over my senses, and it just intensifies the ache in my heart. "I'll see you upstairs."

I hesitate at the top of the stairs. If I turn left, I'll be at my old bedroom. The mattress has been replaced, and the bed is all made up. I should sleep alone. Let him figure out why I'm mad with him.

But big and dramatic gestures aren't my thing, and I don't want to fight with Leo. I turn right, enter his bedroom, and settle on my side of the bed. Leo comes upstairs a few minutes later. The mattress shifts with his weight, and then he puts his arm around me. "Rosa?"

It's an invitation, one I've taken every time he offers it. Any other day, I'd turn around and kiss him. He'd tell me I'm wearing too many clothes, and I'd challenge him to do something about it. And we'd end up making hot, passionate love.

But tonight, I close my eyes and pretend I'm asleep. And because I have my back to him, he can't see the tears that roll unchecked down my cheeks.

31
LEO

Do I notice that Rosa is awake?

Yes.

Do I know she's pretending to be asleep?

Yes.

Does it send a quiver of fear through me?

Of course it does.

You're being dramatic, I tell myself. She's tired, that's all. My relentless nightmares have been waking her up every single night. She just needs rest.

But as the days count down to our wedding, I become afraid. Everything starts to fall apart. We still sleep together, but Rosa has stopped initiating sex. When I kiss her, she kisses me back. When I part her legs and rest my thumb on her clit, she still moans deep in her throat, her eyes glazed. She gives every sign that she's enjoying herself in bed.

But she doesn't give me a coy look through her eyelashes and ask me if I want to sexy wrestle. She doesn't grab my arm as I walk by and drag me down for a kiss. She doesn't pull me into a room, unbuckle my belt, drag down my pants, and give me the hottest blowjob of my life.

And God, I miss it.

There are a thousand reasons for her behavior. She is extremely busy. This week alone, she had three wedding dresses to finish and seven fitting appointments, each taking more than two hours. This work is in addition to running her boutique, ordering stock, and making payroll. Then there's the sample portfolio she's sewing for Milan Fashion Week. She's only allowed to show eight pieces, and each of them needs to be of the highest quality to satisfy the committee that she has what it takes to participate in the prestigious event. All of this *plus* our own wedding? She's being run ragged, and it's not a surprise she isn't in the mood to initiate sex. Who would be, under the circumstances?

But a gut instinct warns me that's not the reason she's pulled back from me.

All this time, I've taken Rosa for granted. Her

endless optimism, her good-humored nature, her ability to see the best in every situation. No matter how grouchy I was, Rosa always had a sunny retort. No matter how hard I tried to push her away, she was there at my side, a smile dancing in her eyes.

Now, she's withdrawn into herself. She's stopped asking me about my nightmares. It's a logical reaction to my continued refusal to confide in her, yet it fills me with terror. My behavior is driving her away.

It strikes me for the first time that I could lose Rosa.

The nightmares don't stop. I'm increasingly paranoid about Rosa's safety, and I've doubled the guards on her, even though there's no sign of danger.

I neglect work shamefully. Max Guerra has been in Venice for three days, and I've done nothing about it. I haven't demanded that he meet with me and explain himself. I haven't told him that Hugh Tran has no interest in talking to him. Rocco Santini declined our wedding invitation—he cannot risk leaving Lecce right now—and I barely registered it. Spina Sacra appears to be tearing itself apart. Lorenzo Corio, Santini's former second-in-command and new son-in-law, appears to be doing his best to assassinate him. Santini's daughter, Sienna, hasn't been seen since the wedding. Romeo, his son and heir, is dead. He was on his way to the airport when his car exploded. Two other people were with him, the bodies burnt beyond recognition. That's just the highlight reel. The entire region of Puglia is on the brink of an out-and-out civil war, and Valentina's reports have more detail on what's going on, but I haven't read them.

Antonio is extremely worried about the situation. If I were doing my job properly, I would be too. We're far away from Puglia in Venice, but this kind of instability has a way of spreading.

Instead, I'm obsessed with Rosa. I walk her every morning to her boutique, and I pick her up in the evening. I accompany her to her gym and prowl around the exterior until she's done. I installed a tracker on her cell phone and even considered installing cameras in her sewing room to keep an eye on her when I'm not physically there to protect her.

But I refuse to tell her anything. I won't tell her about Patrizia's death; I won't tell her the reason for my fear. No wonder she's pulling away from me. If her brother's safety didn't depend on her going through with this marriage, she already would have left me.

And I'd deserve it.

A WEEK BEFORE THE WEDDING, Max Guerra sends me a message.

> I need to talk to you. It's urgent.
> Meet me at Casanova tonight at ten.

I stare at my phone in utter disbelief. It's seven days until my wedding, Rosa slips a little further away from me with each passing day, and now Guerra wants me to go to a *fucking sex club?* Is he out of his mind?

This is your fault. Max Guerra suggested meeting at Casanova because you're treating Rosa like she's a business arrangement. Even worse, you're treating her like she's a business arrangement while sleeping with her. You're acting like a complete asshole.

If I go to Casanova, that will be the nail in the coffin. I can kiss our relationship goodbye.

I stare at my phone for a long time and then get up to find Rosa.

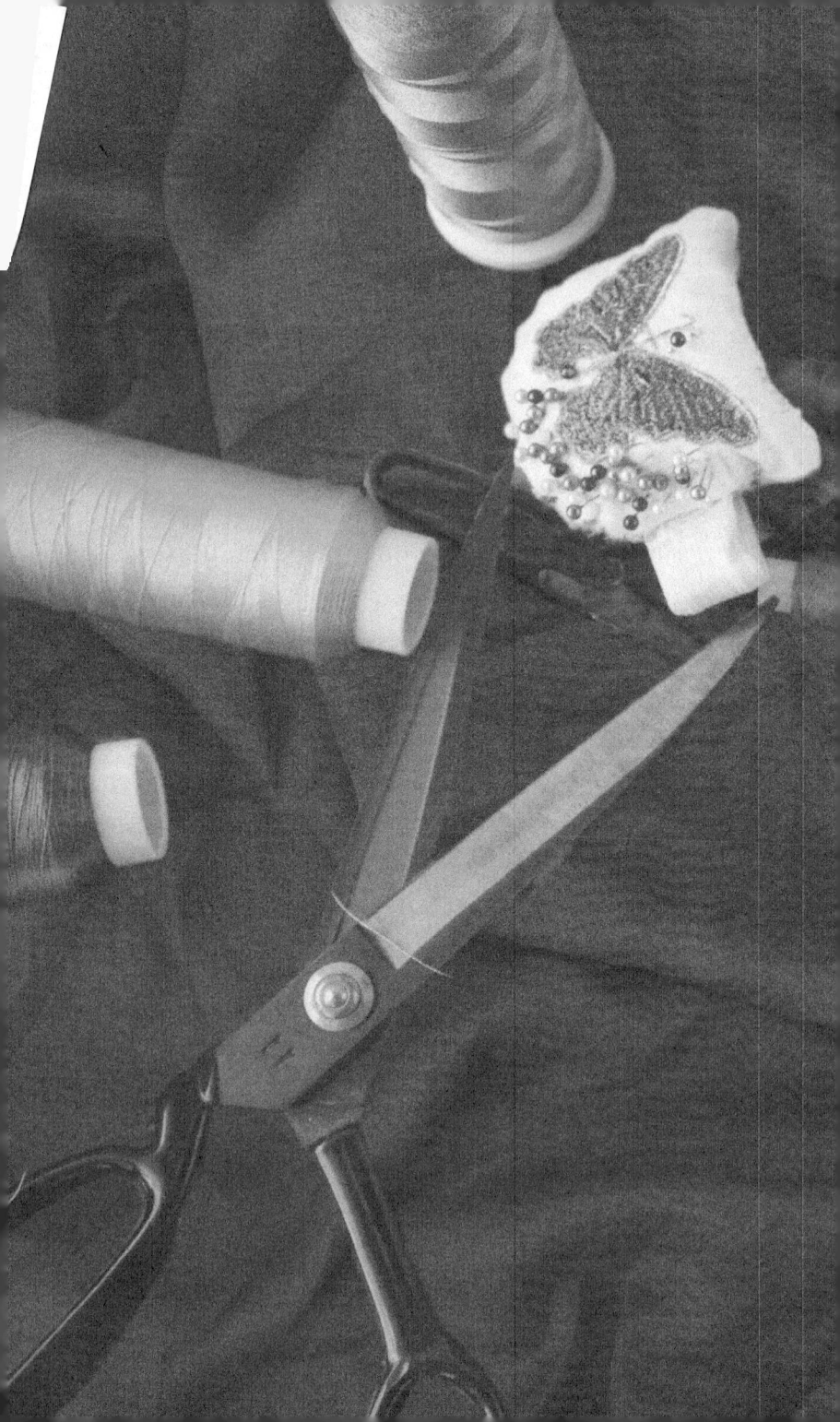

32

ROSA

Am I miserable? *God, yes.*

Should I have a big, flaming row with Leo, where I confront him, tell him I know about his first marriage, and demand to know why he was keeping it a secret from me?

Also yes.

But fear keeps me silent. As we get closer to the wedding, Leo feels as brittle as glass, and that one wrong move from me will shatter him.

Or maybe I'm just afraid that if I push, he will leave me.

I can't make myself confront him, but I'm still reeling, and it's created a barrier between us. He's still having nightmares, but when I try to get out of bed, he won't let me join him. "Stay in bed," he says. "You need the sleep."

And I hate it. I miss Leo. I miss our nightly snack sessions. I miss being close to him, saying outrageous things to make him laugh, and talking to him about everything under the sun. I have only one hope: once we're married, the nightmares will stop, and things will go back to normal.

I cling to that hope with all my might. Because if it doesn't happen, I don't know if I can survive being married to Leo.

A WEEK BEFORE THE WEDDING, I'm putting the finishing touches on my dress when my mother calls. Oh God. My mom is stressed about every single detail of the ceremony and the reception. Last week, she was fretting about favors. Yesterday, she had opinions about the cake. It's not just me she's bugging; it's also Violette. Our wedding planner insists my mother isn't driving her insane, but I'm convinced she's just being polite.

I quite seriously contemplate sending it to voicemail, but that would just postpone the inevitable. I pick up the call and put it on speaker. "Hello, mẹ."

"I just saw the weather forecast," she says. "There's a thirty-five percent chance of rain. What are you going to do if there's a storm?"

I knot off my thread and start to hem the satin with tiny invisible stitches. "The hotel will move us inside."

"Are you sure?" she asks dubiously.

"Yes." I move the needle in and out. "I asked Violette about it, and she assured me she has a plan."

"I think that woman just says whatever she thinks you want to hear. I told her we had to have xôi gấc on the menu, and she didn't even ask me what that was."

It's a good thing she can't see me roll my eyes. "Violette lived in Hanoi for six months; she knows what it is."

"I didn't know that." Sticky rice-needs sorted, she moves on to the next item. "Your gown looked tight on you."

Serves me right for inviting her over to see it. "No, it didn't. It fits perfectly."

"You should be watching what you eat," she continues, ignoring my words. It's not as if I do this for a living or anything. "You're not twenty-one anymore. You can't eat cake all the time. You'll put on weight, and then Leo won't be interested in you."

Leo walks into the room just as she says that, and he hears her. He strides up to my phone, his expression annoyed. "That's never going to happen, Elaine," he says, his voice clipped. "Rosa can eat all the cake she wants. Nothing's going to change the way I feel about her. We need to go now; she'll call you back." He hangs up before she can react. "I probably shouldn't have said that," he says to me, though there's no real regret in his voice.

"I'm not annoyed." There's a lump in my throat. *Nothing's going to change the way I feel about her.* After days of tension between us, this simple sentence makes me want to burst into tears. "What's up?"

He looks uncomfortable. "This is going to sound bad," he says. "But I need to go to Casanova."

My heart sinks. "The sex club?"

He raises an eyebrow. "You know it?"

I don't think that's the relevant question right now. "Are you going there for your bachelor party?"

He gives me an incredulous look. "You think I'd go to a sex club for my bachelor party? God, no. It's a work thing. Max Guerra, a guy who works for Ciro Del Barba, wants to talk to me there."

Max Guerra. I sit up. This is the guy Hugh mentioned, the one who started working for Rocco Santini. It was his investigation into the missing ten million euros that made Romeo panic and blow up Hugh's car. If I remember right, he had some kind of superhero nickname. Oh, right. The Consultant.

How can I get Leo to tell me more about Guerra without setting off his suspicions?

"At Casanova?" I ask skeptically.

He sighs. "Guerra probably picked that location because recording devices aren't allowed in the club. Or maybe he's just being a jerk. Who knows? But he said it was urgent, so I should probably go see what it's about."

He's going to a sex club. There will be women there, beautiful women who will flirt with him, laugh with him, touch him... Jealousy rears its ugly head and swallows me whole. "Okay," I say tonelessly.

"Would you like to come with me?"

I jerk my head up. "Really?"

"You might enjoy it." His lips tilt up in a smile. "I know I'll have more fun with you there."

My mood lifts. A warm glow goes through me. Leo could have just told me he was going out. He didn't have to tell me where he was going, and he certainly didn't have to invite me. But he did. He wants me with him at the club.

And my heart—my crazily hopeful heart that looks for every sign that Leo cares for me—leaps with joy.

"I'd love to. What should I wear?" A sudden, alarming thought strikes me. "Wait, I don't have to wander around naked, do I?"

"Hell, no," Leo says emphatically. "Definitely not. But there is a floor show, and the performers will be wearing very little. Will you be shocked?"

His tone is teasing. This exchange between us feels like how it was before the nightmares—before I found out he's been married once—and *I've missed it.* "I won't be shocked," I reply. "Maybe I'll be turned on."

"Will you?" His fingers slide down my cheek, and my body comes to life. "Turned on enough to play at the club?"

"With you?"

He fixes me with a fierce look. "Yes, with me. If you think I'm going to share you, principessa, you're wrong. When it comes to you, I'm a possessive asshole."

Sex with Leo at Casanova. My cheeks heat. I'm definitely intrigued, and he can hear it. A sudden wave of lust hits me, temporarily washing away the doubts of the previous week. "I'm a definite maybe."

His eyes flare with heat. "Good," he murmurs. "I have to meet with Guerra at ten. It's eight now. Can you be ready in thirty minutes?"

That'll give us a little over an hour there. And the sooner I get dressed, the more time we'll have. "Absolutely."

I DECIDE that a little black dress is probably appropriate sex club attire. Who am I kidding? I have no idea what to wear, but I'm not going to sweat it. I trust Leo to warn me if I'm wearing something that makes me stick out like a sore thumb.

I own three little black dresses. I pull out one I made it five years ago when I was experimenting with my style. The leather bodice is strapless and corseted, and the skirt is three layers of black tulle dotted with black sequins. I try it on, and it still fits. Resisting the urge to call my mother and gloat, I get to work on my makeup. I forego my usual caramel brown and reach for a blood-red lipstick. I apply three layers of mascara and work in a glittering bronze eyeshadow. By the time I'm done, I've used twenty-five of my thirty minutes. I decide to leave my hair down, quickly slip my feet into a pair of black high heels—Leo's going to get another opportunity to mock my shoes—and head to the living room.

Leo's already there, waiting for me. I take in what he's wearing, and my breath catches. His suit is black linen and fits perfectly, but that's not what draws my attention.

Underneath his jacket, he's wearing the shirt I made for him.

I swallow the lump of emotion in my throat. I can't cry—tears would wreck my carefully applied eye makeup. "Nice shirt," I say instead, keeping my voice light. "I don't mean to brag, but it fits you perfectly." I walk into the room, feeling the weight of his gaze on me. "What do you think?"

He stares at me for a long moment, his eyes hot and dark. "Every man in Casanova is going to want to fuck you," he growls.

"Will they?" It doesn't matter. There's only one man I want, and that's the one standing in front of me. "I'm flattered."

"They will." He pulls a small box out of his jacket pocket and opens it. Inside, nestled on the black velvet, is a pink teardrop diamond surrounded by two rows of tiny white diamonds. "They can look all they want, but they can't touch." I lift my hair out of the way, and he fastens the necklace around my neck. "You're *mine*."

When he touches me, I feel breathless. My heart gallops in my chest, and my knees go wobbly. "I believe your precise words were, 'I'm a possessive asshole,'" I quip. "And this possessive thing works both ways, orsacchiotto mio. Nobody gets to touch you either."

He gives me a strange look. "You haven't called me that in days," he says after a long pause. "I've missed it." Then, before I can react, he holds out his hand to me. "Shall we?"

Leo and I sign in at the reception desk. A woman dressed in a white shirt and black slacks goes over the club rules and takes our phones from us. "No recording devices inside the club," she says. For additional security, we pass through a metal scanner, and then we're inside.

It takes my eyes a minute to adjust to the lighting. At first blush, Casanova doesn't look very different from an upscale nightclub. The atmosphere is moody and adult. Golden chandeliers drip down from a tall, black and gold painted ceiling. A bar lines one end of the space, with mirrored tiles on the wall behind it. Comfortable seating areas with plush couches dot the right of the room. Music plays through hidden speakers, loud enough to encourage dancing yet low enough to allow conversation. A handful of couples have taken the invitation and are on the dance floor, randomly lit by flashing strobe lights.

And then the lights flash against the wall, and my mouth falls open. A couple is doing it in a glass-fronted room. The woman's back is pushed against the wall, her skirt bunched up at her waist, while the man kneels between her legs, eating her out.

Right there, where everyone can see. Some people look, their eyes lingering. Others act like this is no big deal and barely give them a second glance.

Oh. My. God.

A shiver rolls down my spine. I can't tear my eyes away. The strobe light illuminates them in flashes, and my imagination fills in the rest. The way he's kneeling reminds me of the first time Leo and I made love. It reminds me of how Leo demanded that I put my fingers on my clit and show him how I liked to be pleasured. Then his tongue followed...

Three people occupy the next room. A woman in a leather harness wearing a strap-on dildo fucks a blindfolded man bent over a bench. As I watch, the third person—another man—approaches the man over the bench and pushes his cock in his mouth. My eyes widen. This is very much outside my experience, but rather than being shocked, I'm becoming very, *very* turned on.

Leo notices. "Do you want to watch, principessa?" he growls into my ear. "Or do you want *to be* watched?"

My breath catches.

"Liam's new invention," Leo continues. "Glass-fronted private rooms. You can adjust the opacity from inside." His hand moves to the small of my back. "I made us a reservation."

He's looking at me like he's expecting me to balk, but a sudden recklessness fills me. "I'm in."

"And here I thought you'd be shocked." He laughs under his breath. "You always surprise me, principessa. Let's go play."

We have to head back out to the reception area and then through a corridor to the right to reach the private rooms. I follow Leo on shaky legs. I'm aroused and also nervous. I've never done anything like this before, not even close. Plus, it's been a couple of days since Leo and I have made love, which doesn't sound like a lot, especially if you consider the fact that I was a virgin until a few weeks ago, but it feels like an eon.

At the door, Leo's eyes search my face. "Second thoughts?"

My pulse is racing. I take a deep breath and steady myself. What am I afraid of, anyway? Leo would never push me further than I'm ready to go. He'd never, ever toss me into the deep end of the pool. I'm freaking out because this is a sex club, but really, I'm thinking about this all wrong. I get to have hot sex with my gorgeous soon-to-be husband. And if the people in the club see occasional flashes of it, so what?

"None," I respond, sweeping into the room ahead of him.

He laughs again and follows me inside. It's a small space, barely four feet wide and ten feet long. The decor is sparse—just a narrow bench and a wooden chair. And, of course, the glass wall in front of me.

From this end, it's clear, not opaque, and I can

see the other attendees perfectly: the white-shirted waiters moving through the crowds, carrying trays of drinks, the strobe lights, everything.

Okay then. This is really happening. I'm really doing this.

Leo turns me to him. His gaze sweeps over me, slow and thorough, and by the time he's done, I'm hot all over. "We can control the opacity of the glass," he says. "You decide how much you want the people outside to see."

I can either tiptoe into this experience, or I can forget about everyone else and enjoy myself. Option B, please. "No," I respond. "I don't want to decide." I jump off the high wire, absolutely secure in the knowledge that Leo will be there to catch me. "You control it."

"Are you sure?"

"Absolutely. You're in charge." I give him a look through my eyelashes. "Would you like me on my knees, Signor Cesari?"

He growls in his throat. "Ah, principessa. You drive me wild." He backs me into the room until my butt hits the glass. "You say stop at any point, and this game ends. Understand?" I nod, and he leans forward, his arms on either side of me, caging me in.

He bends his head to my neck, his lips making me shiver. "Are you wearing panties?"

What kind of question is that? "Of course."

"Show me," he orders, his warm breath tickling my ear. He takes a step back, but his eyes stay on me. "Lift up your skirt and show me."

Oh. My. God. Everyone on the dance floor is going to see my ass. I have my back to the window, yes, but in a way, not being able to see their reaction is almost worse.

And yet... My insides clench with need, and my nipples are tight, aching buds of arousal.

I suck in a breath and bend, lifting the layers of tulle up. My panties are black lace, the fabric sheer and the cut skimpy. Leo studies them for a long moment, his expression maddeningly neutral. "Take them off and give them to me."

I gulp. This isn't for the faint of heart. My heartbeat races as I move to obey. I wriggle out of the panties and hand the scrap of lace to Leo, letting go of my hem once I'm done. He puts them into his pocket without comment and frowns. "Did I give you permission to let go of your skirt?"

A current of electricity jolts through me. I once told Valentina that Casanova wasn't my thing. I didn't understand the appeal of a man barking orders at me and expecting me to obey. But I do now. As long as we're in this room, I don't have to make a single decision—Leo will make them for me. I don't have to think—he'll handle it. It should be confining, but it isn't. It feels freeing.

"No, Signor Cesari, you did not." I lift the skirt back up and drop my eyes. "I'm sorry."

He positions the chair in the middle of the room and settles himself in it. "Kneel," he orders. "Facing me. Spread your legs wide. I want to see you."

Cheeks flushed, I sink to my knees, this time taking care not to lose my grip on my skirt. He smiles in approval. "Very nice," he purrs. "Such a good girl. Do you like this, principessa? Do you like knowing that everyone in the club is transfixed by the sight of you? If I push a finger into your pretty little cunt, would I find you wet?"

At the reminder that people are watching, fresh heat fills my core. "I have no idea," I murmur.

"Liar," he accuses. "Do you know what happens to liars, Rosa?"

"No."

"They get punished." He pats his lap. "I was planning to take it easy on you, but I've changed my mind. Come here, principessa."

He pulls me down on his lap, my back to his

chest, making me face the window. I'm acutely aware that everyone on the other side of the club can see my naked pussy. Somehow, I don't care. My attention isn't on the strangers outside—it's on Leo.

"Spread your legs wide," he orders implacably. "I want everyone to see who you belong to." He shoves his finger in me, and my muscles clamp down around him. "Whose pussy is this?"

Need explodes through me. "Yours, Signor Cesari," I pant.

He pulls his finger out and holds it in front of my lips. "You weren't sure if you were wet?" he asks, his voice rough. "Here's the proof. Taste yourself."

My face feels like it's on fire. My body, too. I part my lips and suck his finger greedily. This is so wicked, and I'm loving every moment. "Leo," I whimper. "I want..."

He's hard. I can feel the thick bulge of his erection against my ass, and I grind down on it, desperate for more. I want him to bend me over the bench and fuck me, just like the leather-clad woman in the strap-on was doing with her partner. I want him to ram into me so hard I scream. I want it to *hurt.* I want to replace the heartache of the last few days with this cleaner, sharper pain.

"Yes, principessa," he growls, his fingers gripping

my hips. "Tell me what you want." His hands move up my body. He tugs my bodice down, freeing my breasts from their corseted prison, and he slides his thumbs over my swollen, aching nipples. I moan, stirring restlessly on his lap, and he pinches them hard. "Sit still."

You try sitting still, I want to retort, but being a smart-ass doesn't seem in the spirit of the game, so I hold my tongue and stay as motionless as I can as Leo tugs and tweaks my engorged nubs. It's an impossible task. Pleasure rampages through my body, while on the other side of the glass window, people dance, heedless of the storm building up inside me. Somehow, the forbidden nature of what I'm doing makes everything even hotter. What do they see in between flashes of strobe light? I'm sitting here on Leo's lap, legs splayed open, grinding against his cock. Can they see how much I need to come? Can they see how close I am?

Leo dips two fingers into my soaked pussy. "Ask for permission, principessa," he says harshly, his breath hot against my ear. "If you want to orgasm, I want you to beg."

A full-body shiver runs through me. I have no shame about begging. I left that behind the moment I stepped into this room and placed myself in Leo's control. "Please. . ." I plead, my muscles clenching around him. "Please let me come."

Leo rewards me by pulling out his fingers and thrusting them into me again, his thumb grazing over my swollen, sensitized clit. "Is that the best you can do?" he asks conversationally, and then he adds a third finger.

I bite back a scream. The burning stretch is delicious, and I'm like the rat in the cage that will take the hit of pain for the pellet of pleasure. "Do that again," I gasp.

"What, this?" He thrusts in, hard and deep, and I throw my head back as sensation storms through me. "Is that what you want me to do?"

"Please," I whimper as he fucks me with his fingers, his thumb rubbing my clit. "Please, please, please. . ." It's a chant and a babble rolled into one, a desperate plea for release. My legs kick, and my toes curl. "I need. . . I can't hold it back. . . please. . ."

"Come for me, Rosa."

His words push me over the edge. Shivers wrack my body, and I shatter with a muffled cry. He doesn't stop. He keeps thrusting into me, over and over, savoring every little flutter, every last aftershock.

Leo's still hard. I haven't initiated sex for days, not since I found out he was married before. It's a self-preservation strategy, one I've been clinging to with increasing desperation. But I just let him make me come in front of a roomful of people, and I suddenly realize it's too late to protect my heart. I've already given it to him.

I can't bring myself to say the words. But we're in a sex club, and I don't need words. I grind into his ass. "You took care of me," I whisper. "Let me return the favor." I slide off his lap and onto my knees. "Please?"

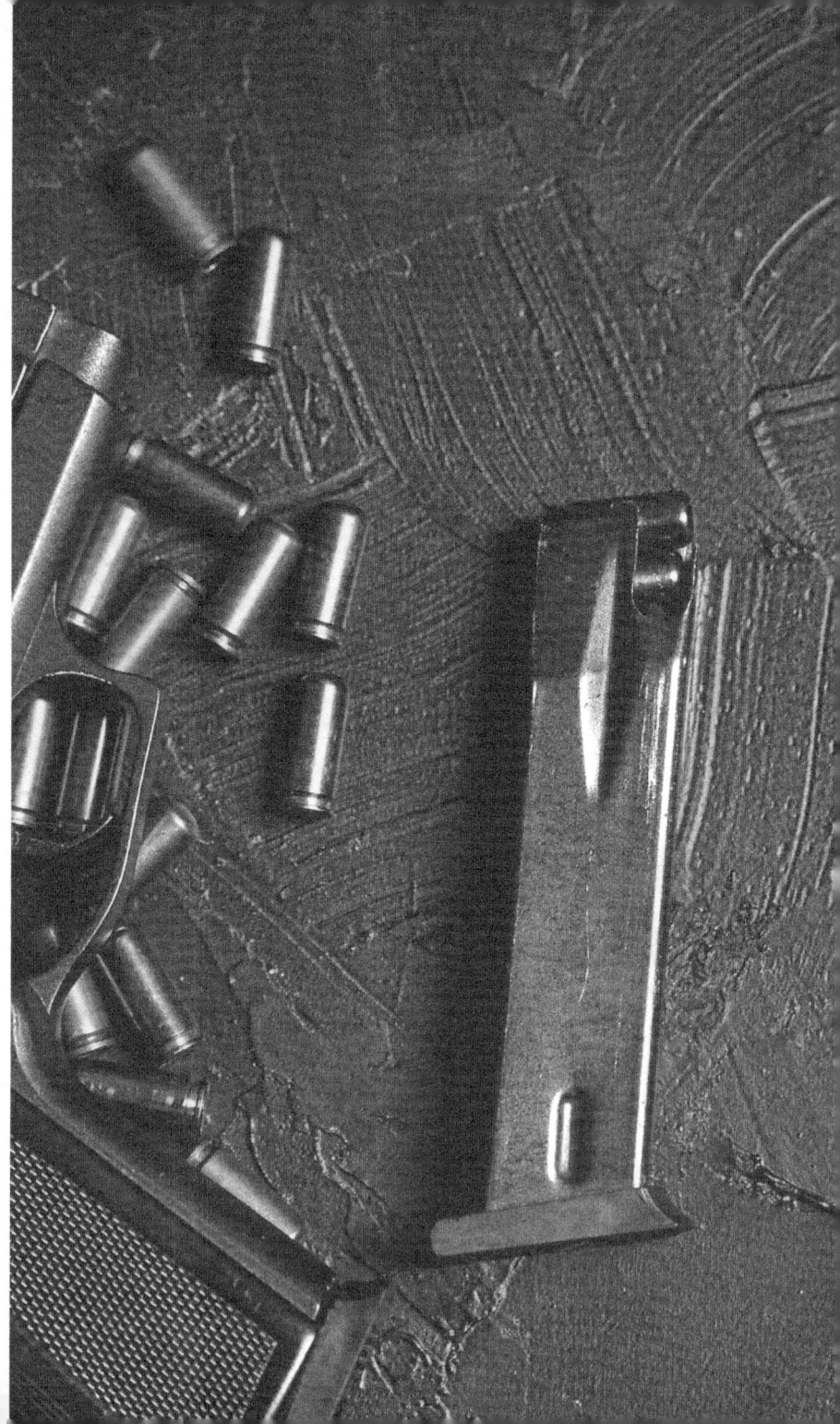

33

LEO

Oh God. She's looking at me through her lashes, and fuck. Desire rages like a river of lava in my blood, but it's more than just need. This is Rosa, and it's never just been about sex with her.

I don't want her mouth on my cock. I lift her up, push her down on the bench, unzip my pants, roll a condom on, and thrust into her wet heat. I'm not going to last. I'm too raw, too uncontrolled. Everything is too close to the edge. The wedding is in a few days. My life is dangerous, and I'm dragging her down with me the way I did Patrizia. I thrust into her, hard and brutal, and she gasps, her body throbbing around me. My ears are filled with the sound of her moans. I breathe in, and the smell of her perfume assaults my senses. She's in my dreams, in my blood, and in my heart.

I'm in love with Rosa.

The realization sends my release rocking through me. I throw my head back and drive deep, my cock jerking inside her as I erupt.

I TAKE off the condom and throw it in the trash. There's a box of tissues on a shelf, and I offer it to Rosa. She takes it from me with a smile of thanks. "Could you do something about the window tinting?" she asks. "I know it's weird that I'm okay with people watching me come but not with the clean-up part, but here we are."

I give her a puzzled look. "Nobody can see us. The glass is opaque. You didn't know that?"

She blinks in surprise. "No. I thought people could see everything."

As if I'd let a roomful of strangers leer at my wife.

"I would never throw you into a scene like that without prior discussion, *principessa*. I thought you knew it was a roleplay."

She laughs bemusedly. "I definitely did not know that," she says. "It's probably for the best. It was hot in the moment, but I'm not sure how I feel about public sex."

"Hang on. You told me to control the window without knowing what I would do? Why?"

She shrugs. "I trust you, Leo. You would never do anything to hurt me."

I trust you. She says those words as if they were no big deal. As if what she's saying was perfectly obvious. And her matter-of-fact tone shatters the last walls around my heart. I take a deep breath and tell her everything. "I fell in love with the girl next door when I was sixteen."

Rosa looks up.

"Her name was Patrizia. She was. . . " I wait for the old grief to rise to my throat, but the ache feels muted. "She laughed a lot. She had stars in her eyes and dreams in her heart. When she was six, she wanted to be an underwater explorer. At ten, it was a gondolier." I smile at the memory. "It was the striped shirts they wore. She loved them. By the time she turned fifteen, she had it narrowed down. She was either going to be a detective or a teacher."

Rosa laughs softly. "She sounds like a lot of fun."

"She was." I stare at nothing. "I started working

for the Mafia when I was thirteen. At first, I acted as a lookout. Sometimes, as a messenger. People don't really pay attention to kids, and Domenico Cartozzi, the old padrino, was not above using that to his advantage. I was good at what I did, and I started to move up the organization. By the time I turned twenty, I was part of his inner circle."

We're sitting in a darkened, private room in a sex club, watching a roomful of dancing strangers through a tinted glass window. An incongruous setting for my darkest secrets.

"You have to understand. We were poor growing up, both Patrizia and me. Money was always tight. And I burned to change that. I wanted to make my mother's life easier, and I wanted to give Patrizia everything. It didn't matter to me that Domenico was vicious and unpredictable, chaotic to the extreme. It didn't matter that everyone walked on eggshells around him. My ambition made me blind."

"What happened?" she whispers. "Because something did, didn't it?"

"Yes. Domenico got into a fight with a Russian outfit. They paid a protection fee to transport drugs through Venice, but he decided it wasn't enough. He doubled the price, and when they wouldn't pay, he arranged to have their shipment intercepted by the carabinieri." My voice is flat. "The Russians fought back. In the resulting shootout, Nikolai Smirnov, the Bratva heir, was killed. His father, Gregor, discovered Cartozzi's betrayal and wanted to send a message." I swallow hard. "On my wedding day, the moment Patrizia and I finished exchanging vows, a hired gunman entered our church and opened fire. Patrizia died from a bullet meant for me."

"Oh God, Leo." Tears well up in Rosa's eyes and spill down her cheeks. She wraps her arms around me, enveloping me in her softness. "I'm so, *so* sorry."

"She bled out right there in the church," I continue, forcing myself to relive that painful memory. The hail of bullets that met Patrizia at the church. The look of confusion in her eyes as she clutched her stomach. The red, *red* blood spreading over her white wedding dress. "She died in my arms on what should have been the happiest day of my life."

She swallows a sob. "Oh, Leo," she whispers brokenly. "I wish I knew what to say."

I cup her cheek and kiss her on her lips. I'm upsetting her and should stop, but the dam has burst open, and I cannot hold back the flood of words. "I was responsible. I didn't pull the trigger, but I might as well have. I put her in danger the day I went to work for Domenico Cartozzi." I sit on the chair and tug Rosa on my lap. She's crying for me, and it breaks my heart. "I also took a bullet that day. I was in the hospital for three months. When I got out, I tracked down the gunman, Luigi Ferlito, and killed him." I squeeze my eyes shut. "He had a wife and a child. I wanted to kill them too."

"But you didn't." There's no doubt in her voice. She's utterly convinced of my ability to do the right thing.

"You sound so sure of me."

"I was there when Angelica was kidnapped," she replies. "I saw the look in your eyes. You didn't hurt them, Leo."

Rosa believes in the innate goodness of people. "I wanted to," I reply. "Not the child, never the child. Children are always untouchable. But Ferlito's wife. . . I wanted to kill her. I wanted to put a bullet in her brain with every fiber of my being. I was ready to pull the trigger."

"What stopped you?"

"It wouldn't have brought Patrizia back." I tighten my grip on her waist. "Killing Ferlito was justice. Killing his wife would have been vengeance. Besides, there were other targets, people who deserved to die.

While I was recovering in hospital, the situation with the Russians had become an all-out war. I stayed long enough to ensure we won, and then I went to Cartozzi and announced I was out. I was still a nominal member of the Mafia, but I was no longer part of his inner circle. And there I stayed until Antonio Moretti came along and took the throne from him."

She's quiet for a long time. "You've been dreaming about her death," she says. "That's what the nightmares are about?"

"It's not her death I'm dreaming about, principessa. It's yours. Night after night, I dream that a gunman interrupts our wedding and kills you. When I'm not with you, I have guards shadowing you. Against her better judgment, I've made Valentina hack into the cameras at your gym. I've even gone so far as to plant a tracker on your phone. I'm trampling all over your privacy and your autonomy because I'm a paranoid fucking wreck. I love you. If something were to happen to you, I would shatter."

She twists around to stare at me. "Say that part again," she whispers.

"Doubling guards, cameras in the gym, tracker on your phone."

She punches my arm. "Not that part. The other part."

I intercept her hand before she can punch me again and bring it to my lips. "I love you. I think I've loved you from the day on the beach when I told you that the only way you could save your brother was by marrying me, and you replied that it wasn't a hardship because I was easy on the eyes."

Tears roll down her cheeks. "Well, you are," she says. "I wasn't lying about that." She brushes them away with the back of her hand. "I love you too. You probably already know that, though, because unlike you, I wasn't being inscrutable."

I feel a smile break out on my face. *She loves me.* I just told her I was responsible for Patrizia's death, and she's not running away screaming. She's sitting on my lap, her head nestled into my neck, and *she loves me.* I feel like the luckiest guy in the world. "You're not worried about the risks of being married to me?"

She answers my question with one of her own. "Why do you work for Antonio Moretti?"

"Cartozzi lurched from conflict to conflict," I reply. "He was like a toddler throwing a tantrum. So many people died because of him. So many innocent people's lives were ruined because of his hubris. It's easy to fight. Any idiot with a gun and a grievance can do that. It's a lot harder to maintain peace. I work for Antonio because he never loses his temper, and he's never erratic. But most importantly, he realizes how destructive war is, and he'll do everything in his power to avoid it."

"There's your answer then," she replies calmly. "You didn't kill the wife of the man who murdered your bride, Leo. And you broke Simon's wrists, but you left him alive. Justice, not vengeance. That's why I'm not worried." She makes a face. "Besides, it was Hugh's actions that sucked me into your world, not yours. If I'm going to be mad at anyone, it should be him."

Full of surprises. Every single time. "And you're not angry with me?"

"For what? Because I found out through Annalisa that you were married before? Because you wouldn't tell me about the nightmares?"

"You knew about Patrizia? Why didn't you confront me?"

"I was hoping you'd tell me yourself. And you did." She kisses me gently. "Leo, I can't even begin to put myself in your shoes. Your wife was murdered at the altar. Nothing in my life even comes close to the trauma you've suffered. Of course, I'm not angry with you—I have nothing to be angry about. As for the guards, if you feel like I'm in danger—"

"You're not. The guards, the cameras at the gym, the phone tracker—that's my paranoia. Spina Sacra is tearing itself apart, and they have too much going on to bother with us. You have no reason to be afraid."

She studies my face. "But Max Guerra is here, and he's connected to them, isn't he? How does he fit in?"

Something niggles in the back of my head. "Who knows?" I reply. "Guerra's an enigma. I thought he was working for Santini, but then he said he works for Ciro Del Barba, but that story doesn't ring true either. Valentina compiled a file on him. The guy's a lone wolf, and he doesn't stick around. He wanted to talk to Hugh, but he wouldn't tell me why. He thought Hugh knew something."

"He wanted to talk to Hugh?"

"Yeah, he showed up in Venice a couple of weeks ago and then left almost immediately. Now he's back. Maybe he's concerned about Spina Sacra's impending destruction. Santini's fending off assassination attempts, his son is dead, his daughter is missing, and the organization is on the verge of a civil war."

"Wait, what?"

Have I concealed the truth from her? Not intentionally. But maybe subconsciously, I was afraid that if she found out how big a disarray Spina Sacra was in, she'd start asking questions. Questions like: if they're on the verge of a civil war, are they really going to bother to come after Hugh? And if they're not a threat, do we really need to live together? Do we even need to get married?

"The son is dead?" she continues. "When did that happen?"

She looks disturbed by the revelation. My principessa has a tender heart. "Sometime last week. Monday, I think. Why?"

"No reason. What time is it? Aren't you late for your meeting with Guerra?"

"Probably." I reach into my pocket for my phone and make a face. The club took it away, and now I don't know the time. "I better try to find him. Will you stay in Liam's office until I'm done?"

"Who's Liam?"

"The manager. Irish guy. Trustworthy." I frown. Liam Callahan is a good-looking man. "But if you tell me he flirts with you, I'll break every bone in his body."

"I'll get right on that, orsacchiotto mio." She rolls her eyes. "You do remember I love you, don't you?"

I smile at her. I probably look like a lovesick fool, and I don't even care. "It's still sinking in. Tell me again."

She laughs, stands on tiptoe, and presses a kiss on my lips. "I love you, Leo Cesari."

"And I love you, Rosa Tran. I'm the luckiest guy in the world. Anh Yêu Em."

She takes a step back and stares at me in disbelief. "Did you just say I love you in Vietnamese?"

"I looked it up on the Internet. I might have butchered the pronunciation."

"You did, a little," she says, laughing at me through tear-filled eyes. "But I love you for it."

34

ROSA

Liam Callahan gets me settled in his office. He offers me a drink from his refrigerator, shows me where the snacks are, and tells me he has to go down to the club floor. That's okay with me; I could use some alone time.

For a few minutes after he leaves, I bask in the afterglow of Leo's revelations.

Leo loves me. I want to sing and dance around the room like a Disney princess, giggle from sheer delight, and also bawl my eyes out. I don't do any of those things, however. I sit in the extremely comfortable armchair in Liam Callahan's office and eat his chocolate.

Thinking about Leo's first marriage makes my heart hurt. Leo loved her. I could hear it in his voice when he described every career that Patrizia wanted to pursue in her life. Underwater explorer, gondolier, detective, teacher. She sounded fun, adventurous, and imaginative. I'd have liked to meet her.

You'd have been so jealous of her that you'd want to claw her eyes out.

No wonder Leo didn't want to talk about her. No wonder our impending wedding brought his trauma back. No wonder he's been wound so tight. Annalisa warned me I was going to have to be patient, and now I understand why.

And I'm determined to do everything in my power to make sure he's okay.

I don't like being shadowed by guards, and the cameras and phone tracker are flat-out nuts. But Leo recognizes that, and I'm sure that once we're married and his nightmares cease, he'll back away. He might call himself a possessive asshole, but he's not controlling. He might walk me to and from the gym, but he's never once stopped me from going.

I finish eating my chocolate bar. Swiss dark chocolate with flecks of almonds and dried cranberries—delicious. I look around the room for something to do. While Liam's office has a refrigerator filled with chilled water and prosecco, there are no books or magazines in sight.

Oh shit. Romeo Santini. I've been so happy that Leo loves me that I've totally forgotten about everything else. I need to talk to Hugh, tell him the news.

Their last conversation... My heart sinks when I remember Hugh's harsh words. *We're done,* he said to Romeo. *I owe you nothing. Whatever we had is over.* Hugh was justified in his anger—of course he was. Romeo Santini blew up his car and tried to kill him. But no matter how much he denies it, I'm pretty sure my brother loved him. And now Romeo's dead, and that's always going to be their last conversation.

That's not the only reason I need to talk to Hugh. When Leo bared his heart to me, I couldn't stop thinking about the secret I was keeping from him. By not telling him about Romeo's threat, I'm just adding to his trauma. He's dead now, and my brother is no longer in danger. It's time to come clean.

I reach into my purse for my phone before remembering that the woman at the reception confiscated it. Muttering a curse under my breath, I head downstairs. The same woman is still there, which makes sense—it's probably only been an hour since we got here. "Can I have my phone back?" I ask. "I need to make a call."

"You can't use your phone in the club," she reminds me, reaching into the cabinet behind her and handing me my phone. "You need to step outside. The reception is terrible at the front of the club, but it's better at the back. If you go around the building, you'll get to a patio with a couple of picnic tables. That's the employee break area, and the coverage is pretty decent there."

I smile. "Thank you." I head in the direction she pointed. When I reach the patio, I turn on my phone and call my brother. To nobody's surprise, he doesn't pick up. Unlike me, Hugh always screens his calls. It's deeply annoying. "Hey, it's me," I say when the phone beeps for me to leave a voicemail. "Pick up the damn phone. I need to talk to you urgently about Romeo. Call me back as soon as you get this."

I hang up, then send him a text telling him to call me urgently for good measure. Then I sit on the picnic bench and wait. With any luck, Hugh's at home, not out clubbing with his friends, and he'll call me back within the next five minutes.

Then I hear a footstep. Before I can look up to see who it is, a knife is pressed to my throat. "Don't move," a man's voice says from behind me. "Or you'll get hurt. On your feet, Rosa Tran. You're coming with me."

35

LEO

Finding Max Guerra isn't as simple as you'd think. I head to the club floor, and at least a dozen people intercept me on my way to the bar. Half of them offer congratulations on my upcoming marriage, and the other half want to know why I'm in a sex club less than a week before my wedding. "Rosa's here with me," I grit out to the third person who poses the question, resisting the urge to wring his neck. "Obviously."

"What time is it?" I ask the bartender when I finally get clear of people.

"Nine fifty-five," she replies. "What can I get you to drink, Signor Cesari?"

If I wanted proof that Liam Callahan only hires the best, here it is. I'm not a member of the club, and

I haven't been to Casanova in *months,* but she still knows my name. "Just a Perrier, please." Instinct tells me I'm going to need all my wits for my conversation with Max Guerra, and my brain is already fuzzy. I'm riding high on a wave of euphoria. I told Rosa everything, and she didn't recoil from me. She told me she loves me. Thrice, in fact. Yes, I kept count. I thought she'd leave me when she found out the truth, but all my fears were unfounded.

I settle at the bar and scan the crowds for Guerra. Five minutes go by, then ten. At the twenty-minute mark, I lose patience. I pay for my drink and stride to the front. "Can I have my phone?" I ask the employee at the reception. "I need to check my messages."

"Of course, Signor Cesari," she replies. She gets my phone from the cabinet behind her. It's one of those old-fashioned apothecary cabinets, rows of small wooden drawers, perfect for storing small electronic devices. But the drawer she pulls my phone from is empty.

"Did Rosa already come downstairs for her phone?"

"She did," she replies. "Signorina Tran stepped out to make a call, and I suggested the back patio. It has the best reception." She smiles warmly. "Would

The Fixer

you tell her I love her designs? The dress I bought from her boutique is my favorite item of clothing."

Rosa went outside? I stifle my instinctive alarm. I'm being ridiculous. Yes, there are no guards on her tonight, but Venice is a safe city, and we're not at war. I have nothing to be afraid of. "She'll be delighted to hear that," I reply. "How long ago was this?"

"It's only been a few minutes."

"I'll join her there then," I reply. My footsteps quicken as I head around the building, and I'm practically running by the time I get to the back.

But when I reach the patio, she's not there. Her phone is, however. It's lying face down on the ground, the screen cracked.

And I know that something very, *very* bad has happened.

I'M TRYING to unlock her phone when Max Guerra rounds the corner. "Sorry I got held up," he says. "Elana told me you were out back—"

A veil of rage rolls over me. I grab the front of his jacket and slam him against the wall. "Where is my wife?" I say through clenched teeth. "What the hell have you done with her?"

"What?" Guerra starts to fight back on instinct, and I knee him in the groin, a vicious, brutal kick that makes him double over in pain. "I don't know what you're talking about."

"Bullshit," I hiss. "You think I believe you? You sent me a message, luring me here. You knew I wouldn't come to a sex club a few days before my wedding without Rosa. I walked right into your little trap, didn't I?" I lift him up by the collar and press my forearm against his neck. "You shouldn't have come back, Guerra. That miscalculation is going to cost you your life." His eyes bulge as I choke him, and his legs kick out. "Where is Rosa?"

"I. Didn't. Take. Your. Wife."

Then, three things happen at once. Liam Callahan runs around a building, a club bouncer right behind him. Cormac. Big bruiser of a guy. Cormac tears me away from Guerra while Liam restrains Max.

And Rosa's phone starts to ring.

I grab the device. "Hello?"

"Leo?" Hugh Tran says. "Is Rosa there?"

"No. She's gone. She's been kidnapped." I stare at Guerra, hatred in my eyes. "Don't worry. I'm going to get her back. Even if I have to break every bone in this asshole's body."

Hugh inhales sharply. "Romeo," he says. "In her message, Rosa said she needed to talk to me about Romeo. If that fucker touched my sister—"

"It's not Romeo Santini," I snap. "He's dead."

Max Guerra looks up from the ground. "No," he says, wincing with pain. "He's not. That's what I wanted to tell you tonight. The timing of Romeo's death was a little too convenient, so I ordered a DNA analysis on the corpses. It wasn't him. The asshole faked his death."

"Why?" I demand. Then the niggle in the back of my head builds to a crescendo. I've never mentioned Max Guerra to Rosa before tonight. I've never told her he was connected to Spina Sacra. When I asked her to come with me to Casanova tonight, I just said he worked for Ciro Del Barba.

But in the private room, Rosa asked me how Guerra fit into the mess in Lecce.

She already knew.

And the only person she could have found that out from is her brother.

"Tell me everything," I growl into the phone. "Tell me everything *now*."

Ten minutes later, Antonio, Dante, Valentina, and Goran have joined me in Callahan's office, as has Hugh. We've reviewed the recording from the security camera at the back of the club, and we've confirmed that Rosa's kidnapper is indeed Romeo Santini.

Hugh Tran has told us enough to piece together the whole sordid mess.

Rosa's brother stole ten million euros from Spina Sacra because Romeo Santini asked him to. When Max Guerra discovered the theft, Romeo was forced to act. He knew that if Hugh was questioned, he'd implicate him. So he tried to kill Hugh by blowing up his car.

When we paid off Rocco Santini, the mafia boss stopped giving a shit about the missing money. But Romeo didn't. He still wanted the ten million euros, and so he called Rosa and threatened her.

Rosa wanted to tell me about it, but Hugh talked her into keeping it a secret until the wedding. "It was a stalemate," he says to us. "It was the only thing we could do. We weren't part of the family until Rosa officially got married to Leo. You couldn't protect us."

That's quite possibly the stupidest thing I've ever heard out of his mouth. I'm not the only one who thinks so. "What does that have to do with anything?" the padrino snaps. "The deal was done. Romeo Santini can't touch you without forfeiting his life, and he would have known that."

"But I thought—" Hugh begins. Then he sees the expression on my face and shuts up.

"Forget Hugh's utter stupidity for the moment," Dante says. "Romeo threatened Rosa the week after she got back from Lecce, but after that, he laid low. Why kidnap Rosa now?"

Max smacks his head. "Because of me," he groans. "He must have been watching me, damn it. I forced his hand by coming to Venice. Romeo thinks I work for his father. He believes that if I discover that he was the mastermind behind the theft, I'd tell Rocco, who'd then personally kill him. That's why he couldn't let Hugh talk to me."

"So he kidnapped Rosa to persuade Hugh to keep his mouth shut?" Antonio turns to Rosa's brother. "If that's the case, you'll be hearing from him any moment now. Valentina, we need to trace that call."

Valentina jumps to her feet. "I'm on it." She squeezes my shoulder on her way out. "We're going to find her, Leo," she says. "You're not alone."

Dante gets up as well. "There's only one thing I don't understand," he says, looking at Guerra. "Where do you fit in all of this? You're not from Puglia, and you have no connection to Southern Italy. Why are you involved in an internal Spina Sacra matter?"

The other man hesitates. I start to unbutton my cuffs. "My wife made me this shirt, and I don't want to get blood on it," I growl. "But if you do not answer Dante's question, I will beat you to a bloody pulp; consequences be damned."

Max nods tightly. "I don't give a shit about Santini, father or son," he says. "But I'm in love with Sienna Santini. When Rocco sold her to Lorenzo Corio, he sealed his death sentence. As for Romeo—"

He never gets a chance to finish his thought. Hugh's phone rings just then. He answers with a shaking hand. "Romeo," he says. "What do you want?"

It's been twenty minutes since Romeo Santini

took Rosa. My principessa is in the hands of a man who feels like he's backed into a corner. Romeo cannot harm her, else his life is forfeit, but desperate men make mistakes. Fear threatens to choke me, and I squash it deep down inside.

I need to hold it together. For Rosa's sake.

Liam has a map of Venice on his wall. I walk up to it and draw a circle around Casanova. "Santini has a twenty-minute head start on us," I say. "This is our search area. It's a lot of ground to cover. Let's narrow it down."

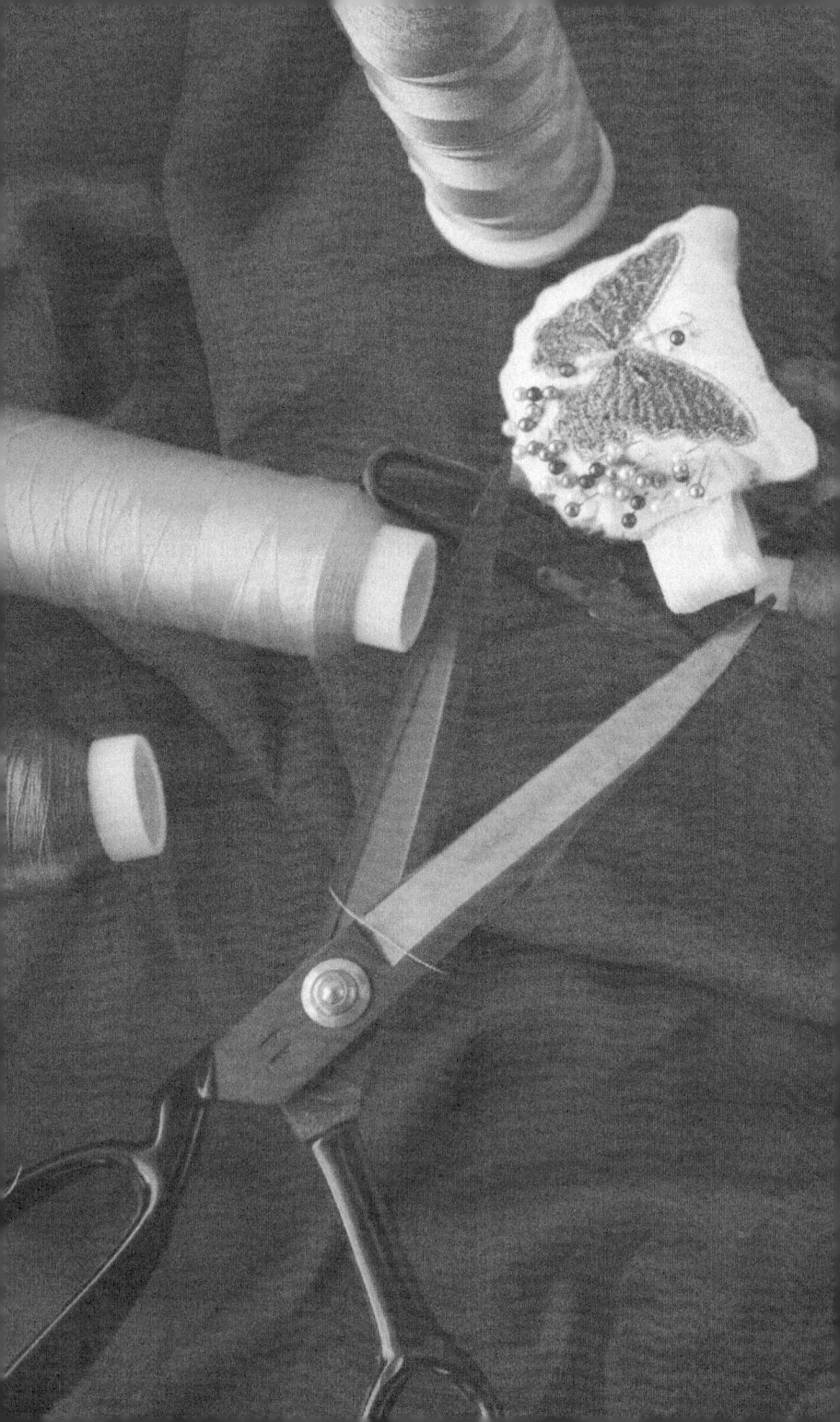

36

ROSA

My assailant drags me down an alley. We don't go far. Less than five minutes from Casanova, he pulls me to a stop in front of a small, squat building that's no bigger than a garage and hands me a key. "Open the door," he says, the knife still at my throat. "If you scream, it'll be the last thing you do."

For three years, I've been taking MMA lessons. I should know what to do in this situation. I should be able to wrestle free. But I can't remember anything I've learned. I'm terrified, and my mind is blank.

With trembling fingers, I unlock the door, and he pushes me inside the pitch-dark room. My knees hit something—a couch—and I collapse onto it. He shuts the front door behind him and locks it, and then he turns on a light.

And I see him clearly for the first time.

He's young. *So young.* My kidnapper is just a boy. He's tall, skinny, and doesn't look a day over eighteen.

"I'm sorry," he says. He stares blankly at the knife in his hand and sets it down on the coffee table, then slumps into a chair across from me. "I'm so sorry. I really need the money, and Hugh won't listen. I didn't know what else to do."

I can't lunge for the knife. Even if I could stop trembling, I'd never reach for it before he does.

Then his words sink in. "You're Romeo Santini?" I ask disbelievingly. "But you're dead."

"No. That was supposed to throw them off my scent." He runs his hand through his hair, his expression bitter. "Not that it worked. Guerra ordered a fucking DNA test, the asshole. Any moment now, my father's going to get the happy news that his son and heir is still alive."

I thought Leo was brittle, but he has nothing on this guy. Romeo Santini is practically vibrating with tension. His jaw is clenched, his eyes hard. He picks up the knife and starts to flip it in his hand. Tip, handle, tip, handle, the movement restless, *danger-*

ous. Any moment now, he's going to slice his fingertips into ribbons.

"Why wouldn't your father be happy that you're alive?"

Romeo laughs, and there's a definite hysterical edge in that sound. "Because I'm trying to kill him," he says. "Three fucking attempts so far, and none of them have succeeded. If only Hugh. . . " His voice trails away on a choked-off sob. "Who cares? Lorenzo and my precious papà will tear each other to shreds, but it's too late for Sienna, and it's too late for me."

I can't tear my eyes away from the blade. "Why do you want to kill your father?"

He laughs again. "Didn't Hugh tell you? When I was fourteen, Rocco Santini decided I was done with childish things. I was a man and needed to act like one. He had me brought to a basement room." He swallows convulsively. "There was a boy there, tied up in the corner, bruised and bloody. His name was Edoardo. He was the gardener's assistant. My father was a prick, and my mother had died in childbirth; the household staff were all terrified of my father and wary of me. Edoardo wasn't. Apart from Sienna, he was my only friend."

I have a dreadful feeling that I know where this story is going, and I don't want to hear the rest of it.

"My father handed me a gun," Romeo continues tonelessly. "He told me that Edoardo was a spy from a rival family, caught stealing our secrets. And the punishment for that kind of betrayal was death. He stepped out of my way and told me to shoot my friend."

"What happened then?" I whisper.

"My big sister found out somehow. She was two years older than me and a thousand times braver. She burst into the basement, snatched the gun from my hand, and shot Edoardo herself. My father was furious. He whipped her bloody as punishment for interfering, and then he whipped me for being a coward. He sent Sienna off to boarding school, and I wasn't allowed to have any contact with her for the next two years."

He takes a deep, shuddering breath. "Six years," he says. "For six years, I've bided my time. I learned all about the inner workings of his business. I pretended to be the dutiful heir. Then the asshole married Sienna off to his second-in-command. She begged him not to, but he sold her like property to keep himself in power."

My voice is very quiet. "Why did you ask Hugh to steal ten million euros from your father?"

"Assassins aren't cheap," he replies. "It was the only way to save Sienna. I had to take out both my beloved papà and my new brother-in-law."

I push away the twinge of sympathy I feel for Romeo. "And Hugh," I add, my tone caustic. "You forgot his assassination attempt."

He plucks the blade out of mid-air. "I love Hugh," he says. "I fucked up, and he will never forgive me, and I don't blame him. But nothing I did changes the way I feel about him."

"That makes perfect sense." I fold my arms over my chest, suddenly acutely aware that I'm wearing a leather bustier and a flimsy skirt. "You love my brother, so you blow up his car and kidnap his sister at knifepoint."

"He wouldn't listen," Romeo grits out. "Don't you understand? Sienna hasn't been seen in *days*. She might already be dead. I can't afford to fail again. If there's even a chance she's alive, I have to succeed in my next attempt."

"You told Hugh you needed the money. You never told him why. He wouldn't have kept it from you if he knew the truth."

"I was trying to *protect* him. Don't you understand? Knowledge is dangerous, and the wrong secrets will get you killed." He starts to juggle with the knife again. "None of this was supposed to happen. My father should have been dead before anyone found out the money was missing. Then Guerra came along and fucked everything up."

He picks up his phone. "I don't want to hurt you," he says again. "All Hugh has to do is give me the money. Then I'll leave Venice, and none of your family will ever hear from me again."

As much as I want to hate Romeo, I can't. He's just a badly frightened boy who's trying to save his big sister. I can't say I'd do anything different in his shoes.

Romeo calls Hugh and makes his ransom demand. When he hangs up, he gets to his feet, opens a closet, and puts a shirt on the coffee table in front of me. "You look uncomfortable," he says. "Do you want some water?"

"I'm okay."

Time passes, slow and viscous. Romeo fiddles with his phone, plays with his knife, and prowls around the room. I stay on the couch, hug the shirt to me, and try not to worry. I should have stayed put in Liam's office. I should have never left. I can't imagine what Leo's going through right now. This is straight out of his nightmares, his darkest fears brought to life.

My fear jerks me out of my passivity. "You need to let me go," I tell Romeo. "If it's money you want, I can help you."

"How?"

I unclasp the necklace Leo gave me. "This is a pink diamond," I tell Romeo. "I'm sure it's worth a few million euros." I slide my engagement ring from my finger. A pang goes through me as I do it, but jewelry can be replaced, and right now, Leo's my priority. "The ring cost two million." I put both pieces on the table in front of me and push them toward him.

"It's not enough."

"It's a start. Let me go, and I'll make sure Hugh sends you the rest. You have my word."

He stares at me for a long moment. "You're serious, aren't you? You really mean it."

"I really mean it. All I want is for my family and friends to be safe. You can understand that, can't you? All you really care about is your sister. We're not that different, you and I."

He opens his mouth to say something, but before he can, the front door crashes open. Leo bursts into the room, his gun pointed straight at Romeo Santini.

He came for me.

"Put down your fucking knife and kick it to me," he says to Romeo, his voice cold as ice, "and step away from Rosa, or I will shoot. And I never miss."

Romeo complies, and Leo swings at his face. The other man goes down, clutching his nose. More people rush into the room, people I don't recognize. They hoist Romeo back on his feet, ignoring the blood trickling down his face, and cuff his hands with heavy-duty zip ties.

As for Leo, he just looks at me. He sees that I'm unharmed, and his shoulders slump with relief. I see the aftermath of terror in his eyes, and I ache for him. He's at the edge and could fall over into the abyss, and I need to hold onto him and tug him to safety. But I have no idea how to do it.

"You found me, orsacchiotto mio," I whisper, "How?"

Then, a faint light twinkles in the inky depths of Leo's ocean-blue eyes, and he comes back to me. He steps into the room and holds out his hand to me. I lace my fingers in his as he tugs me forward. I fall into his embrace, my lips tilting up for the warmth of his kiss.

"I got lucky, and I had help," he replies. He picks up my engagement ring from the coffee table and slides it on my finger before kissing the palm of my hand. "But most importantly, principessa, it took me a long time to find you. And now that I have you, I'm not letting go."

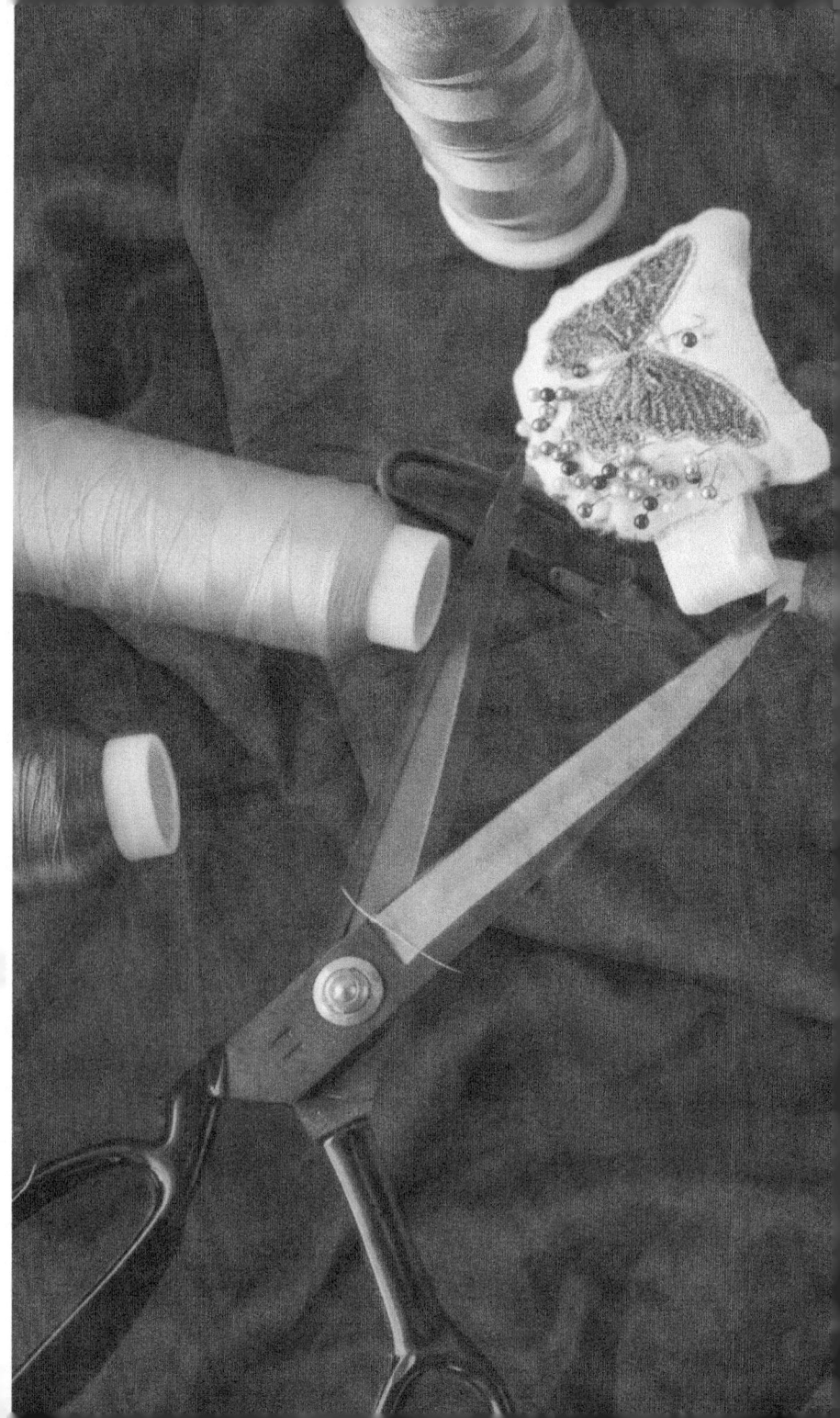

37

ROSA

I thought Leo would stay and deal with Romeo Santini. He is the Venice Mafia's enforcer, after all. But he doesn't. Never letting go of me, he says something to one of his guys—Goran, I think—and then he looks into my eyes. "Let's go home, principessa."

Home. Now that Leo mentions it, being back home sounds amazing. I want nothing more than to be in bed with Leo, safe in his arms, a warm blanket covering both of us and keeping the outside world at bay. It's slowly starting to sink in that my ordeal is over. The adrenaline that kept me going drains away, and I start to shiver, so I pull the shirt Romeo Santini gave me tighter around my shoulders.

Leo's eyes follow my motion. "No," he says, his eyes darkening. "Not his shirt. *Mine*."

The possessive edge in his voice sends a thrill through me. God, I want him. I want to fold myself into his arms and stay there. I want him to throw me down on the bed and loom over me, his weight holding me down. I want to feel him against me, skin on skin. For the last few days, home has been filled with strained silences and unsaid words. Tonight, at Casanova, we made a major breakthrough, but then I was kidnapped. *Enough*. I want to replace all of that with a fresh start. I want to luxuriate in my soon-to-be husband, wrap myself in the cloak of his love and stay warm. I want Leo's palazzo to be transformed by our happiness.

He undoes the buttons and drapes the brown cotton shirt I made him around my shoulders. It smells like Leo, a mix of cologne and man, and it takes me back to that beach in Lecce, only a few weeks ago, where he done the same thing for me.

Always protective. Always caring. *Mine*.

"I love you," I whisper. I'm clinging to him and can't seem to stop. I don't want to. He's the love of my life, and I'm never going to let him go.

His eyes soften. "I love you too, principessa," he replies. He tips his thumb under my chin and tilts my face up, and he kisses me, soft, sweet, and tender. We're in full view of his men, all of whom are doing a heroic job pretending not to watch, but Leo doesn't seem to care, and neither do I.

"When I thought I lost you. . ." His voice trails off, and he pulls me into his body and buries his head in my shoulder. "I can't survive losing you, Rosa. You are everything to me. *Everything*."

I swallow the lump in my throat. I don't want to tell him how much he means to me—*I want to show him*. "Let's go home."

"Of course." He sweeps me off my feet and into his arms. I wasn't expecting that. I squeal in surprise and instinctively wrap my arms around his neck. "You might warn me if you're going to do that, orsacchiotto mio," I say, my cheeks flaming. His people are openly watching us now, grins on their faces, and I just know Valentina is going to call me tomorrow morning, teasing me about how my fiancé cannot seem to keep his hands off me.

"Afraid I'm going to drop you?"

"Of course not. But I'm perfectly capable of walking."

A shadow passes over his face. "I've done a terrible job of taking care of you so far, Rosa," he says quietly. Seriously. "Let me fix it."

"There's nothing to fix." Leo hasn't done a terrible job of taking care of me, quite the opposite. He takes care of me every single day. And I'm still amazed at how quickly he found me. Less than two hours after Romeo made his ransom call. There are thousands of apartments in Venice—how did he even manage it?

And I'm at least partly to blame for this situation. Leo told me to stay inside the club, and instead of heeding his warning, I went outside. No matter what happens next, my kidnapping is going to have an aftermath on Leo. He's going to have more nightmares, *and it'll be my fault.* If carrying me through the streets of Venice is going to make him feel a little better, then I'm going to put my embarrassment on hold and let him do it.

When we get home, Leo takes me straight upstairs to our bedroom. "You want to shower?"

A hot shower sounds *amazing*. "Yes, please," I reply. "Join me?"

"Absolutely." He carries me into the bathroom, sets me down, and helps me out of my clothes. I adjust the taps until the water is at the perfect temperature, watching him surreptitiously and greedily as he strips naked.

Then we tumble into the shower. We stay there for a long time. Leo washes my hair and soaps my back, and I cling to him, hot water raining down on us. "You must have been terrified," he says, stroking me, his voice promising murder.

"I was," I admit. "Even worse, I kept thinking I should be able to fight him off. All the classes I've been taking, all my time in the gym, but when it came to the moment of truth, I was frozen. So embarrassing."

"You have no reason to feel embarrassed, tesoro. He had a *knife*. If you'd been hurt. . ." He clenches his eyes shut. "It's selfish of me to be thankful you didn't try to fight him, because then he didn't have the opportunity to hurt you. If that had happened, I don't know what I would have done."

I stand up on tiptoe and kiss him. "He didn't hurt me," I say firmly. "You found me. I'm perfectly fine, as you can see." A wicked thought occurs to me. "But just to be sure, you should check every inch of my body."

. . .

LATER—*MUCH later*—the topic comes back to Romeo Santini. I'm wearing my favorite pair of pajamas, and Leo tucks a mountain of pillows around me. I feel like I'm in a pillow fort. He also insisted I needed a hot drink, which is why I'm cradling a mug of cocoa with a huge dollop of whipped cream in my hands.

His mother used to make him cocoa when he got caught in the rain.

"I should have told you about Romeo," I say softly. "I shouldn't have kept it a secret from you. I'm sorry I did."

He kisses my shoulder. "I don't blame you for not trusting me; why would you? I was an asshole to you."

"No, you weren't," I contradict immediately. That's a bullshit narrative, and I'm not going to let it slide. "You were never mean to me. *Never.* And I always trusted you. I didn't know what to do. Romeo said that if I warned you, he'd kill my family."

"I know. Hugh told me." His expression turns grim. "And I'm going to kill Santini for that. Among other things." He takes the cocoa from me and sets it down on the bedside table before lifting me on his lap. "I didn't do a very good job of protecting you, principessa."

"That's nonsense. You told me to stay inside the

club. I'm the one who went outside so I could get a phone signal. And besides, you found me." I trace the scar on his cheek. "He's just a kid, Leo. He was going to let me go."

He grunts. His expression doesn't exactly invite me to continue, but I don't let it stop me. "I feel sorry for him."

"Typical Rosa," he says wryly, shaking his head. "You get kidnapped at knifepoint, and instead of being angry with the person who did it, you feel sorry for him. Why do you care what happens to that bastard?"

I tell him everything Santini told me. "Think about it, Leo," I whisper. "Think about being a child in that home. No mother, no love. A father who demands that you kill your only friend when you're fourteen to prove you're a man. What a childhood. That poor boy. All he had was his sister. Tell me you don't feel a little sorry for him."

He makes a face. "Damn it, fine. I do. I didn't have much growing up, but my mother loved me. I knew that as surely as I knew the sun rose in the east. She would do anything to protect me. But as shitty as his childhood was, Romeo is an adult. One who tried to kill your brother."

He's not wrong. "I'm not going to pretend I

forgive him for that. But you know something, Leo? I don't think he'll ever forgive himself either." I stare at the diamond on my finger. "I offered Romeo my engagement ring and my pendant if he'd let me go. I didn't want to, but—"

"You did the right thing," he cuts in. "You think I care about the diamonds? You are worth more than some damn stone. Jewelry can be replaced. People can't."

I squeeze his hand. "He was going to take me up on it—I'm absolutely sure he was. He didn't want to hurt me anymore than I wanted to be hurt." I lean on Leo's shoulder. "I understand why Romeo did what he did. Tell me, if it was your sister sold off to an abusive alcoholic, what would you do?"

"I would burn the world down to protect what's mine," he says flatly. "That's never going to change." He lifts my hand and presses a kiss into my palm. "And that's exactly why I'm going to kill Romeo Santini."

I take a deep breath. Leo is ready to kill Romeo, but I know he'll regret it if he does. This is the same man who couldn't bring himself to kill the wife and child of the assassin who murdered his wife. Leo lives by a code. Romeo isn't an innocent—far from it —but he's a victim. His father is the true villain here.

But I'm not going to ask Leo to spare him. In the end, this is Leo's world, and his decision to make. "I love you, Leo, and I trust you. I haven't done the best job showing it, but I really do. Whatever you decide to do, I'm okay with it."

I kiss him and feel his cock stirring against my ass. "Want to search me again?" I ask hopefully.

He laughs softly. "Are you sure you're not tired? It's really late."

It *is* really late, so late that the sky is turning light. It's five in the morning, and if I had any sense, I would forgo sex and catch up on sleep.

But then Leo kisses my hand again, stares at the ring on my finger, and growls, "My wife."

And I come undone.

I want Leo. My soon-to-be husband, the love of my life, *orsacchiotto mio*. Sleep can wait.

38

LEO

Two days later, I'm summoned to a meeting in the padrino's house.

I don't want to be here; I don't want to leave Rosa. I'm afraid to let her out of my sight. The only reason I left is because Dante and Valentina personally offered to stand guard at my home. But I know my reaction isn't healthy. "How do you go on?" I asked Valentina on my way out. "How do you let Angelica ever go on a play date again?"

In response, she gave me the business card of her therapist. I'm going to call him as soon as the wedding is over. I'm lucky, so very lucky. I'm getting married to an amazing woman. But she deserves to be with someone whole, someone who's got their shit together. I'm too much of a selfish asshole to let her go, but therapy? I can do that.

Max Guerra is seated at the conference table, as are Antonio and Dante. Ciro Del Barba is here too. Why? Not a clue. I'm about to find out why he's involved in this matter, and I have a strong hunch I'm not going to like it.

We get to the point pretty quickly. "You've probably already figured out why I needed to talk to Hugh Tran," Guerra says. "I had to know what Romeo Santini was up to. Why did he want ten million euros, and what was he planning to do with that money? I thought Tran would know."

"If you wanted to know why Romeo wanted ten million euros, why didn't you just ask him directly?" Antonio says in exasperation. "That certainly would have been a lot less complicated for everyone."

Guerra steeples his fingers. "You would think so," he says. "But it's not that simple. Romeo has always played things close to his chest. Even Sienna wasn't sure if her brother just wanted to kill Rocco for the power. But I thought Hugh would know."

"He didn't," I say, an edge in my voice. If Guerra hadn't come back to Venice, Rosa would have never been kidnapped. "Hugh knew nothing. Romeo never told him why he wanted the money. He just said it was important."

"I miscalculated," Guerra admits. "But I've taken steps to fix this mess. You'll be happy to know that Rocco Santini was killed in his home this morning. Lorenzo Corio was stabbed last night." He takes a deep breath. "We need Romeo."

"No." The reply bursts from my lips. "No. Romeo Santini kidnapped my wife at knifepoint. He broke the treaty his father signed. His life is forfeit." I lean forward and stare at Guerra. "His life is mine."

Ciro Del Barba, the Kingmaker, speaks for the first time. "You owe me a favor, Leo," he says. "I'm calling it in."

I stare at him in utter disbelief. "Are you fucking kidding me?"

"You know the price of doing business with me." His voice is quiet. Almost regretful. "That's the deal we made. A favor for a favor. And this isn't something that will compromise your loyalty to Moretti. He doesn't care if Romeo lives or dies."

"No."

"I warned you," Antonio says to Ciro, his voice cold and precise. "I warned you about his reaction. You know what your problem is, Ciro? You think we're all puppets, ready to dance to your bidding."

He turns to me. "Spina Sacra finds itself without an heir," he says. "Sienna Santini is the obvious choice, of course, but those idiots are too hidebound to bend their necks to a woman. Guerra will marry Sienna next week. But he isn't from Puglia. They won't accept him either. They will, however, accept Romeo."

"Romeo Santini is an out-of-control child," I snap.

"He is," Guerra agrees. "When he is king, Sienna and I will be his regents."

"And if he is unwilling to be minded?"

Guerra's voice is very cold. "You will find that I am prepared to go to extraordinary lengths to protect the woman I love."

"So there we have it, Leo," Antonio says. "That's the choice. You can have your revenge. You are owed. Not a single person here will dispute that." He glances around the room, daring anyone to voice a protest. They don't. "But if you kill Romeo Santini, there won't be a clean succession in Lecce. There will be war."

Rosa once asked me why I worked for Antonio Moretti, and I recall my reply. I work for Antonio because he never loses his temper, and he's never erratic. But most importantly, he realizes how destructive war is, and he'll do everything in his power to avoid it.

My answer comes to haunt me now.

Goddamn it. "This isn't fair."

"No," Antonio agrees. "It isn't. Welcome to my world."

I take a deep breath. For a moment, I rage at the choice I'm going to have to make. If there was any fairness in this world, Romeo Santini would die. But I'm going to be forced to let him go. Not because Ciro insists on collecting his favor but because they are right. War is a thing to be avoided at all costs.

And then Rosa's face pops up in my mind, her voice in my ear. *I love you, Leo, and I trust you.*

After that, it's easy to let it go. I leave my anger, my fear, and my trauma behind in that conference room. Because no matter what happens to Romeo Santini, I'm marrying Rosa in five days. And that's the only thing that really matters.

I get to my feet and stare down at Max Guerra. "Your welcome in our city is revoked," I say coldly. "And if I see either you or Romeo Santini in Venice again, you're dead men."

Guerra's head snaps toward Antonio. The padrino gives him a bland look in return. "You heard Leo," he says, also getting to his feet. "Take Santini and leave. And Ciro? Consider all favors owed to you repaid."

Rosa is in her boutique. I tried to insist she stay at home this week, but she was having none of it. "I have a business to run, Leo," she said, my stubborn principessa. "And a collection to design. Besides, there is nothing wrong with me."

I nod in greeting to Annalisa and turn to my soon-to-be-wife. Less than a week, and we'll be married. *I cannot wait.* "Can you step away for an hour?"

"Yes, why?"

I wink. "It's a surprise. You'll find out soon enough."

"You know how I feel about surprises," she says, trying to frown and failing miserably.

"You love them?" I tease.

"I do," she admits sheepishly. "Where are we going?"

"Nice try, principessa."

I take her to the beach, of course. We walk along the water edge until we find a quiet spot. Then I take her hand. "When I proposed to you the first time, I didn't want to get married," I say quietly. "After

Patrizia's death, I was afraid of love. Of finding it again, of losing it. I was sure I could keep you at arms' length." I smile wryly. *What a fool I'd been.* "But the problem wasn't that I didn't care; it was that I was afraid to. I told you that this was a business arrangement and nothing else. I even lied and said that I wasn't interested in you."

"I remember," she whispers.

"I was wrong." I slide the ring off her finger and get down on one knee. "Rosa Tran, I love you. You make me smile every single day, and I want to spend the rest of my life with you. I promise that no one will work harder to make you happy than I will, and no one will cherish you as much as I do. Will you marry me?"

A tear slides down her cheek. I wait for her to respond, more nervous than I've ever been in my life. I don't have to wait long. "Yes," she says, a wide and happy smile breaking out on her face. "Yes, yes, yes."

I slip the ring on her finger once again. But this time it's real, not pretend. And this time, it's forever.

EPILOGUE

The day of our wedding dawns bright and clear. Rosa's father insists on taking me out for breakfast. We end up at an English-style pub. "It's a family tradition," he says over a pint. "Elaine's dad took me to breakfast on the morning of my wedding. Told me what to expect on the wedding night."

I nearly choke on my beer.

Ben digs into his plate of eggs and bacon with relish. "I better get started, I guess. When a man and a woman love each other very much—"

Oh God. He's not serious, is he? He doesn't actually think Rosa and I have been celibate all this time? Then again, she's his *daughter*. If he chooses to bury his head in the sand, I can't say I blame him. "Ben, I'm begging you, please stop talking."

He gives me a long look. "Leo, are you implying that you and Rosa already have. . . " Then he dissolves into helpless laughter. "Your face," he chokes out. "You should have seen your face."

It takes a minute for my heartbeat to return to normal. "Haha," I say sourly. "Very funny, Ben. Positively hilarious." Okay, it was pretty funny. He totally had me convinced. "I know where Rosa gets her acting skills from," I tell him with a grin, clinking my beer against his. "And her sense of humor."

We talk about cars after that. Ander's garage, the Bugatti he's working on, how difficult it can be to find parts. The conversation moves on from there to their upcoming trip to Hanoi this winter, the number of tourists in Venice, and how nice the weather is today. We're just getting to leave when Ben says, "We never did thank you, Elaine and I, for saving Hugh's life."

I stiffen. "I don't know what you're talking about."

Ben fixes me with a look. "Leo, I'm not an idiot. Banks don't give cars as bonuses to entry-level employees. My daughter never mentions a boyfriend, then you show up. Suddenly she's engaged, and the two of you are getting married in a month. And we all have to leave Lecce within the week?" He shakes his head. "I'm not going to lie, I was very concerned. But the more I see you two together, the more reassured I am. I think you'll be very good to her, Leo, and I think the two of you will be very happy together."

That'll teach me to underestimate anyone in the family. "Thank you, Ben. I know we'll be."

I STAND at an altar under a trellis draped with red silk and gold tulle and decorated with garlands of white roses and jasmine. Behind me, the ocean glitters like a million sparkling diamonds.

My friends are here, sitting on the chairs arranged in front of me. We've eschewed the typical bride and groom's seating, and instead, everyone sits together. Annalisa sits next to Elaine, Ben, and Hugh. Antonio and Lucia are talking to Alina, while Tomas is doing his best not to stare at her. Dante and Valentina are smiling at a story that Angelica is telling them. Joao and Daniel are both glued to their phones.

Then, the music begins, and everyone turns to the bride.

Rosa walks down the aisle, a vision in white. She holds my gaze as she makes her way toward me, a smile on her lips. She's wearing her hair down, and as she nears me, the wind blows a strand of her hair into her face, a familiar gesture that makes my heart swell.

I take a step toward her and tuck it behind her ear.

I thought I would be afraid today. Afraid of the past, afraid of what might happen. I thought I'd be on edge, waiting for someone to burst upon us and start shooting.

But when I see Rosa, all I feel is joy.

I take her hand, and we step up to the altar together. We exchange the wedding vows we wrote, and then I'm kissing her, pouring all the love I feel for her into my kiss.

We're going to spend the rest of our lives together. She's going to call me her teddy bear to make me laugh, and I'll retaliate by calling her principessa. We're going to share a bed and come together in passion. We'll lie on the beach, stare at the waves, and spend hours talking about our present, our future, and everything under the sun. And I hope that one day, when it's time, we'll build a family together.

The future stretches in front of me, bright and filled with promise. I take Rosa's hand in mine, and we step forward into it. Together.

Thank you for reading The Fixer.

More Leo & Rosa?! I've put together some bonus content exclusively for my newsletter subscribers. There's a great deleted scene where Leo visits a button store with Rosa **with disastrous results!** Plus Rosa's Milan Fashion Week debut & Leo & Rosa's wedding vows! Sign up to read it by scanning the QR code below or going to: https://taracrescent.com/bonus-the-fixer/

Want more Venice mafia?

Lucia and Antonio fall in love in **The Thief,** which kicks off with Lucia stealing a painting from Antonio. Read this mafia hero+art thief heroine romance with second chance vibes today!

Valentina and Dante banter, hack, and stab their way to love in The Broker. Enemies-to-lovers, with a mafia hero and a single mom hacker heroine? Yes please.

The next book in the series features **Tomas & Ali,** and will be out summer 2024. My newsletter is the best way to find out when it goes live, so sign up by scanning the QR code above.

ABOUT TARA CRESCENT

Get a free story from Tara when you sign up to Tara's mailing list.

Tara Crescent writes steamy contemporary romances for readers who like hot, dominant heroes and strong, sassy heroines.

When she's not writing, she can be found curled up on a couch with a good book, often with a cat on her lap.

She lives in Toronto.

Tara also writes sci-fi romance as Lili Zander. Check her books out at http://www.lilizander.com

Find Tara on:
www.taracrescent.com
tara@taracrescent.com

ALSO BY TARA CRESCENT

CONTEMPORARY ROMANCE

Venice Mafia

The Thief

The Broker

The Fixer

Hard Wood

Hard Wood

Not You Again

The Drake Family Series

Temporary Wife

Fake Fiance

Spicy Holiday Treats

Running Into You

Waiting For You

Standalone Books

MAX: A Friends to Lovers Romance

WHY CHOOSE ROMANCE

Club Ménage

Menage in Manhattan

The Dirty series

The Cocky series

Dirty X6

You can also keep track of my new releases by signing up for my mailing list!

Made in the USA
Las Vegas, NV
16 April 2024